# LONG STEADY DISTANCE

Long Steady Distance
© Helena Hill, 2018
helenadhill.com


Published Jan. 25, 2018 on Kindle Digital Publishing.
ISBN 978-1-9768-5505-4


Cover art by E. Julien Coyne
mhaladiej.com

This is dedicated to strong moms, gentle dads, and compassionate teachers.
~HH

# CHAPTER 1

*LIFE IS THE EXPRESSION OF PROTEINS.*

It's written on the summer-clean blackboard in Harris's familiar scrawl. I stare at the words until I'm no longer seeing them, my mind zooming down into my skin, down into the cells, into the spiraling DNA coded with the instructions to keep it all going…

"You can understand my concern, Mr. Harris," says Mom, bringing me back. We're sitting in plastic classroom chairs, pulled up to the front of the room so we can sit across from Harris at his desk. She eyes the message on the chalkboard, and not in a good way. "I'm very proud of Emily, but isn't this a senior class?"

Harris meets my eyes for one moment. I look down at my lap, shoulders tensing up. I remember Biology 1 from freshman year, learning about the fight or flight response. Harris taught us about species-specific defense responses, taught us that there's also a less catchy third option: fight, flight, or freeze. That last one is what my body always seems to default to.

It's late August, the first day of my junior year. The early morning sunlight streams straight through the windows and into my eyes. In the morning, Harris's classroom basically becomes a greenhouse, between the plants on every available surface and the second-floor east-facing windows.

Homeroom hasn't started yet. Harris isn't even my homeroom teacher. Mom set up this meeting several days ago, when our schedules came out and she saw I was in Senior AP Bio. Which I had signed up for at the end of the spring. At his suggestion.

"I know Emily pretty well by now, both academically and personally," he says. "I'm more than willing to take her into this class as a junior."

Mom pats my hand. I duck my head lower.

Harris does know me well. My first day freshman year I was back in this classroom, and he and Mom and I were having a meeting with the same purpose. His classroom looks the same now, just more dried snakeskins tacked to the wall, more student presence. Notes pinned to the corkboard, posters comparing plant stamens to straws sucking soda. The mice in the terrarium on his desk are different—two grays and one little brown one, instead of the three white ones that had been in rotation back in June. The label on the terrarium still reads Snap, Crackle, and Pop, though. They don't know about their destiny as snake food.

"I suppose I'm more concerned about the curriculum," Mom says once it becomes clear that Harris is not going to bring up the real issue. "I'm obligated to make sure you're giving time to the theory of intelligent design."

"Emily?" Harris says. He has a gruff voice. Thirty-five years teaching and coaching in a public school will do that to a person, I guess. "What do you think?"

Loaded question, Harris. I don't think he wants to throw me under the bus, but this is his career here. "Um…" I say, "I don't know. I don't want to rock any boats."

In the cage, the brown mouse digs deeper into his sawdust mountain in the corner. I'm jealous that he has a hiding place, even if he is going to be meeting Harris's classroom snake Boris eventually.

Harris begins pulling together papers from neat piles on his desk—syllabus, reading list, AP prep info. First day of school, he's ready to go. "I don't want to rock any boats either. Mrs. Ferris…"

"Samstone," my Mom corrects him.

He doesn't know her last name is different than mine. But he continues smoothly. "Mrs. Samstone, AP courses are based on a national curriculum and taken for college credit. What's more, this is a public school. I can only diverge from the syllabus so much when it comes to accommodating a specific religious belief."

"It's not specific," said Mom. It's her passionate voice: soft, but urgent. "All the Old Testament religions have their root in Genesis. And it's a beautiful theory, one that hundreds of reputable scientists support."

My sweaty, nervous feeling gets worse. Harris is an outspoken atheist. When I was in Bio 1, he spent a good ten minutes harping on how "hundreds" of "crackpot outlier scientists" supporting something was "in no way a substitute" for the "complete acceptance as fact by the sum and total of the entire sane scientific community." End of lecture. I stare back down at my lap, tracing the lines on my gray corduroys up and down, up and down.

But Harris is unperturbed. "Still, I really do have to try and teach this course without bringing any religious precepts into the curriculum." His voice is calm, his words rote. "However, individual students can absolutely be accommodated, whether it's excused absences on religious holidays, or maybe an independent study." He hands her a packet of papers.

Mom hesitates, then takes the stack. "I suppose that makes sense... Emily, what do you think about an independent study project? About intelligent design?"

I will do anything to end this conversation. "That seems to be a reasonable compromise," I say to the floor.

The metal chair legs squeak against the linoleum as Mom turns back to Harris. "And you'd be supervising her on this? I'm not familiar with the process."

"Absolutely," he says. It might just be me, but I think I detect a very, very thin layer of irony.

"Well... all right," said Mom. My shoulders relax. "But even if it's not given equal time, I'd appreciate it on a personal level if you at least gave students resources about where to find theories aside from evolution, so they can decide their beliefs for themselves."

"Please don't worry," said Harris. "Intelligent design will absolutely be mentioned in the first unit alongside evolution, even if we aren't able to spend much time on it."

*I bet it will.* Yep, definitely some irony in his voice there.

"I appreciate that," says Mom. She claps her hands against her lap, then stands up. "Thank you for meeting, Mr. Harris. I do have reservations about the course, but I must say I'm very happy Emily has you for class again. I already hear so much about you, and the team."

"Well, that's very nice to say," says Harris. "We're lucky to have her."

"And I do love all these plants in your classroom," she adds.

*Please, please just let's all go to our separate environments where we belong.* "Have a good day, Mom," I tell her.

"You'll be home after school?" she asks.

"Is it okay if I help out with cross country practice?" I ask, sinking lower into my chair.

"Okay. Home by dinner." She kisses me on the forehead, and then walks out of the classroom. "Have a great first day."

There's a very long silence when she leaves. Then the first bell of the day goes off. I jump.

"So, independent study, huh?" says Harris.

"Sorry," I say in a rush. "You don't even have to look at it, I don't want to make extra work for you. I'll just, I'll write something up, and..."

"Emily," he says. "Calm down."

I shut my mouth.

"I'm not going to hold you to this independent study thing unless you buy into it. So, you'll do my curriculum. And you'll do whatever research outside of class that personally satisfies you and that keeps your mother out of my hair." He stares me down. "And I'll sign off on it. That work for you?"

I nod, daring to look at him. "Thank you, Harris."

"Don't thank me yet," he says. "I'm not getting fired over this. You're coming to practice?"

I nod.

"You gonna run at all this year, or just manage?"

"I think I will most likely be staying on the managerial side of things," I tell him. The team is going to be good this year. My brain will be more useful to them than my legs.

Harris gives me a long look, but then shrugs. He's not one to force a point. "We've got a senior woman who just transferred over from Rhizenstein," he says, straightening his papers.

"Rhizenstein?" That's where Mom and I lived before we moved out here.

"Yeah. Sophie Williams." He glances at his email. "Sorry, Tuzarova-Williams. Real track star, but never run cross country. From talking to her dad, I get the impression she's a little undercoached."

I smile. "Is she going to join the team?"

"Yeah. I want you to be her dyad. Take her under your wing."

Immediately, the idea of taking someone "under my wing" has me sweating again. "What do you mean?"

"You know this sport, you know how to pace yourself. She could be near Kari's time by the end of the season. Maybe get close to Christa's with a little discipline."

I don't have time respond before the door swings open, slamming against the opposite wall. "Harris!" yells Jon, his voice cracking with first-day-of-school excitement. Jon is this year's male captain of the cross-country team, one of Harris's favorites because of his fast 5K time (personal record: 15:46) and environmentalist leanings. He's one of my favorites, too.

Right behind him come his ever-present companions, Derrick (PR: 16:31) and Rhys (PR: 16:01). Derrick, spots me and lunges toward me, giving me a terrifying hug. I squeak, and pat his back. "Hi, Derrick."

"Hey Emily!" he says, before leaving just as quickly as he came to throw his arms around Harris in a similarly enthusiastic manner. Rhys gives me a quick nod. I wave, awkwardly, and then start rifling through my backpack like I'm looking for something. I'm not. Rhys just makes me nervous. He's the only person on the team who talks less than me.

"I knew this year was going to be rough," says Harris when Derrick lets him go. "The Two Stooges and Rhys, all in my homeroom."

"You taking AP Bio, Emily?" Jon asks. I nod. He's leaning against Harris's desk like he owns the place. He's in this classroom all the time. All the cross-country kids trickle in and out during the day, showing up if they have lunch or study hall. Harris pretty much lets them do what they want, as long as they sit in the back at his lab tables and don't disrupt whatever class he's teaching.

"Harris, what are we doing at practice?" says Derrick, who has already seized one of the white mice out of the terrarium and placed it on his shoulder.

"Five one-mile repeats, and put my snake food back, please."

"Five? I'm gonna die." Derrick returns the mouse and slings his backpack onto the floor. Derrick drives Harris nuts because if he applied himself even a tiny bit, he would probably be faster than Jon. But he's too busy being "a real P in the A," to use Harris's technical term. Harris has a lot of technical terms.

"Should have shown up to preseason," says Harris. "Not my problem."

A few other seniors begin to trickle in. I gather up my backpack, violin case, and new, enormous Bio textbook. All the trappings of a nerdy tryhard on the first day of junior year, the year that college admissions officers look at with an especially critical eye, according to all the sources (aka my step-uncle Peter, the college counselor Mrs. Keynes, my SAT prep book, etc.) "I'll see you in class and practice," I say to Harris in a low voice.

He nods. "Thanks, Emily. And if you want any research sources for your independent study, you've always got full access to my bookshelf."

Harris's bookshelf at the back of the room is overstuffed, filled with nature guides and out-of-print lab manuals and books by all the great evolutionary theorists going back to Darwin. I'm not going to find anything Mom likes in there, and he knows it. But he also knows that when I show up for my lunch periods, I'm usually back there, in the armchair with the ripped upholstery, devouring yet another book.

The bell rings again. I leave my favorite classroom until lunch.

*

I'm already tired by the time two o' clock rolls around. Time for orchestra, last period of the day. I received not one, not two, but five giant textbooks today, and my backpack is heavier than ever. Since it's the first day, the freshman who haven't figured out where things belong yet are sitting in the first row of the auditorium. I get onto the stage, drop my backpack in the back, and then sit down in the second row of the violin section. The auditorium echoes, the high ceiling and empty audience filling the enormous room with a kind of promise of what we're going to accomplish. All around me, upperclassmen are taking their seats, chattering, laughing, feeling the thrill and the confidence of being back in this familiar place.

Pineridge is the only school in the district—heck, one of the only schools in the state—with enough students (and money) for a full concert band. Or at least most of one. We haven't had a tuba player since my freshman year. We have ten violinists, four violists, a smattering of brass and at least fifteen winds. Jenny Lewis drags her cello back and forth between home and school every day, so we all feel some pressure to try hard.

And then there are the percussionists. It's a different vibe over there, loud and raucous. Except Rhys, who is quietly setting up the xylophone. I give him a little wave, and he smiles. I like when the quiet people play the loudest instruments. He normally plays the xylophone because most of the percussionists aren't much for sight-reading music, but he's pretty good when he lets loose on the tympani.

I sit quietly, setting my violin case on my lap, letting it rest for a moment. I take a deep breath. It's good to be sitting, good to be at the start of a promising year, good to be getting back to group music. I practiced every day this summer, as an antidote to loneliness. I know my playing is sharper, more polished, than ever, but it feels good to be part of something larger than myself again. I close my eyes.

"You ready for naptime, Emily?" a snotty voice says. I open my eyes. My step-cousin Beth sits down in the row in front of me, setting her violin case on the ground half open. It topples shut with a clatter.

"Hi Beth," I say, almost inaudibly. Beth is the niece of my stepfather, Peter. She is the worst person I know. The first time I met her, when we were 12 and 13 respectively, she made fun of me for crying at the end a Disney movie that we had been corralled into watching together while we watched my much younger now-stepsister Rachel at a family event. At Mom and Peter's wedding, she told me I looked stupid in my glasses and you were supposed to wear contacts when you had to look nice, in her stupid dumb voice I had since come to know and loathe.

But she usually limits her nasty comments to one per interaction so long as I don't acknowledge or let her escalate. So I don't. She turns behind to talk to her friend Katrina soon enough.

Mrs. Porco, the band and choir director, walks onto stage. Walks is the wrong word. Sashays is more accurate. As per usual she's dressed in all black with a bold color element. Today, it's a white scarf patterned with brilliantly red poppies. "Wonderful, wonderful. So many bright and shining faces. Welcome, welcome, my friends, old and new."

I can practically hear the eyes rolling. Still, I can't help but smile. Mrs. Porco is one of my favorite people, even though she is quite possibly insane. "Newcomers, welcome to the Pineridge high school orchestra. Now, we will play our signature piece for you as a gesture of welcome."

It's a tradition. We always play the school alma mater at least once per rehearsal and at the end of every concert. I can basically play it in my sleep at this point.

The rest of the first day is pretty much taken up by getting the freshmen into their appropriate sections, and loaning out the ones that don't have their own instruments ones that Mrs. Porco has collected over the years. The time rumbles by in a clumsy, discordant haze. By the time everyone is settled in their appropriate place, we manage to get halfway through our warmup before Mrs. Porco stops us. "My dears, it is the end of a magical, wonderful first day. I want to remind you that we will be holding auditions for section leaders in late October as we start our preparations for the holiday concert and spring showcase."

Beth leans back in her chair, a smile appearing on her face at this announcement. Like me, she's been playing violin since she was a kid. I don't like how she plays, though. Precise note-wise, usually, but just a hair off-rhythm. Or maybe I'm just seeing her through hate goggles. Still, she's more experienced than the rest of the violinists in her year, and as a senior, she's probably the de facto first chair. I might have a shot at second this year, though. The thought makes my stomach quiver with nervousness.

The bell rings. Time for cross country practice. It's weird to be back in school and have my days so filled again. I feel like my head is stuffed full of... stuff. I need a snack. I'm getting hungry and it'll still be two hours before I get home.

Before I leave, though, Mrs. Porco calls to me. "Emily! Wait here a moment, if you please. I'd like a word with you as soon as I distribute these forms!"

"In trouble, Emily?" Beth says as she leaves.

"Very funny," I say, but I'm pretty sure she doesn't hear me because I have this real mumbling problem. I smooth my hands over the velvety ridges of my corduroys and push my hair back behind my ears. I can't be in trouble. It's day one of school, and I'm pretty much a teacher's dream because I do well on tests and can hardly summon the nerve to talk during class, let alone cause any disruption.

Stage left, Rhys is putting the drum set away. He's the stage manager this year, a position which mainly consists of taking out and putting away chairs in the morning and after school. He makes quick work of it, which is good, because practice starts in about fifteen minutes. I walk over while I wait for Mrs. Porco. "Want any help?" I ask him.

He shrugs. "I've got it."

I want to ask him about if he's going to try out for section leader, but I'm sure he will. And we've each used up our three-word quota for our conversations. There's nothing more for me to do but gather up my things and wait for Mrs. Porco to bustle over. "Emily, my dear," she says breathlessly. "I wanted to talk to you about the spring showcase senior solos."

"Um, what about them?" I ask.

"Well, dear, are you planning on trying out?"

My hands get sweaty just at the question. "Maybe?"

"Emily!" Affronted, Mrs. Porco puts a hand to her chest. "It's the spring showcase senior solo!"

For one thing, I have no idea how that amounts to an argument. She's just restating her claim. It's not like alliteration instantly trumps logic. For another, I'm not sure I feel about this. "I'm not a senior, Mrs. Porco. And it's August."

"I'm well aware, but Emily, you'd do well to at least toss your name in the ring." Mrs. Porco smiles. "And ahh, we have some exciting pieces that I'm planning on unveiling..."

"I, just... I'm not a very good performer," I mumble. "I get a little stage fright."

"All the more reason to start preparing now!" Mrs. Porco booms. "Face up to your fears! Do what you love! *Carpe diem!*"

I glance over at Rhys, who fights back a smile as he collapses music stands. Whether or not he had heard the beginning of the conversation, he certainly heard that. "Well, um, maybe," I tell her. "I'll think about it."

"I certainly suggest that you do so." Mrs. Porco beams down at me. "If you play at the level which I am accustomed to seeing you, you'll certainly have a good chance."

I smile, feeling awkward. I give her a weird little half-wave goodbye before I walk down the stage stairs and out of the wide auditorium.

*

I check Harris's phone to get some weather statistics while he drives us to the Ross Golf Park in his minivan. Late August and it's eighty-six degrees with 70% humidity. I don't envy the team. It's one of the reasons I'm happy to be manager. I get to run when I want, and today, I really, really don't want.

By the time we arrive, the team has already crowded into the scrubby shadow of a young elm tree to stretch. Today we're practicing at the public golf course instead of a trail, and there's not exactly tons of shade. But it's a good place to practice: a mile away from Pineridge High School, the perfect distance for a warm-up run for people to gauge how they're feeling and loosen up tight muscles.

While Harris unloads his bicycle from his trunk, Jon and Christa introduce themselves as the men's and women's captains respectively. They start the team off with dynamic plyometric stretches, something we implemented last year with great results.

"All right, everyone," Harris says from his bike once people are gathered and stretching. Since his knees are, in his words, "pure garbage held together by metal screws," he uses a bike to keep up with the team. "We are officially back in the swing of things. If you haven't been showing up to preseason, today's when you're gonna pay for it."

I catch a few uneasy glances among some of the less committed runners. Meg barely showed up, and Anthony's been on vacation for the last two weeks. Preseason's technically optional, but most people show up. People are as devoted to Harris as I am.

Only one girl I don't recognize from preseason. Almost everybody, even the freshmen, come out to at least one practice if they know they're going to run. Pineridge is a good school with a strong cross country team, and the parents in the neighborhood pass on the word.

So this must be Sophie Tuzarova-Williams, by the power of basic deductive skills, a.k.a. not being an idiot. She sticks out among the group like a dark-allele peppered moth in a lichen-rich forest. She's black, for one thing, in the very white school of Pineridge in the very white sport of cross country. She's thin and lanky, which sometimes points to natural running talent. Still, height isn't a perfect correlate. Jay, who's my year, is 6'2" and he barely held onto his number seven spot (the last varsity spot) on the team last fall.

Sophie's hair is a wild dark cloud, and it looks like it might actively be attempting to escape her ponytail with a mind of its own. It's the most noticeable thing about her. Well, that and the way that Jon has abandoned Christa to lead the stretching circle in favor of making his way to Sophie's side. He tries a joke on her. I can't hear what he's saying from my spot under the elm, but I know it's a joke because he follows it up with a wry shrug and then his puppy dog "aren't I adorable" eyes.

She laughs. That I can hear. She has a nice laugh. You can practically taste the pheromones wafting over the air.

And this is the girl I'm supposed to take under my wing? Harris, if we're talking wings, I'm a pigeon and this girl is… a swan. No. A heron—she has long, long legs. Biological accuracy, Emily.

"Mile repeats today," Harris announces. "Doing 'em on the Bowl. The key here is going to be consistency, people. Consistency and mental toughness." Harris talks a lot about mental toughness. It's one of the reasons I'm never going to be a great runner. Or a competitive one, at least.

As far as practices go, this is a brutal one. The sun is hot and somehow heavy. My hair sticks to my neck with sweat, and I didn't even run here. And the Bowl is our most devastating mile course, basically a steadily increasing incline the entire way. On his bike, Harris leads the team down to the bottom of the Bowl. We call it that because it's flat near the bottom but steep near the top. I stay where I am under the elm. It's where they finish the mile, and Harris will want me to take down their times.

Harris's whistle carries faintly over the still air of the golf course. I watch the runners start: first in a pack, then spreading out like marbles rolling down a hill, the guys mostly in front, the women mostly in back. Sometimes, when I look at the team, I don't see people, just a scrolling list of personal records and team rankings.

Jon's in the lead, almost immediately. Rhys is a few yards behind him, but the gap is widening. Then a cluster, then some of the male stragglers, with Christa leading them. She's our resident prodigy, third place at states last year and a top twenty finisher at nationals. And then… Sophie and Kari are neck in neck. Interesting. Kari is easily the most competitive person on the team, and it shows in her running. She's no Christa, but she works hard and she's fierce. I've heard her actually growl at other runners during meets.

If Sophie can keep up with her at meets, it'll be great for our rankings. Christa's PR is 18:57, and Kari's is 20:21. I'm hoping Kari gets under twenty this year, but having a third girl under twenty might win us a state championship.

I check my watch as they disappear behind the hill. A minute forty-six has gone by. Jon will be back in three minutes, twenty seconds, on the dot. I take the time to pick a stray thread off my old watchband. It's beginning to fall apart. It was my dad's running watch, from back when a digital watch that could keep track of a few mile splits was a big deal. It's not nearly as fancy as the one Peter gave me when he was still in his "buy the affection of the sullen stepdaughter" phase. I use both, sometimes, if Harris wants me to take a ton of times, or sometimes I'll use one for the guys and one for the girls.

But when I have to choose, I like my dad's better. It makes me feel connected to him. He died when I was in fifth grade. He was a big runner. Every year our church held a 5k to raise money for one of our parishioners, Mr. Graham, who had ALS. And Dad won the whole thing a couple times. When I was young I used to run in the little kid race. It was one lap around the block our church was on, less than half a mile. I never won. Even then, my legs never moved as fast as I told them to. But I ran the whole way, past some of the boys who blew out of the starting line and then walked half the way. And even when they sprinted past me at the end of the race, my dad told me, "It's okay—a steady pace is the most important thing. Those boys are never going to run a marathon. But you could someday."

That was the last year he ran. He got sick after that. It was a rare, aggressive variant of bone cancer, and he died a year and a half after his diagnosis. Mr. Graham outlived him.

When I started at Pineridge, I decided to join cross country because of my dad. Something he said about the marathon stuck in my mind. Twenty-six point two miles on my own two legs. It sounded pretty good. If I could go twenty-six miles, I could go forever.

The runners are back in view now, Jon still in the lead but Rhys having made up some ground on the hill. He's good on a slope. As they sprint to the finish, I take splits, clicking the watch every time the next person hits the elm tree. Christa clocks in at 6:16, so she's clearly feeling bold. She's a distance runner, not a sprinter, and if she runs a time for the first mile, she intends to keep it up for the next four.

I'm mostly waiting to see what happens in this Sophie vs. Kari faceoff. The point goes to Sophie, who notches 6:28 to Kari's 6:30. That's still fast for Kari. I smile. Some intra-team competition might be a good thing, although Harris really tries to emphasize the whole "team before self" aspect of things.

Kari looks a little winded, but Sophie looks worse. She's covered in a sheen of sweat, and her hair is falling out of its ponytail. She leans over, says something to Jon as she redoes her hair. He grins, broadly.

"Two minutes rest time!" Harris calls out. I set about flipping back through the times so I can record them on my clipboard. My watch is only capable of holding twenty splits. I add in a line for Sophie at the bottom of the roster, which is a real blow to my neatly organized spreadsheet arranged in order of last year's PR. It correlated perfectly with their finish in the first mile. Except Sophie. Who is this girl anyway? Just some other girl Jon's going to be into, and therefore the center of the autumn's gossip.

"All right, everybody, back on the line," says Harris, to groans.

Sophie looks a little apprehensive as she steps back onto the line, but she glances at Kari and puts a game face on. I smile. This will be interesting.

Except she goes on to absolutely tank the second and third miles. 7:05 and 7:17. Wildly inconsistent. Kari is smirking while Sophie leans against the elm tree, panting. Internally, I find myself rooting for her when Harris yells, "Thirty seconds!"

She closes her eyes, steels herself, walks to the line, plants herself right next to Kari.

"And—go!"

She takes a deep breath, bobs up and down once on her calves, and sets off.

I think back to my first practice ever. It was a less brutal one, but I messed it up all the same. We were out in Emerson Nature Reserve on the trails. I fell way behind the pack and took a wrong turn. The sun was low in the sky by the time I heard the then new, now familiar, click click click of Harris on his bicycle. "Emily!" he boomed. "The three-mile loop too short for ya?"

By then I was so tired, I could barely respond, but I hadn't stopped running yet. "I got lost."

"Where the hell is Derrick? He was supposed to be your dyad." Harris was big on the buddy system. He called them dyads, with occasional triads if our numbers were not even.

Harris led me through a shortcut ("Don't tell your teammates," he said. "Jon will go and use the time he saves to climb trees") and we made it back to the tail end of the team stretching. "Derrick!" he yelled.

The lanky boy with curly hair saw me, ran over, and gave me a crushing hug. I would later come to know that this is a common Derrick move. "I was so worried!" he said. "I doubled back and you were gone!"

I was breathing too heavily to speak. My heart was pounding in my ears, and my legs were trembling. I almost fell when Derrick let go. But I was so relieved to be found, to have been missed, that I couldn't get the grin off my face.

I practiced with the team for the next two weeks. I was scared, shy, but it felt like I was part of something. It wasn't until I got to a meet that things started to go sour.

I'm taken back to the present when Sophie pulls herself together on miles four and five, pulling a 6:52 and a 6:35 respectively, and beating Kari on the last one. Once we're back under the elm, everybody sweaty and exhausted, Harris calls for silence. Everyone shuts up. I don't know how he does it, maintaining this crazy respect. Well, I do. He walks his talk. "Not bad," says Harris. People visibly perk up. "For a start. We've got work to do, people."

Derrick lies flat on the ground, gasping like a fish. Sophie and Kari are panting on opposite sides of the circle. Kari stands straight, arms laced behind her head, while Sophie hunches over, hands on her knees. I want to tell her to straighten up. She's never going to refill her lungs that way, and Kari will see it as a sign of weakness.

But I feel clammed up and shy. I stay where I am under the elm.

"Tomorrow's gonna be tough, too, but we'll ease off the gas for Friday." Harris's eyes are bright, despite the firmness in his voice. He's not a smiler, but I know how much he loves this—the opening of a new season, taking a look at who will grow, who will come into their own, who will plateau. "Then enjoy your weekend, because after that we've got a meet every Saturday until states. Now, go run back and check in with your dyad."

Once people are done stretching, they stand up in groups of two and three and start the cooldown jog back toward the school, slowly, almost at a walk. I eye Sophie. So. Taking her under my wing. A first step would probably be to introduce myself, but even that seems insurmountable in the face of this girl from Rhizenstein. I have no clue how to act, or what to say, and even just saying my name feels like too much. Instead, I stay still as though I'm rooted to the elm.

But she spots me watching, and walks over before I even have a chance to be nervous. "Hey," she says, plopping down next to me. "Are you Emily?"

Her voice isn't like I expected. Not that I realized that I was expecting anything. But it's bright, and it's direct. It's a voice that carries a conversation without any fear.

"Um, yes, that's me," I reply, staring at the dirt.

"Sick. I'm Sophie." She holds out her hand, and I take it. For a girl who just ran five mile repeats, her grip is cool and hard. "Harris said you could be my dyad thing. Oh, and that I should talk to you about forms."

As the mature, responsible adult on this team, Harris is technically responsible for all paperwork. But he also knows that I kind of like it and am very careful, so by this point I'm basically in charge of it. "Sure, of course, absolutely," I say, cracking open my clipboard. It's a nice clipboard, a plastic case about an inch thick, so that I have more room for storage inside. At this time of year, I keep blank physical and permission forms in there because people inevitably will lose or forget or spill soda on theirs. Later, I'll keep racing bibs and course maps inside. "Um, you'll need to have a physical by next weekend for the first meet, and your parents are going to have to sign this slip."

"Awesome," she says. "He also said… well, okay, I've never run cross country before, just track. And he said maybe you'd be able to take me on a run this weekend outside of practice? Just to get, like, a tutorial about pacing?"

Harris. Even if I'm not running for the team, he's not going to let me get off scot-free. He just wants kids to run.

"Well, I think that's what he was saying," Sophie adds. "He kept mentioning LSD, though, which, okay, I don't know if that's like a running term or if he just does a lot of drugs."

I smile. All of a sudden, I like her. It's that simple. I don't know what it is—the ease and directness of her, the half-laugh that punctuates her sentences—but I want her for the team. She's going to be important. I knew it about Kari and Rhys and Jon freshman year, I knew it about Terri last year, and now I know it about her.

"LSD is just a running acronym Harris made up," I tell her. "It stands for long steady distance." Technically, long slow distance, but Harris always says steady is more important than slow.

"That is one hell of an acronym," says Sophie. She smiles, leaning back against the tree. She's sweaty, her running shorts bunching around her hips, the shoelaces on her battered Nikes frayed and untied. "So Emily, do you, uh, want to do some LSD this weekend? If you're not busy."

"I'll have to check with my mom," I say, and immediately flush. What am I, ten? "I mean, I usually run on Saturdays, though, so it should be fine. If that works for you."

"Hell yeah, I'm free. I don't know anyone here yet. Gotta make me some friends." It's self-deprecating, but the way she says it, it's like she's confident that friends are an inevitability.

"Hey Sophie! We're running back now," calls Jon. "Wanna come?"

She smiles at me. "I'd better head back—that whole friends thing."

"Of course," I say. It won't be long before she gets enveloped into the team. Which is a good thing, I remind myself.

*

Harris usually drops off as many people who will fit in his minivan after practice. Some of the seniors have their own cars, but for the people who don't live nearby or whose parents don't pick them up, he's willing to let us pile inside. It's always cramped and smelly, but people laugh, joke, and pass around the giant Tupperware container that he always keeps filled with Costco brand trail mix.

Mom's rule is that any driver I get into a car with needs to be over twenty years old, with a family exception for 18-year-old Beth. Since Harris is driving, in the technical sense I am obeying her. Though I doubt she'd be thrilled to know that I'm not wearing a seatbelt, squeezed into the space between the bucket seats in the middle row of the minivan, my backpack hugged in my arms, laughing at Derrick's singalong with the radio station to "Hungry Like the Wolf" where he replaces every instance of "Wolf" with "Derrick." But I can probably just not tell her about that part.

Today I'm third to last to get out, with Danny and Terri living in Harris's same development. He drops me off at Asbury Park, which is about half a mile from my house. "Bye Harris! Bye everyone!" I say, before getting out and breathing in the fresh air.

I cut through the playground, past the picnic shelters, across the dirt running track, before I get to the entrance of Wisteria Manors, the subdivision where I live with Mom, Peter, and Rachel. On the first day of school when I have every textbook with me, this feels like a real slog. But the air is cooling and the sky is a lovely soft orange. It's quarter to six, and the sun is sinking low. Soon it will be dark when I'm getting home.

Wisteria Manors is one of the nicest subdivisions in Pineridge. Big Tudor houses, large yards, well-spaced elegant streetlamps that come on at seven o'clock every night. Beth and her parents live here, too. Our house is on one of the cul-de-sacs, curling off from the main road like a new shoot off a particularly mint plant.

First thing, I drop my backpack and gently set down my violin case on the three steps up to our front door. Then I walk into the garden, careful to step around the strawberries, which have been particularly fragile this summer. Mom and I have been working this garden since we moved in, and this was the first summer that it really took off. We've been pulling tomatoes off the vine every couple of days for the last month. The dogwood that was here when we moved in that Mom loves, loves, loves, is just starting to show signs of fall, a few of the leaves yellowing at the edges. The herb section, carefully layered and organized, with the shade-loving ones growing beneath the shelter of the rhododendron and the sun-lovers taking the edge of the garden, are growing tall. Maybe too tall. Our basil is getting a little overeager. .

I take a few leaves from near the top of our basil, leaving the big ones on the bottom to keep being the solar panels for the plant. There's another tomato that looks just about perfect, so I take it off the vine, leaving behind the ones that are just beginning to redden. The geranium that we transplanted from our old house is looking a little droopy.

Treasures clutched in my hands, I head inside. We don't usually lock the door here, which is a big change from our old house. The foyer always echoes when I shut the door, the high ceilings and ceramic tiles acoustically dramatic. Still, I can smell dinner being cooked, which is impressive given the size of the space.

I leave my backpack by the door and walk through the living room into the kitchen, where the warm smells get stronger. Mom is at the stove and Peter's at the table with the Wall Street Journal. Rachel sits on the floor between the island and the sink, coloring next to her beloved stuffed animal Horsie. As soon as she sees me, she pushes herself to her feet and hugs my legs. "You're home!" she says, and squeezes tight.

I laugh. Rachel is my little sister. Stepsister, technically speaking. Based on biological destiny, I should probably hate her given that she shares zero percentage of my DNA and occupies approximately 99.98% of Mom and Peter's attention, but she's five and she's adorable and even a prickly well of internal snark like me can't say one thing against her. "Hi, Rach," I tell her. I ruffle her hair as I set the tomato and basil down on the counter. "You going to try one of our tomatoes tonight?"

Rachel wrinkles her nose, lets go of my legs, runs away from me. "Yuck!"

"Only nineteen days left until the fall," I call to her. "You promised to try at least one summer tomato."

And she's gone. I miss being young.

Mom smiles at the interaction. She stands over a cutting board, chopping onions. The smells of cooking fill the kitchen. I know this recipe; it's her chicken cacciatore. Peter's favorite. "How was practice?"

"It was great. I think the team's going to be strong this year. Also, I think the geranium isn't getting enough water."

Mom sighs, scratches her forehead with her wrist since her hands are covered in onion juice. "It's been a little hot for geraniums. I almost wonder if we should bring it inside."

"I'll water it again after dinner," I say. "Rach, want to help me set                                    the                                    table?"

When we first moved in, Rachel was three. Her mom died right around the same time my dad did. She's almost six now, and we're just starting to introduce chores. It's pretty cute. She carefully puts nice cloth napkins under all the forks while I do the rest of the table.

Peter puts his paper away before dinner starts, though he doesn't help Mom bring over the food or pitcher of water. I feel a little stab of resentment. Peter has made dinner exactly once since I knew him, and that consisted of ordering a pizza when Mom had a late afternoon dentist appointment, which I know for a fact Mom didn't even like because it had banana peppers, which she hates.

"Hi, Emmy," he says as he serves chicken cacciatore onto everyone's plates. "How was day one?"

I've been trying to adjust to the nickname, but I kind of hate it. I'm really more of an Emily. "It was all right."

"How was biology?" Mom asks while she's cutting Rachel's chicken.

"It was fine. Harris added intelligent design to the syllabus," I say, the lie coming smoothly, without my even thinking about it. "I think we'll cover it Wednesday."

"In my opinion, it should really be more than one class, but I suppose there's a lot of material to cover," Mom said. "Do you know what you're going to do for your independent study?"

I put a big bite of chicken in my mouth to give myself a second to think. "Um, I think probably about the status of intelligent design in science today. Like you said, some people back it up and I think that could use some analysis." Keep it boring, keep it light.

"I look forward to reading it," Mom says, and I feel a little stab of guilt. Or resentment. Or both.

"Sounds a little too complicated for me," Peter says, and laughs.

Here's the thing about Peter: he's not a bad guy, if I look at things in an objective sense, even if he can't get it through his balding head that I do not like being called Emmy and that Mom is not into spicy or pickled foods. He's nice to her, mostly, I think. I see him giving her kisses on the cheek here and there; they seem to like spending time talking after work. He's sweet with Rachel. When they got engaged, he started pulling out all the stops in terms of trying to get his stepdaughter-to-be (a.k.a. me) on his side. I got a new violin and a professional-grade trainer's watch out of it. I don't mind him, not really. But we haven't exactly done much in the way of one-on-one bonding.

Mom met Peter Samstone when I was in seventh grade, in a Christian support group for widows and widowers. They got married the summer before I started high school. Mom changed her last name to Samstone, but I kept mine Ferris. The elapsed turnaround time from my dad's death to Mom walking down the aisle with Peter was two years, seven months, and four days.

I don't know if it's just that I'm getting older or getting used to it or what, but I've been thinking more and more about Mom and Peter's marriage, and—I don't know. I mean, Dad used to make dinner sometimes, and Mom worked part-time until Dad got sick, and... I don't know. This pristine little life with the housewife mother and stockbroker father we have now feels fake, like we fell into a magazine ad in *Good Housekeeping* or something.

But it's my life right now, and it's my family, even if it's hastily patched together with duct tape.

Dinner gets better once we turn the focus to Rachel. She has one more week of summer vacation before kindergarten starts, and she spent it running around the backyard while Mom gardened. I feel a little pang of jealousy—I remember getting to be outside with Mom all day, learning everything about the garden and all the plants—but it's ridiculous to be jealous of a six-year-old. And it's nice to see Mom smiling.

As soon as Mom is clearing the plates and Peter is back into the paper, I stand up. "Thanks for dinner. Is it okay if I go water the geranium?"

"Go ahead," Mom says.

I snag our watering can from underneath the sink and go outside. Now that it's cooled off, it's beautiful outside, the scorching hot practice feeling far away. And the garden is the one part of the house that really feels like home. When we moved in, Mom didn't change much, I think mostly out of respect for Peter's dead wife. This is the one place where we've made a mark.

I kneel down by the droopy geranium. "It's okay, little plant," I tell it. When I'm done watering, I lean in to whisper. "I don't really like it here either."

I'm not a hundred percent crazy to be talking to the plants. $CO_2$ is important for their growth. Also, usually it makes me feel better. But it's the beginning of the year. It's a two-day week. Tomorrow's Friday, and then running with Sophie on Saturday. At least I'm starting the year off with at least one social engagement. Even if it is just Harris forcing me to be friends and get a bit of cardiovascular exercise.

I sit with the geranium for a few more minutes, until it's too dark to see. I can put off homework a little longer. I'll spend the rest of the evening practicing violin. It's going to be a busy fall.

# CHAPTER 2

I'm at the northeast trailhead of Emerson Nature Preserve, my absolute favorite trail and ideal for an LSD run: varied inclinations, smooth pathway, cute chipmunks running across the path every so often to distract you when you're exhausted. The best part is the overlook at the top of the hill, though. I want to see what Sophie will think of it.

She's late for our run. It's 3:07 by my watch, and I'm shifting from foot to foot with nerves. Also, with cold. That's lake effect for you. It's fifty degrees, a sharp and unpredictable downturn from the summer weather of the beginning of the week. It'll be ideal once we start running, but in my shorts and my dad's threadbare cotton long sleeve from the Columbus marathon, I'm getting goosebumps up and down my legs.

"Hey," says Sophie, jogging toward me. "Sorry, sorry I'm late. Parked in the lot and couldn't figure out what to do with my keys. I'm always like, paranoid that they'll get stolen if I leave them under the mat or something."

"Where'd you leave them?"

She pats her breasts, and there's a faint jingling sound. "This is why Einstein invented sports bras."

I laugh too loudly, and stop too abruptly. "Um. You ready?"

She doesn't seem to notice how much of a spaz I am. "Lead on, manager."

We don't speak for the first few minutes. The beginning of a long run is always strange. My body rebels against the effort it knows is coming, and my breathing and footsteps and heartbeat are ragged and out of sync. But I know that the inner freak-out will subside as I ease into my pace. By the time the trail flattens out after the initial ascent, I'm in rhythm, feeling loose and happy, enjoying the sound of the trees rustling in the chilly wind.

Sophie's struggling a little, though. She keeps pulling ahead, checking herself, and slowing down. "Sorry," she says. "I know I'm supposed to be pacing myself off you."

It's the first time I've seen her look doubtful. For some reason, that makes it a little easier for me to talk to her. "It's okay. You're a lot faster than me. But Harris really wanted you to get some slow reps at some long distances so you could start to learn to pace yourself."

She nods, slowing down once again. And I'm definitely going a little faster than is totally comfortable, but it's such a perfect day that I feel like I can do it. We'll meet in the middle. "Wanna know my trick for pacing?" I ask.

"Yeah," she says.

"Match my breathing," I tell her. "Just focus on that. Let me set the pace. Your rhythm will come." Even if my short legs can't match Sophie's loose, loping stride, if she's focusing on the rhythm of her breathing, slowing it to match mine, her body's going to slow down, too.

The storm yesterday blew a lot of leaves around. The fallen ones make a damp carpet beneath our feet on the path, releasing earthy smells as we run over them. One breath. Another. Another. It's easy. We start a long descent, one that'll take us alongside the brook.

"How long is this trail anyway?" Sophie asks once we're in stride.

I smile. "Don't worry about it."

She misses a step. "You saying that kinda makes me worry about it."

32

"Harris has a theory that there are two mental skills a runner needs to build up," I tell her. I don't know when I got so didactic about running. Maybe it's nice to have someone that all this accumulated knowledge will benefit.

"Okay," says Sophie. On the downhill, her breathing has eased, but she's taking very small steps so she doesn't lose me on the hill. I make a mental note to tell her to open up her legs on the downhills in competition. She'll be able to blow past other runners.

"The first one is the easier one for most people to understand. It's sort of like, the competitive edge, whether that's with yourself or against another person. And developing that kind of... fire will help you a lot in races. Like if you can tell yourself to go harder and actually get your legs to work harder, your heart to pump faster, your lungs to get more oxygen, that's a skill." I'm breathing hard from the talking and the running. This is why I usually run alone. "The other skill is kind of... Zen. It's the feeling of being able to run forever without any kind of worry about when you'll stop. And that's what we're working on here."

"Hence not telling me how much more we have to do?" Sophie says.

I glance at my watch. We've been out here for around nine minutes. We're going to pass my first mile marker, the pointy rock at the first bend in the brook, very soon. This is faster than my usual pace, but essentially a crawl for Sophie. "Yes. Hence."

She laughs, which makes me feel good. I don't think of myself as particularly humorous. "This is some deep shit," she says.

"If it makes you feel better, I have a good stopping point about three quarters of the way through."

"It does, actually," she says.

We're at the brook. I spot the mile marker. One mile down, five to go. I hit my dad's watch for the split. Nine minutes flat. I already know I'm not going to be able to make it the whole distance at this pace, but might as well keep it going for now, at least meet her in the middle.

Mile two is almost entirely along the brook. "This is a really nice trail," says Sophie.

"Yeah, I come out here a lot."

She looks at me intently for one moment. It's a wide, easy part of the trail—she won't be able to do that once we hit the rocks in mile five. "Can I ask you a question?"

"Uh, yeah."

"Okay, sorry if this is nosy, but like... you seem like a pretty reasonable runner... why don't you run for the team?"

It takes me a long time to figure out what to say. I push my sleeves up. It's starting to feel warmer.

"I mean, no worries if that's like a sore subject or something," says Sophie.

"No, I just...I'm slow. I like running but I don't really like competing very much." It's hard to explain. She doesn't know me, doesn't know that it's the only way I get to feel close to my dad. If I'm focusing on other people, I can't hear his voice, can't calm my brain down to nothing. When I'm competing, it makes it about other people.

"Oh, that's chill," she says. "I get that."

"Really?" I think of her final mile repeat from the first practice, gunning for Kari.

"Yeah. I mean, I get pretty competitive with running stuff, but not really in my day to day life." She laughs. "Not good enough at anything else."

"Did you run at your old school?"

"I ran track for a couple seasons. We didn't even have a cross country team though." She laughs again. It's a nice laugh. Very self-effacing. "My dad likes running, though, so I used to run with him before his knees got too bad. We'd only ever go a couple miles, though."

That gives me a little pang. But it's nice to have something in common with her. "My dad liked running too."

"Oh yeah? His knees go bad too?"

"He died five years ago," I tell her.

"Oh, shit. That sucks. I'm sorry," she says.

"It's okay."

The rest of mile two, we run in silence. It's nice—some people feel the need to talk all the time when running. Like Meg on JV. Who, to her credit, is very kind. But she talks incessantly whenever we run together way behind everyone else at practice. I end up spacing out half the time. But Sophie and I—we're doing okay. I feel focused, and I'm definitely getting tired, but I feel like I can push through. We pass the mile three marker, right after the trail starts back up the hill.

It's a little surprising to me that I'm the next person to speak. But I'm genuinely curious. "Um, do you like Pineridge so far?"

"Uh... kind of." Her form on the hill is not great. She's a little hunched over. She'll need to learn to lean into it while keeping her shoulders back. Little flyaways from her ponytail flop up and down in rhythm with her steps. "It's very different. I mean, it's good for my brother, so I like it a lot. I just miss my friends. But people have mostly been nice. Especially the cross-country team. It's just... yeah. Different."

"I used to live over in Rhizenstein," I tell her. "Before high school, though."

"Oh yeah? Whereabouts?"

"South side," I tell her. That was when Mom and I lived with Nana after Dad died.

"I have a lot of friends over there," Sophie says. "I like it. Little rough though."

Nana had kept her place locked and deadbolted. Mom always laughed that it was like Fort Knox in there. "Yeah."

"Why'd you move?" she asks.

"My, uh, mom got remarried."

"Cool," she says. "Cool, cool."

She's breathing a little hard. We've been going uphill for a couple minutes now. I haven't been on this trail in a couple months. I forgot that the middle of this run is pretty brutal. We fall silent for a few minutes, but she slows down as I do, pacing herself off my footsteps. "How we doing on mileage?" Sophie asks, in between breaths.

We're just getting to mile four. The rocky part. "Just focus on where you're putting your feet," I tell her, as I take the lead, over roots, around rocks. I know it well. "This next part, the terrain is tough."

"Dude, they don't teach you this in track," she tells me.

"Trail running is great for ankle stability." I hop a fallen tree, slippery with moss. "And it's great for developing mental toughness, like I was talking about. You really have to focus, it should be a mental workout too…"

And of course, I'm so busy telling her this that I catch a rock on the toe of my sneaker and fall. The heels of my hands hit the ground first, catching my weight in a painful scrape against the ground. A sharp rock gets me right in the shin.

Sophie, who's just behind, leaps aside to dodge me. "Holy shit, Em," she says. "You okay?"

My embarrassment is way more intense than the pain in my hands. I push myself to a kneeling position. "I swear, I've never fallen here before."

"Well, that in itself is impressive." She offers me her hands. Normally, I'm not so much with the physical contact, but there's something very natural, very easy about the way that she grasps my wrists, avoiding my hurt palms, and pulls me lightly to my feet.

"Want to walk for a minute?" I ask. It's not good for training, it's not good for pacing, but we're almost to the overlook and I still feel so humiliated that I don't know if I can run.

"Yeah, I'm dying over here."

The wind is back, and it's cold, but it feels good against my hot skin. "We're almost to the top of the hill," I tell her. "We can stop and see the overlook."

My hands are really smarting by the time we reach the top, but the view is almost enough to forget them. On one side of the path, the hill is steep enough that it looks out over the whole forest. The trees spread out below us, mostly green, still, but some just beginning to redden, promising the autumn. Beyond the forest is the highway, and beyond that, the train tracks. Rhizenstein is on the other side, visible as tightly knit blocks of gray houses in the harsh, cloud-blocked sunlight.

Being able to see so far like this makes me feel safe. It makes me feel something like a promise. Sophie hasn't said anything. Part of me is worried that she's going to be underwhelmed, but that worry disappears as soon as I look at her. Her face is like—it's soft, like she's looking at something beautiful and she appreciates it. Or maybe I'm reading too much into her expression. "What do you think?" I ask.

"Is that Rhizenstein, or…"

"Yeah."

"It looks very beautiful from here," she says. "Lot more beautiful than in person." She crosses her arms, hugging herself. She's in a t-shirt, and it's cold. We're wind-exposed, and we've stopped running, giving our sweat a chance to do its job and cool us down.

"That's… um… yeah. Stuff usually looks prettier from far away."

"Yeah, when you can't see any of the cracks." She smiles, a little. This one doesn't totally reach her eyes.

A train whistles, long and low, before I see it come around the bend on the tracks. "I like hearing the train."

"It used to wake me up sometimes," she says. "Now I miss it a little,                                                                 though."

I know what she means. I want to tell her that I understand, somehow. This is a weird feeling. It's like… I care that she knows that I'm not just some spoiled rich kid from Pineridge, even though that's the life I'm leading. I care that she knows that I think about this stuff too. But I don't really have words for it when I look back up at her.

She turns to me. "Ready to head back?"

"I, uh… yeah. We're almost there."

The run back is quieter. This part of the trail is as steep downhill as it was going up, and the wind feels a little colder. My hands hurt, and my mind whirs, not nearly as calm as it normally is on the tail end of a long-distance run. Also, pacing Sophie—even her slow, LSD pace, one that is probably half her race speed—makes me feel like I'm about to die.

But even though I have a stitch in my side and I'm gasping for breath, I'm excited. I'm compiling a list of things I want to tell her. Push into the uphill, then just open her long legs and relax on the downhill. She can get some rest that way. When she feels like her lungs are flagging, focus on her form. She's tall and strong, and if she pumps her arms and stays on her toes, she'll be moving at a good clip even if she's not pumping her legs at top speed. And most of all, be confident, because if she can run six miles, casually, without trying, like we just did, she'll be just fine during a race.

But when we finally reach the trailhead where we started, everything I want to say dies in my throat. I'm breathing hard, and when I look up at her after we've stopped, she's tall and pretty and I don't feel knowledgeable anymore, just like an awkward teenage girl who's never quite been able to keep up with girls like Sophie. On the trails, or just... in life.

But she looks at me, and smiles. "Holy shit," she says, bending over, her hands going to her knees. "How long was that?"

"Six flat," I tell her.

"*Miles?*"

"Yeah. Um, you shouldn't really bend over." It's so much easier to talk to her than it is to most people, to tell her this stuff that I've been thinking about for so long. "Gotta open up your lungs."

She mimics me, lacing her hands behind her head and straightening up. We stand there together, getting our breath back, until I go over to a tree to stretch my calves. "Hey Emily," she says.

"Yeah?" I resist the urge to tell her to stretch, too. There's a thin line between helpful and bossy.

"Thanks for, uh... I don't know. Helping me out with this stuff. I know Harris asked you to and I just like, uh... appreciate it."

I smile. The elm leaves whisper above me in the wind. "We're dyads. It's my job."

"You need a ride home?" she asks when we're leaving.

I'm exhausted, and I really, really want one. "I'm okay," I tell her. "I live nearby." It's only a partial truth, but the complete truth—that Mom won't let me ride in cars driven by other teenagers—is a little humiliating.

"Okay. Well, thanks again."

"Anytime," I say, and I mean it.

*

The next morning, Rachel climbs into my bed like she always does on Sundays. "Hey Emmy," she says, her little-girl voice high and lilting. "Momma Ruth says it's wake-up time."

I grab my alarm clock and hold it up to my face. The red glowing numbers read 7:45. "We don't have to leave for church for another hour, Rach."

"But we're having family breakfast!" Rachel snuggles up next to me, still wearing her pajama set with the elephants on them.

I close my eyes again, flopping back down against the pillow. After yesterday, I'm sore, and though my hands feel better, my shin is still throbbing from where I hit it against the rock. The idea of getting out of bed and sitting through church makes me feel like crawling under the covers and never getting back out.

Rachel pulls up one of my eyelids with one of her fingers. "Emmy," she says in her sing-song voice. "Come on..."

Rachel is honestly the sweetest, cutest kid, way sweeter or cuter than I ever was. She's got big blue eyes and sings to herself when she plays with Horsie, her favorite stuffed animal. As much as I resent anyone standing between me and sleep, I can't be mean to her. She was only three when her mom died, and she's just old enough that it's still confusing to her. But against all odds, she likes me, and I'm not going to not try and be a big sister to someone who needs it.

I put on my glasses, pull the covers over us and say, "Well, maybe we'll just hide up here instead."

Rachel giggles, delighted to be a part of the conspiracy. I enlist Horsie as a sentry, and we make plans to start a new civilization in our world of Blanketonia, until Mom comes in. "Girls? Breakfast," she says.

"We're not here!" says Rachel.

"Then what are these lumps?" Mom asks, and proceeds to sit on us. Rachel laughs and laughs. "C'mon, time to go. Daddy's already eating."

Rachel runs downstairs, holding Horsie by a foreleg. Mom sits on the edge of my bed. "Ready for breakfast?"

I nod. "Mom, I'm really tired."

"That was a long run yesterday," she says.

I ask something that I already know the answer to. "Do I have to come to church?"

"Emily..."

"Can we at least go back to our old church? At some point?" I ask. I really, really do not like Peter's church.

Mom squeezes my knee over the blanket. "At some point. I miss it, too. But Peter feels that our current church is a friendlier environment for Rachel."

I don't doubt that. There's less fire and brimstone at Peter's church. But still, I turned out fine, right? This merged families thing is tricky sometimes. "Do I have to go?"

She gives me a look. Church is mandatory in the Ferris-Samstone household, even if there's only one Ferris. I resign myself to an hour spent staring uncomfortably at the ceiling. "Is there gardening club after?" I ask.

"There is. Would you like to stay for it with me?" she asks. "Your notes on the tomato plants are great."

I nod.

"Good. Come eat breakfast." She lets go of my knee and leaves my room. With a final, longing glance at the sweet, fluffy lumps of my pillow, I follow her.

*

Later, once we're in the pews and Pastor Dan is at the front strumming his guitar, I'm sitting in the shiny wood pews feeling sore in my legs, Mom on my left and Mrs. Partridge, the oldest parishioner, on my right. I stare up at the arched ceiling. This church is a lot larger, a lot grander than the one Mom and Dad and I used to go to, which had a congregation of about fifty and an old, old preacher named Father Reynolds who wormed his way into my head with his readings about the fires of heaven and the wrath and glory of God.

Now that we're at a Baptist church, we have a pastor instead. Pastor Dan is an altogether different character. He has about three hundred parishioners, with about two hundred at any given service. He begins to sing.

*Jesus loves me*
*This I know*
*As He loved*
*So long ago*

At the old church, people were so quiet you could hear the eaves slowly settling. Everyone had their eyes closed. Dad would nod along with Father Reynolds, and later, after he was gone, Mom would hold my hand during the sermon and let me follow along with the reading in her beautiful old Bible.

This is... different. Pastor Dan leads the chorus, a beatific smile on his sweaty face. He always looks like he just ran a marathon. Except he's not in very good shape, so maybe he looks more like one of the JV freshmen boys who haven't quite lost their puppy fat and struggle to run a 5K under thirty minutes.

Still, Rachel loves it here. She's only just started going to Sunday school here and she already can't get enough of it. It makes me feel like a curmudgeon for not liking it.

I stare up at the giant wooden cross, remembering the very graphic crucifix in Grandma's house from when Mom and I lived with her after Dad died. Those were weird days. I was kind of morbid. One time, I told Grandma I was angry that God let Dad die, and she admonished me. *You should never be angry at God. Everything has a purpose.* Grandma had scared me sometimes, with all her bedtime tales about little children who didn't love God and suffered for all of eternity.

*Taking children*
*On His knee.*
*Saying, "Let them*
*Come to Me."*

We're still on this song?

In a way, those days were nice, though. It was me and Mom (and sometimes Grandma when she wasn't being scary) against the world. Anytime I confided my fears to Mom, she was quick to comfort me with the fact that these punishments were only for sinners and nonbelievers, people who didn't love God, people who weren't trying to do the right thing. She always answered all my questions. "Why do flowers only bloom in spring?" I asked her once when we were out in Grandma's garden, weeding the bare fall flower beds.

"God made it so," she told me. "We'd never appreciate their beauty if it was easily found."

Anytime I told her I missed Dad, she told me he was watching over me, and he had died because it was part of God's plan. She said it was our sacrifice, one that we were making for a benefit that we couldn't see as part of some greater plan.

Thinking about it now makes my stomach feel a little queasy. I haven't felt good about God since we moved here, haven't felt like I was talking to anyone but myself when I prayed.

Mom married Peter when I was 13. That was when we moved into the big house in Pineridge, with him and Rachel. After that, it didn't seem like Mom wanted to answer my questions as much, especially when they got harder. I was fixated on Buddhist babies in China who never learned about Jesus, imagining that they were being torn to pieces for all of eternity in hell. And then we went to this church, where everything was a little softer, a little nicer... but it made me wonder which was right. The new church? The old church?

Neither?

Pastor Dan puts down his guitar an interminable number of verses later. "People, let's talk about the power of our Lord, Jesus Christ."

*Let's talk about the power of evolution,* Harris had said Friday at the beginning of class. It was the first week. Of course we were talking about evolution. *You cannot discuss any biological concept without viewing it through the framework of evolution. The tiny little chemical flip of a gene from one setting to the other can have radical consequences, and when those consequences are passed down from mother to daughter, parent to child... the consequences get preserved through time.*

I love being back in Harris's class. Freshman year, when I was shy out of my mind and tongue-tied, I looked forward to his class every single day. Except for lab, when I had to work with Delia O'Shea, who spent more time on her phone than on maintaining our potato growth experiment. But this year my lab partner is Jon, which I'm already excited about. He loves Bio and he loves Harris, so it's pretty much going to be the greatest thing ever. We can nerd out together. I'll have a friend, even if just in those fifty minutes every day.

"Our father, who art in heaven..." I'm startled back to the present by deep sound of the parishioners all saying the Lord's Prayer. I quickly look down, assuming a more reverent pose, and jump in at *hallowed be thy name.* Mom gives me a stern look.

I feel a little ashamed. This is the part of church I feel like means something: hundreds of people saying the same words, echoing up to the rafters, sending their hopes and fears out into the universe, personal yet all together. It almost feels like being on a team, the way cross country does.

But then Pastor Dan starts reading from Leviticus and I lose interest again, not liking the honeyed tones he reads with.

I let myself space out again, into more comforting things: back into Biology, back into cross country, back into the woods of yesterday.

*

Gardening club is always a huge relief after church: It involves getting outside and talking about something aside from Jesus. And maybe it should bother me that a not unsubstantial part of my social life is sitting in the church garden, drinking coffee and arguing over whether Mrs. Derrow's passiflora will survive the particularly dry summer we just had. The passiflora argument is only one of a million little tiffs that these women have back and forth with each other. The subtle down-talk they give to each other always provides serious drama.

It's usually six or seven women, plus or minus one or two floaters. Me and Mom and Aunt Gretchen are here, as is Beth, unfortunately. Then there's Mrs. Partridge, who is a thousand years old and has forgotten more about vegetable rotation than I'll ever learn. Mrs. Glenwood, the church's youth events coordinator. Mrs. Derrow, who turns up her nose at almost everything. And finally, in the sunny spot sits Mrs. Thompson, the de facto leader and president of the group.

This group meets every other week, after church and after the post-church fellowship of tea-drinking and conversation. When it's nice out, we sit in the church garden, which is maintained by volunteers—mostly these women. It's hands down my favorite part of this church.

I'm perched on my folding chair, right in front of the Japanese maple. I leaf through our gardening notes from the week. Things were relatively calm, although the storm yesterday knocked a couple tomatoes off the vine prematurely. A small tragedy. Our zucchini hasn't done as well as usual this year, but our squash is just beginning to blossom—another sign of fall.

Mom and Gretchen sit on either side of me. Aunt Gretchen is the one who scored mom (and me, by extension) an invite to this club. She is Peter's brother's wife. She usually drives us home after this, since we live in the same subdevelopment and since Peter and her husband have better things to do than sit around and wait for their wives, I guess. Gretchen is better than her daughter, and bound by the laws of Step-Family Obligation to be nice to me. Still, her personality is as bland as the thumbprint cookies she always brings along, which are always so dry that I find half the crumbs in my bra later.

Beth sits on her other side, on her phone. I do not get the impression that she is a willing member of gardening club.

"Parsley," says Ms. Glenwood, yanking me from my reverie. "Yesterday's rain practically drowned mine." Ms. Glenwood is always harassing me to Socialize™ with the other teens. Still, she's nicer than Mrs. Derrow.

I never talk much at these meetings—my fear of public speaking has a pretty generous definition of what constitutes "public." But I like to listen. And Mom and I pretty much kick butt when it comes to keeping a healthy, productive, and (for lack of a better word) pretty garden.

True to form, Mom is already explaining our solution to that problem. "We plant our parsley under the rhododendrons since it doesn't need much sun. That way it's protected from the rain," says Mom.

I'm paging through our spiral-bound gardening notebook, which is dirt-streaked and water-bloated, trying to find the exact page where we diagrammed out the front yard at Peter's when we first moved in. The parsley isn't with the rest of the herbs, but keeping it underneath the rhododendrons lets it fill a shady patch that would otherwise be bare dirt, freeing up the sunnier part of our herb garden for the lavender and sage that need plenty of sunlight.

These are the kind of details we try to write down every day, or at least every week. Back when we lived with Grandma was when Mom first started teaching me about this stuff. I always was asking her how she always predicted what would happen—the weather, the insects, the wilting hydrangea. She told me that you could never figure out a pattern by looking at just one thing, or for just a little while. "But if you look every day, and you write down what you see, after a while, you'll start to see patterns that you never would have noticed if you were just looking at one plant, or one day, at a time. Everything is connected."

And this is the woman who barely allowed me to take AP Bio.

Still, I kind of get it. She taught me that a garden isn't just a collection of plants in a yard. It's a whole little world, where everything affects everything else, and the connections affect the other connections. It's where she finds God. I used to find him there, too. I don't know what happened.

Eventually, the conversation turns to tools. Specifically, gardening benches. "I went to Flower Power, but the only bench they had was much too small for me," says Mrs. Thompson of the gardening store favored by the ladies in the Pineridge Mall.

"And it doesn't even have a shelf," adds Gretchen, who would walk through a fire if Mrs. Thompson told her to.

"You know, I got my bench at a tiny little hardware store out in Rhizenstein," says Mom. "It's one of my favorite places."

"Oh, but Rhizenstein," says Mrs. Derrow. "That's, um, a bit of a drive." She, of course, is apparently willing to drive thirty minutes just to church since she lives way out in Whispering Pines, so the thin disguise over her snobbery doesn't exactly ring true. "Maybe we can ask Flower Power if they'll order a few for us."

For some reason, the comment makes me think of Sophie. Something about the way Mrs. Derrow's nose wrinkles, just the tiniest bit, at the thought of the poorer half of town, the way Sophie's laugh had been more like anger than mirth on our run. I don't really want to know what she would say about gardening club. It makes me feel a little weird. Plus, I'm still so sore from our run yesterday that I feel sort of like I'm slowly dying.

They discuss the summer-fall transition for a little while before Beth says, "Mom, can we go?" without looking up from her phone.

"She is growing up so beautifully," Mrs. Partridge says faintly from her chair. I grin.

Soon, we say our goodbyes. I try not to let Mrs. Derrow's comment stick in my brain. It was just one of a thousand nasty little things she says. But I'm thinking about it, and thinking about the way Sophie's face changed when she looked at the train smoking through Rhizenstein, all the way home.

# CHAPTER 3

Peter always listens to the Christian rock radio station when he drives. It starts playing the moment he turns the key in the ignition. This is something that Mom and I have agreed to privately hate. It's not that she doesn't like Christian music. But she thinks Carrie Underwood making a million dollars for singing "Jesus, Take the Wheel" makes her a less sincere musician than, for example, Bach, who said that "Music's only purpose should be the glory of God and the recreation of the human spirit." Mom loves classical music, always plays NPR when she's cooking dinner, often lingers outside my bedroom door while I'm deep into practice mode.

But it was Christ that said "Judge not," so Mom doesn't judge, and I just try not to complain. After all, Peter is the one driving me to school to catch the cross-country bus at five thirty in the morning. I don't mention the music. Even if hearing these soupy opening violins and guitar strummings makes me feel like beating the car radio with my Team Manager clipboard until it fizzles out into blessed silence.

"It's just about time we thought about getting you your learner's permit, hmm, Emmy?" Peter asks.

I ignore the detested nickname in favor of pleading a pre-existing case. "I really want to, but Mom says not till I'm eighteen."

"Well... it's her decision..." he says, but his wistful look back at our house and his stifled yawn suggest real weakness in his feelings on that subject. I file that information away for later use. We don't speak for the rest of the ride. The streetlights are still on, the sky a gray blue that doesn't happen anywhere in nature except the early morning clouds.

The bus is already in front of the school when we pull up. I glance at my watch. 5:29. Excellent. "Thanks, Peter," I tell him, before I ditch him for the bus.

The team is clustered in the back rows, mostly asleep. Derrick is talking, though, obviously. "How long's the ride?" he asks me as soon as I enter.

"Hour forty-nine," I tell him. He groans, and pulls his hoodie over his face.

Harris walks onto the bus and nods at the driver. "Everyone have their dyads?" he asks. Sleepy murmurs of assent from everyone. I glance behind me, looking for Sophie. She and Jon are in the very back seat. He whispers something in her ear. She doesn't say anything back, but a little smile steals over her face and she rests her head against his shoulder.

"Emily," Harris says from right beside me. I jump. He's at his usual seat right behind the driver. "You have the racing bibs?"

"Yep," I say. Racing bibs are the numbers we'll pin to the runners so that the officials can identify the placement of the race. I heft the team duffel bag, running through the rest of my mental checklist as I walk down the aisle toward the runners. First aid kit. Timer, on my watch. Extra timer, in the duffel. Extra metal pieces to replace any broken spikes in people's racing shoes, in a little bag in my backpack. Four empty water bottles—I'll fill them at the course, or they would be too heavy to carry. An emergency bunch of bananas and salt tablets in case of cramps. An Ace bandage to wrap Derrick's hamstring, stuffed into the pocket of my jeans.

Once we head out onto the highway and my checklist is complete, I trace out the Seyton course on my clipboard. The map they sent Harris is a bad photocopy of last year's map, which itself was a bad photocopy. But unless they changed anything, it'll be the same as always: two long loops around a cornfield, with a downhill finish near a pumpkin patch. It's not an exciting race—no hills to see what people are really made of, no forest terrain. Just a grass path between a fence and a cornfield.

That makes it a good first meet. It's the first one we go to every year. I put away my clipboard and close my eyes against the highway going by outside. There's a reason I remember Seyton clearly. My very first meet freshman year was this very meet, at this very time. Which was also my last meet, as a competitive runner.

I was standing in the starting box with my other teammates, mostly girls who have since graduated. But Kari and Terri were both there for their first meet like me, along with Christa and Laura, who were sophomores at the time. My arms were covered in goosebumps and my teeth were chattering. I was shivering in my uniform, which was partially from the fifty-degree morning but also from embarrassment about the tight suit and real fear about whether I could finish the race before the boys' race started. The noise was unreal. It was just an early-season cross country meet, but we were surrounded by the starting boxes of the girls from forty other schools around Northeast Ohio. All around me were girls who seemed bigger, stronger, wiry, not at all afraid. Including my teammates. I felt like I was the only one freaking out. They were just all laughing about something Harris had said, which I hadn't been paying attention to because I was too busy trying not to throw up on my new uniform.

I ran. Not in the race. Before the starting gun could even go off, I ran back to the bus, which was locked. And I waited there for two hours while the girls' and boys' races both happened. All I could think about the whole time was my dad, wondering if he would have been disappointed in me. He had died close to three years ago at that point. My thoughts about him weren't as constant anymore, but when they came on, they came on strong.

On the bus ride back, I sat by myself, too embarrassed about my freak-out to talk to anyone. Harris came over and sat down in the seat across the aisle. "Wanna tell me what happened back there?" he asked.

I was still so scared of him then. "I'm sorry," I said, horrified to find myself fighting tears. "I don't think I can do this."

"Do what?"

"Race, or… I'm so bad at this. I don't want to be in the races." I couldn't explain it then. How running at my own pace felt right, but looking at the other girls and knowing I would be tested on how well I could do against them made me feel sick. I didn't want to be watched in a competition that I knew would crush me. I stared at the seat in front of me so he wouldn't see the tears dropping onto my lap. "I have to quit the team."

"Hey, hey," said Harris. I wondered if anyone else could hear him. "Emily, you're a fine runner, and a good teammate. We want you to be a part of this team."

My tears were spilling over. "But I can't race, I just can't."

Harris shrugged. "If you feel that way, then sure. But so what? There are plenty of other things to do on this team aside from racing. You can practice, there are team dinners, there's some administrative stuff I could use help with, some team management…"

This is the moment I remember the most clearly. I looked up at him, and he smiled. Harris isn't a big smiler, so it still stands out in my mind in this weird intense clarity. "Look," he said. "I just want to get kids running, and teach them how to be part of a team, all right? It's okay with me if you don't race."

That was two years ago. This is my third trip to Seyton. I don't even have my sneakers. I'm not here to race. I'm here for the team.

*

Four other buses are parked in the lot by the time we pull up. It'll be full by nine. Harris likes to show up at least an hour early, which the team moans and complains about. But a good warmup is a good warmup and a good warmup takes time. There's not a single cloud in the sky, and the cornfield looks like it's made of actual gold, which is quite bucolic, I must say. It smells the same here every year, wet damp plants in the morning dew.

Harris is off the bus first, then, me, with my clipboard and my duffel bag of supplies. Sophie's off next, yawning. She was asleep the whole ride, her head resting on Jon's shoulder. "Need a hand with any of that, Em?"

I smile. We've been talking during every practice, and I've been giving her every pointer I can think of. She's good—really good—at integrating them into her running form and pacing. Her mile repeats were within ten seconds of each other this week. Not sure when she got so nicknamey with me, but for some reason, it doesn't bother me. Em is casual, maybe even tough. Not like Emmy. "I have everything balanced," I tell her. "Um, you could maybe help with the tent if you feel like it."

She gives me an absurd salute, and follows Harris to the rear of the bus, where he retrieves his bike and the bag of tent poles and canvas. All the sleepy minions follow us to find somewhere to set up our tent.

Now that I don't run races anymore, I love cross country meets. While Jon and Anthony argue over whether the tent should face north or west and Rhys quietly sets it up himself, I hand out the racing bibs. I help Terri pin hers on her back, and tell Laura I'll help her replace a broken spike on her racing shoes, and remind myself internally to make sure that Derrick warms up for at least 30 minutes so he doesn't tear his hamstring again.

"Varsity women, you're up first," says Harris over the chatter of the now mostly-awake team. "Once you get your number go take a run. Not too hard, just get a little sweat going. Half mile out on the course and back."

Sophie changes from her flip-flops into her same battered pair of Nikes. I hope she has a decent pair of racing spikes to run in. The terrain isn't particularly unpredictable, but when the women's race starts at eight, the grass will still be slick with dew. Not something I want anyone running on with anything less than half-inchers.

"Emily," Derrick calls, "Wanna give us a hand with the tent?" He's finally helping Rhys, but it's really a four-person job, one for every pole.

It ends up taking nearly the entire time the varsity girls are gone to set up the tent. We've lost a screw, which means one of our poles won't stay in its expanded, locked position and frees up the team to make no fewer than four "screw" puns. It takes twenty minutes of searching, and two trips back to the bus, to find it (before it turns out that it was in Harris's fanny pack.)

"God, you guys are slow," Kari sees fit to inform us when she jogs in from her warm up. She usually goes fast, hard, and alone on warm-up runs, claiming that that's the best way to psyche herself up. I don't doubt it. Kari is a little crazy, and prone to dishing out trash talk. But there's a reason that she's been number two on our team since we were freshmen (and has her eye on Christa's number one spot after she graduates.)

Sophie and Christa follow behind, chatting amicably, and I don't know, after our run, part of me is kind of hoping Sophie will give Kari a run for her money. The rest of the varsity girls roll in just behind: Laura, Terri, Tess, and Emma (23:03, 23:31, 24 flat, 24:12 respectively). Julie, formerly number seven (and last) on varsity, sits somewhat glumly under the tent in her new JV uniform. Sophie's taken her spot in the top seven.

Every minute, the course is more crowded, louder, and more awake. The anticipation in the air grows and grows. I'm not even a part of it, and it still makes my stomach twist with nervous excitement.

Harris checks his watch and gets on his bike. His knees are bad enough now that he always brings the bicycle to get around at meets. "Time to start heading to the starting line." He turns to me. "Emily, once they're started, I'm going to need you to get the mile one splits. I'll be able to get out to mile two for those, and I should be able to get back to the finish line in time to get race times, but just in case, can you make sure you're there for the end of the race?"

I nod. I've already planned the route I'll take to get from mile one to the end of the race. One of the reasons cross-country is interesting is because courses tend to dip in and out of the woods, and so while some portions of the race are crowded with cheering spectators, other parts are just the runners and the trees. But it's usually easy to get from one mile marker to another if you don't have to obey a winding course. Although this has resulted in me scrambling and sliding down steep hills in the woods trying to beat the runners to the finish line so I can collect race times more than once.

I grab the garbage bag I use to collect peoples' warm-up sweat suits. The runners will wear them until the last possible moment before the race starts. A cold body at the starting line is a recipe for disaster.

The runners follow the biking Harris down the hill. I follow behind them, jogging to keep up, all the way to Pineridge's starting box. Illegible numbered lines on the ground designate where each school's team is supposed to stand at the start. "All right, women," Harris says to the runners. "The start is on an uphill and it's muddy out. But after that things flatten out quick, so give it your all on the start. Really get up on your toes. You'll have to get ahead of the pack right away," he adds, looking directly at Christa. "Trail narrows up fast. Emily, anything to add?"

"Um, the finish is on a downhill, so... go all out when you see the end." I shrug, noticing the little things I always do about these runners: Terri cracking her knuckles, Christa's deep, calming breaths, Kari's twitching quadriceps. Sophie bounces from one foot to the other, her arms crossed across her chest. Everyone else is wearing the team sweat suits we got last year. But Sophie wears a pair of faded flannel pajamas over her legs, and nothing at all over the thin racing top. She's gotta be cold. I mentally note that we need to reorder team gear.

"Pants off, then a strider." says Harris.

Almost immediately, a deluge of sweatpants descends upon me. I shove them into the bag as quickly as I can. Terri grins, balling hers up and tossing them into my arms. "Ah, yes, another year of the sport where an old man can order a bunch of teenage girls to take off their pants."

Harris rolls his eyes. "Strider, now."

The girls take off. Sophie turns to me, struggling to pull her pajama bottoms off over her shoes, her eyes wide and panicked. "Strider?"

"Just a short run, fifty yards or so, sprint form but about half-speed. Look, they're already finishing up." Sophie nods, hands me her pants, and goes after everyone at an all-out sprint to catch up. I smile, shake my head. She's still wearing her muddy Nikes.

"You're doing a good job with her," Harris says while everyone jogs back.

"She's really good already," I tell him.

"Sweatshirts off, then another strider," Harris announces. Jackets and sweatshirts come my way. I shove them all into the garbage bag, which, after many uses, does not smell awesome. I'll leave everything out in the tent later for everyone to collect.

The team does another strider, Christa in the lead, calm and composed, wearing long-sleeved spandex under her shirt, Kari all clenched energy. Sophie, her shoulders bare and her arms covered in goosebumps, looks completely miserable.

"You okay?" I ask her in a low voice when they're back.

She shrugs, tugging the end of her ponytail with one hand. "I'll be fine once we start running."

"This is dumb, but, um, just smile. Endorphins and all that." I try to smile at her myself, but seeing her nervous makes me feel nervous, too. Plus, someone in a Seyton jacket is walking to a step ladder about twenty meters in front of the starting line. The tension in the air rises.

She takes a breath, and smiles, but it doesn't quite reach her eyes. "Smile. Okay."

In that moment, I forget my own anxiety. All I want is for her to do well. I lean in close so nobody else hears. They're all focused on their final pre-race routines, anyway. Christa asks Harris a question, Laura says a prayer quietly to herself. "And... if you don't know how to pace yourself, just beat Kari," I whisper to her.

Sophie smiles again, a real one this time. "Got it, manager," she says.

"Good luck," I tell her, before following Harris away from the starting line. I wait next to him on his bicycle, among all the other coaches, watching the start. I hate the few seconds before the starting gun. It's loud, and it's sudden, and there's just so much buildup.

I squeeze my eyes shut for the bang, but then the runners are off, and it's like relief. Almost immediately, I lose sight of our runners in the crush of people. Our girls know how to start a race—and I'm hoping Sophie is following Kari, who has a great start.

"Mile one mark if you don't mind, Emily," Harris tells me before turning around on his bike to head toward mile two. I speed walk off toward mile one, course map tucked under my arm just in case I need it (I don't), bag of clothes slung over my shoulder. I deposit them in the tent on my way to the mile marker.

By the time I get there five minutes later, spectators are clustered at the mile marker: a few parents, some teammates, and many other coaches, all waiting for the runners to pass by. Jon, Rhys, and Derrick are among the small crowd, so I make a beeline for the three senior guys.

"How we lookin'?" Jon asks me, hands in the pockets of his sweatpants. Like Sophie, he's not wearing a shirt over his uniform one-piece. Sweat coats his face and arms. The day is already warm, and based on their race starting in (I check my watch) forty-seven minutes, the boys should be in the middle of their warmups.

"Pretty good," I say. "No one at this meet is going to be able to touch Christa. And if Kari has a solid race and Laura and Sophie do okay, women's team might have a shot at taking the meet."

Derrick grins. "Who's gonna finish first, Kari or Sophie?"

I shrug. "If the mile repeats this week were any judge, it'll be close."

"Ten bucks on Sophie," Derrick says. "Good thing, too. Kari's head could use a little deflating."

"I'm asking her to homecoming," Jon says, running a hand through his curly mop of blonde hair and grinning.

"Kari? Are you kidding?" Derrick asks.

"Sophie, duh."

"Already?" Rhys says, amusement cracking through his impassive face.

"Dude, that's like six weeks away. That's a huge tryhard move." Derrick adds. "Hey, Emily, do you have any water?"

I reach into my backpack for one of the squeeze water bottles, waiting to hear Jon's answer. "She's new," he says. "I bet she'll be glad for the offer. I'd want friends if I were her." He smiles. "Plus, did you see her in that unitard? Damn."

I roll my eyes.

"There's a lady present, Jon." Derrick laughs. "How long's it been?"

I glance at my watch. "Six eleven. Christa should be here any... there!" Christa's in the lead, to nobody's surprise, at least not among us Pineridge kids. She passes by with her gaze straight ahead, her footsteps carefully measured, her red running spikes hitting the ground in steady rhythm.

"Six thirteen, six fourteen," I call to her. "Go Christa!"

I love these moments. I don't feel like an awkward teenage girl. I feel like a manager. I'm focused on the team.

It's a good twenty seconds before anyone else passes. None of the next three runners are from Pineridge, but they come in as a pack of three right around six minutes forty. Kari comes gunning along at six forty-five, her face a fierce mask.

"She's booking it," says Derrick, his face appreciative. "Hell yeah."

"There's Sophie!" Jon calls, and gives the signature birdcall that he uses to cheer his teammates. It's loud enough that people around us turn and stare.

I click my stopwatch for her mile split without looking at the time. She looks like she's in okay shape breathing-wise, but her legs are slick and dirty, and her uniform wet and grassy all the way down the front. "It's slippery!" she gasps when she sees us.

"You're doing great, Sophie," I say, but she's already gone, pounding after Kari, disappearing around the bend. Only then do I look down at her mile one time. Six fifty-one. Good, but for someone in standard running shoes running her first ever competitive 5K? It's amazing.

We watch as the bulk of the runners begin to flow past, now in groups of five and six and ten. I mark down the rest of the mile times for the women's team—Laura, Terri, Tess, Emma, in that order—as soon as I catch sight of the green spandex uniforms in the crowd.

As soon as Emma disappears (7:39), I turn to the guys. "You should finish your warmup," I tell them, clicking through mile splits on my watch until I locate what I'm looking for: the time of day. "There's less than an hour before you're on the line." And I have to meet Harris at the finish line, not babysit senior boys. Plus I want to see the end of the race.

I end up getting waylaid by skinny but fast freshman Greg for a few minutes, who is in the middle of a minor freak-out due to the detached flapping sole of his racing spike right before the start of his first varsity race. Those shoes are a hand-me-down from his brother who graduated last year, and they are falling apart. Some quick duct-tape action on my part clears that right up, but I'm panting when I get to the finish line eighteen minutes into the race. I find the gentle downhill slope where the finish line is located, and spot Harris on top of his bike immediately. "How were the mile two times?" I ask.

"Solid. Christa's not trying to break any land-speed records, but I don't want her killing herself this early in the season. Sophie and Kari are neck in neck. Are the boys warming up?"

"Yup, even Derrick."

"There's Christa!" Harris says. He cheers her to the finish, his deep voice booming above the crowd, then turns to me. "Nineteen twenty."

I record her time on my clipboard. "I love that taking it easy for Christa is still sub-twenty," I say.

Harris nods. "I want her sub-eighteen by the end of the season. She could be top half, maybe top twenty at natties."

Nobody else at this meet is under twenty minutes, though one of the women from the host school Seyton comes close. Then I spot Sophie and Kari at the top of the hill, right next to each other.

This is big. It's down to the final sprint. Kari's mouth is twisted into a grimace. Sophie looks tired, but her long legs chew up the ground a lot faster. "Sophie's got this one," Harris says.

I agree, until she skids on the wet grass and hits the ground hard. By the time she scrambles back up to her feet, Kari has crossed the finish line at 20:27, a fifteen-second PR for her. Sophie jogs the last twenty feet and crosses at 20:33.

I glance at Harris. He's wearing an expression of uncharacteristic glee. "We need to get that girl into a pair of spikes," he says. "Emily, give me that clipboard and go make sure Sophie's okay, looks like that spill hurt."

I hand over the supplies and run off to find Sophie. But I find Kari first, sitting on the ground about fifty feet away from the finish line with her head between her knees. "You okay, Kari?" I ask, placing a hand on her back.

She ignores me. *Drama queen*, I think, but a fifteen second PR is seriously impressive. "Nice race," I tell her before dropping my other water bottle at her side and leaving to find Sophie.

The JV squad is probably off watching the rest of the women finish before they get started on their warmups. The men'll be off with Jon, who has some weird pre-race ritual for the varsity boys that I don't know anything about. When I finally find Sophie kneeling in the tent, she's alone, pawing through the first aid kit with shaking hands. "Hey," she says, glancing up when I come in.

"Here, let me do that," I say, partially so she'll stop destroying my carefully organized bandages, but also because she's a sad sight, her right arm crooked at an awkward angle, bleeding from the elbow.

She flops back, breathing hard, blades of grass plastered to her legs and arms. "Shit," she says, while I grab two Band-Aids and an antiseptic wipe. "That was really hard."

"You ran a great race," I tell her. "Harris is really happy."

She shrugs. "I slipped like four times on this stupid wet grass. I should have slowed down at the finish, I could tell I was going to fall. But..." She laughs a little, and lays back against the ground. "I wanted to beat Kari. Oh, well. Ashes to ashes."

"Can I see your elbow?" I ask. She raises it. "You need a pair of racing spikes," I tell her.

"I don't need anything fancy," she says.

"It's just so you don't slip. And they're way lighter than your shoes. Honestly, they'll take a good thirty seconds off your time. Maybe more, considering how much you fell today."

Sophie hisses when I wipe her elbow with the wipe. "I mean, it's no big deal. I'm happy with my time. What'd I get, like a twenty thirty? That's good, right?"

I unwrap the Band-Aids, and carefully arrange them over the scrape in an X. "Don't get me wrong, your time is fantastic," I tell her, and then lower my voice as I smooth out the bandages. "But Kari gave everything she had to beat you today. In spikes, she's not gonna be able to touch you."

Sophie grins, and sits up. "Maybe I'll have to find a pair then. Um, will you help me?"

I smile. "Of course."

All seven of the varsity boys show up then, finished with whatever Jon's thing is. "Shit! Did we miss the finish?" Derrick says when he sees us. "You won, right?" he asks Sophie.

"Kari got it," says Sophie.

"By approximately eight seconds," I point out. "Sophie would have gotten her if she hadn't slipped. She's going to dominate next time."

Jon turns on his full-force smile. "That's great, Sophie," he tells her. She smiles back. How can she not? Jon's sensitive-boy charm is adorable, in a strictly objective sense.

I roll my eyes, and get my trash bag ready for the boys' race.

# CHAPTER 4

I'm in Harris's room during fifth period. It's technically my lunch period, but I hate the noise and the fluorescent lights of the cafeteria. Harris has a study hall this period and pretty much all the cross-country kids who have lunch or a free period tend to crash it. Jon and Tevyn (a clarinetist in concert band and a sprinter with track in the spring) play Scrabble and loudly argue over whether "yar" is a word. Harris helps a couple of the non-cross country freshmen with their Bio 1 lab. Greg plays with Boris the snake.

I sit in the back of the room at a lab bench, eating the peanut butter and banana sandwich Mom made me this morning and poring over Harris's well-worn copy of *On the Origin of Species*. I'm completely absorbed, pausing every few minutes to copy passages into my notebook. Neither Mom nor Harris has brought up the "independent study" project again, but I've been taking it seriously. So help me if I want an education.

Because this stuff... it's exciting. Ever since we moved to Pineridge, ever since we started going to this new church, the feeling that I got in church— reverence, wonder, the sense of the world out there being larger and stranger than I could ever comprehend— all that's been gone. Until Biology. Until I started learning from Harris about a primordial soup, where little floating chunks of protein simply existed as functions of the temperature and different atoms colliding into molecules into animals... until one of them happened to be one that would replicate itself.

Because some of the questions I used to ask Mom might have better answers. "If God created everything, did He create Himself?" I used to ask.

Mom would look at me. "What do you think?" she would ask me back.

"I don't know, that's why I'm asking you," I asked once, petulantly.

She laughed, ruffled my hair. "I believe that there's an answer, but I think it's something that we can't understand. We're so, so tiny compared to God's might. It would be like asking an ant in our garden asking how the garden was created. It can't comprehend any of that, but it lives in the garden and it understands its little function, tiny but important. We're like ants. We might not be able to comprehend God, but He loves us anyway, and we can trust in that."

And that was comforting, but I'm still pushing for answers, and here, in these biology textbooks talking about how something can arise from nothing and life can arise from non-life by combining repeating replicating pieces... it's beautiful. In a different way. It's vast and dizzying, thinking of billions of years, of long points of stasis and punctuated equilibrium, but it's making me feel like there might be answers out there, somewhere.

So for my independent study, I'm writing a report about different theories of how the universe began. And rating them. Intelligent design is not currently winning.

"Hey, Harris."

I look up right away. Sophie's leaning in the doorway to the classroom, hair spilling out over her fading hooded sweatshirt. Jon stands up right away, leaving Tevyn to give himself 18 points for yar (triple word score, I guess), and goes to hug Sophie.

I look back down at my book, suddenly annoyed. I suppose, ostensibly, it's sort of cute. Jon really seems to like her, and it's not that hard to see why. Sophie's just... interesting, and not in a bad way. She dresses differently, she lets her hair run wild, she says exactly what she's thinking in words and phrases that nobody else at Pineridge uses. But it's mostly in the way she carries herself that she's unusual. There's just this sort of Pineridge...attitude she doesn't have. Little bad things don't seem to stick to her; she shrugs them off with a laugh and a joke.

Jon asked her to homecoming right after the race at Seyton, and according to popular rumor on the team, she had accepted. Much to the delight of the team's gossip mongers, they've even left after practice together a couple of times since in Sophie's battered Oldsmobile.

Ugh. Teenage romance always makes my skin crawl a tiny bit.

To my surprise, however, Sophie merely gives him quick hug before walking back to my lab bench. Jon follows her. "Hey, Em," she says, "I have a huge favor to ask you."

I place my pen inside the book so I don't lose my place, then close it. "Um, sure."

"I'm gonna go buy spikes after practice today. Harris said you could help me figure out what kind to buy." She shrugs, grinning. "I have no idea where I can buy them. Also, like, what they are."

"Oh. Running spikes are just ultra-ultra-light shoes with metal spikes coming out of the bottom. There are different lengths of spike depending on what you're running on. So you won't fall over four times in a race, even if it's slippery. But it's the weight that really changes the race. They're like six ounces whereas standard tennis shoes are close to a pound, which means you're using up significantly less ATP to take a step. Over three miles, it matters. A lot. Around a thousand pounds different." I take a deep breath, realizing I haven't breathed at all during that monologue.

"Damn, I don't think I've ever heard Emily talk that much," Jon says.

Sophie punches him gently in the arm, then looks back at me. "Why don't we wear them all the time?" she asked.

"It's a psychological boost during the race," Jon says sagely.

I suppress the urge to roll my eyes. Jon's an excellent runner but I wish he wouldn't show off when he doesn't know what he's talking about. "That and, more importantly, they have zero ankle support. You can hurt yourself in them if you're not careful. Wrong kind of spike, wrong kind of terrain... It's better to train in sneakers and save these for when you need to perform."

Sophie's face betrays her concern. "Okay, um, so where should I look?"

"Well, you could always go to Dick's or pretty much any athletic store. But there's this great running supply store out on 229 that'll have a really wide selection. It's a small business, everyone there really knows what they're doing."

"*You* seem to really know what you're doing," Sophie tells me. "I wish I could just take you along and have you point at the pair I should buy."

"Well, um, I could..." For some reason, I blush. "I could come along, if you need help finding the place."

Sophie smiles, then. It's remarkable how expressive her face is, how it changes from concern to confusion to amusement all within a moment.

"Good idea. Emily's really good at this stuff," Jon says. "I'd come along, but I have an environmental club thing tonight."

*Nobody invited you*, I think to myself. Then I wonder why I've been so irritated by Jon lately. He's a pretty good friend and a great lab partner.

"We'll just have to get along without you," Sophie said, ruffling his hair. I fiddle with the dust jacket of my book. "So, Em, are you free tonight after practice?" Sophie adds, turning to me. "If you're not, we could go another time. Seriously, thanks for helping me."

"No problem," I mumble, "um, today's fine." I realize I'm going to have to lie to Mom if I'm going to drive out there with just Sophie. Well, practice today is a quick one. I'll just tell Mom it ran late.

"Awesome." Sophie flashes me another one of her full-faced smiles. "You're amazing. Okay. I've gotta get back to my study hall, Thompson is a hardass. He thinks I'm in the bathroom. Anyway, I'll see you later."

"Bye, Sophie!" Jon waves.

"Bye," I mumble, and open my book back up.

\*

"Oh my God," Sophie says as we walk into the store.

I understand. Elite Runners, despite its humble appearance as a tiny store out in a strip mall on 229, is stuffed: with shoes, with gear, with customers in levels of fitness varying from the overweight guy in his fifties who's probably trying to whip himself into shape after a scare with his heart next to the lady whose calves look like they're carved from granite. Bruce Springsteen is playing on the speakers, and yes, it's *Born to Run*, which was also playing the last time I was here. I inhale deeply. I love the smell of rubber and plastic.

I haven't been here since last year, when Harris asked me to pick up some supplies for the team my freshman year. Mom waited on a bench outside while I wandered for what felt like hours, finally asking some questions of one of the salespeople once I had worked up the nerve. It's fun to think about how much more I know about running—about good form and lactic acid buildup and shoe variations and calf muscles—now versus then.

Sophie's eyes are big. She runs a hand through her hair, which is sweaty after practice. I'm tired, too. I ran with the team today. It was an easy one, a 5K in the nature preserve out by Black Lick, so I ran cleanup with Steve, one of the JV boys who is half injured with a light ankle sprain.

"Pretty cool, right?" I say to Sophie.

"Damn, this is a lot of stuff just for running," she says.

"Some of it's dumb, but some of it's actually useful," I tell her. We poke around for a few minutes, classifying things as dumb or useful. There are the special elastic shoelaces (dumb), the water bladders that fit in a backpack (expensive but useful), the neon rain jacket with reflective stripes and breathable fabric for running at night. "This is hideous," she says.

"That one's both dumb and useful," I say. "Gotta stay safe. Want to try some spikes on?" I ask.

We find a bench, empty except for some piled shoeboxes spilling out with tissue paper. I grab a size measurer. "I'm like a nine," Sophie tells me.

"I just want a super exact measurement. In centimeters. Length and width. Um, want to take off your shoes?"

She slips off her Nikes, which I have yet to see her not wearing. "How long have you been team manager?" Sophie asks as I take her warm foot in its green sock and press it onto the measuring pad.

"Um, since freshman year. I started out just running with the team but, um, well, Harris let me switch over to managing because of my... not liking races."

"That's dope," she says. "You're really good at it."

I duck my head, smiling behind my hair while I take the measurements. "I've learned a lot. Harris trusts me with more stuff now. And he knew me from freshman Bio, especially after all the stuff with my mom." Why can I not shut up? "Um, your foot's really narrow."

"What stuff with your Mom?" Sophie asks.

"Um... my family is really religious. And when my mom looked at my syllabus, she got kind of mad, and basically marched in and demanded that he teach intelligent design as an alternative theory." It still makes my face burn to think about it. "So he did, for, you know, thirty seconds. Same thing happened again this year for AP Bio. But it got my mom off his back, and surprisingly he does not hate me."

"He loves you," says Sophie.

I shrug, but internally I smile. I know it's true. The first test we took in freshman Bio, we had to write a short essay explaining the process of natural selection within the context of a non-human species. On the top of my crammed, unnecessarily detailed essay about the convergent evolution of cacti and euphorbias, he'd written *You really get it.* "Mostly he was just being nice. He liked me in class, and he knew I hadn't really made any friends outside the team, so he let me stick around even though I didn't want to race."

"I'm sure you had other friends," Sophie says as I take her other foot and flip the measuring pad around.

"I mean, I wasn't like a pariah or anything, I was just like... absurdly shy. I could barely talk to people." Her left foot's a little smaller than her right foot. "Still not great at it."

"You're talking to me," Sophie points out.

"Yeah, but you're..." I hesitate.

"What?" Her eyes are amused.

I look back down, take back the measuring device. "Different. I don't know. Like, different than most of the irritating people at Pineridge. It's fine." I stand up. "Um, I have you sized, I'm going to go grab a bunch of pairs for you to try on... you can wait here, I guess."

I don't look at her face, but I can hear the smile in her voice. "Sure thing."

I rush away. This whole making friends thing really leaves a lot of room for embarrassment. I find one of the employees and report Sophie's measurements, and he retrieves several boxes from the back closet. The whole time I'm waiting for him, I try to take deep breaths. Why am I so nervous? I think that it's just for once I want to be friends with someone.

The lanky guy comes back with five shoeboxes—one under each arm, three stacked in his hands. It's a bit more than I can manage, so he follows me back to Sophie so that I don't cause an avalanche of shoes. "Do you need any information on these?" he asks.

Sophie glances at me. I shake my head. "Nah, we're good," she tells him.

To my relief, he leaves. I sit beside her on the bench. "Okay, we've got a bunch of different brands and makes here. I know you like your Nikes, so here's a spike they make that I know Christa really likes..."

She takes one out of the tissue paper and rests it on her lap. "Hey Em," she says. "You want to come back to my house for dinner?"

"What?" I ask.

"After this. I mean... I need to thank you for all this somehow." She starts putting on the shoe, pausing when she realizes that the toe is stuffed with tissue paper.

"I mean, it's no big deal," I mumble, but I'm smiling. "Uh, sure, yeah, I'd like that. I just need to call my mom." *And lie to her a little.*

She pulls her phone from her pocket and tosses me hers. "Go for it," she says, unlacing the track spike. "I'll start trying on."

I walk her phone out of the store, dialing our house phone number from memory. Mom does have a cell phone that Peter bought her, but half the time she just leaves it plugged in on her nightstand.

She picks up on the third ring. "Samstone residence."

It's always weird that I live at the Samstone residence, even though I still have my dad's last name, Ferris. "Hey Mom,"

"Are you at practice, Emily?"

If I say I'm at Elite Runners she'll want to know how I got out here and I'll have to tell her I let Sophie drive me. "Um, yeah. My friend Sophie invited me to dinner at her house after... can I go?"

Mom pauses. "I haven't heard of her... who is she?"

"She's new, and... I don't know, Mom, she doesn't have a ton of friends yet." Which is also a lie, Sophie is well liked and whatever's going on between her and Jon is really skyrocketing her popularity, at least on the team.

"How are you getting there?"

"She lives close to school, we're walking." How far could she possibly live from the school? Although we're a good thirty minutes from Pineridge right now.

"Is she a good person?"

Mom. Always cuts to the core of things. But I'm not lying when I say, "Yeah, Mom. She's... she's great."

"Okay... well, make sure you say thank you to her parents. And call if you need a ride home."

By the time I get back inside, the floor around Sophie is strewn with tissue paper. She's got a Nike on her right foot and an Adidas on her left, with the Saucony box in her hands. "Help?" she says. "What am I supposed to be looking for?"

I laugh. "Let's see how those Adidas do on a jog around the store."

Sophie smiles. It's enough to make the guilt fade from my stomach.

\*

The sun hits us right in the eyes as Sophie takes the exit for Pineridge and goes west down Evergreen Street. She reaches over me so she can rummage through the glove compartment. "Want some sunglasses?" she asks.

"Sure," I say. She drops a pair in my lap, putting on her own. I perch them on my nose, over my regular glasses. They're bright orange plastic, with lenses so scratched that it's hard to see, but I like them anyway.

"My car's name is Patricia, by the way," says Sophie. "Patricia Junior, PJ for short."

I laugh. "Who was Patricia Senior?"

"She was my neighbor back in Rhizenstein," Sophie tells me. "She was old as fuck and not super nice but I mowed her shitty lawn for literally ten years. And then when her son put her in a—what do they call them? Old folks' homes?"

"Assisted living?"

"Yeah. She gave this to me. Well, she told her son to, anyway. And PJ's got like a couple hundred thousand miles on her but she's pretty great. And she came with all the Tears for Fears cassette tapes I could ask for, so that's always fun."

I don't even know what Sophie's talking about half the time, but I like listening to her anyway. We're in a part of Pineridge that I don't know very well, out near the edges. The developments are smaller here, the houses a little closer together, no garages. Sophie turns into one called Fox Run. "Home sweet home," she says, a little sarcastically.

"It looks nice," I tell her, although it looks pretty much like any other development in Pineridge, but smaller. Like my street, the houses follow a mirror image pattern, with the ones on the left reflecting the ones on the right other than the occasional touch of personalization—a yellow door, a garden gnome.

"It just really freaks me out how everything is exactly the same. Very Stepford. But like..." She pulls into a driveway, puts the car into park, pulls out the keys, leans back in her seat. "It was for the best. The high school wasn't gonna be a good fit for my brother, he was way too smart for that dump. And the cross-country team is better here. For lots of reasons." She smiles at me before she opens the door.

I follow her out of the car with a goofy grin.

We walk around the house and into the tiny backyard. Her family's one defection from uniformity is a large set of wind chimes hanging next to the back door. "We've already had our neighbors on the left complain about the wind chimes," Sophie informs me as she pulls out her keys and unlocks the door. "I mean, Christ, what are you even doing with your life."

She holds the door open for me, and I'm greeted by a blast of opera music. All of a sudden a little nervous, I walk inside. The entryway goes directly into the kitchen. Inside, the air is warm with stove heat and steam. On the table, glass jars and wine glasses stand in a crowd. A painting leans against the wall, not yet put up. A man is singing along to the aria at top volume and adding salt to a pot of boiling water.

"DAD," Sophie yells over the music. "CAN EMILY STAY FOR DINNER?"

Sophie's dad looks up, startled from his reverie, and reaches up to the top of the cabinets to turn down the stereo volume. "Sorry hon, what'd you say?"

He looks a lot like Sophie. Although technically, genetically speaking, I suppose Sophie looks a lot like him. He has the same lanky build and mild expression, although his skin is much darker and his hairline is receding. He gives me a friendly smile. I smile back. Something about this small kitchen, half unpacked but filled with music and good smells, feels warm and homelike to me in a way that I haven't felt in a long time.

"Dad, this is Emily," Sophie says. "She's the manager of our cross-country team and she just helped me buy dope racing spikes, so I figured we could have her over for dinner."

"Hi Emily," her dad says. "I'm Ed. Dinner's just roasted squash and pasta tonight, I got caught up with work. But you're more than welcome to join us if you like."

"I like squash," I say, having trouble getting enough volume into my voice.

But Ed hears me, and smiles. "Good."

"We waiting on Mom?" Sophie asks.

"She's on her way."

"Cool," says Sophie, and leads me out of the kitchen and into the living room. Behind us, the music volume goes up once again. The living room smells like fresh paint. It's full of boxes, most empty, some still taped shut and clearly full. The walls are beige, but one has several patches of color with paint cans stacked below, with different colors clearly being tested out. "Sorry, it's a work in progress," says Sophie.

"No, don't be sorry! I love your house," I say. "And your dad seems awesome."

"He's a big dork," says Sophie, but her voice is full of affection. "He's an illustrator, which is pretty cool but also not a huge source of cash, so my parents tend to do the whole gender role reversal thing in terms of breadwinning and housework."

"That's nice," I tell her. I remember when Mom worked part-time. Dad was always the one who worked full time, but it seemed like they shared more responsibilities. With Peter, she seems to have traveled back to the 1950's, and sometimes I can't tell if it makes her happy or sad. Both, maybe.

The front door opens, and a tiny white woman with graying red hair walks in. "Sophie," she says in a tired voice, and begins speaking an unintelligible string of words that I realize after a moment are in another language.

Sophie responds in English. "Yeah, I got them," she says. "They were like forty-five dollars. Mom, this is my friend Emily from cross country."

The woman sets her briefcase down and extends her hand to me. "Hi, Emily. I'm Katerina," she says, in a musical accent. "I apologize for the mess."

There are so many things I didn't expect about Sophie's mom that it takes me a second to respond. "It's totally fine," I tell her, and shake her hand. She's about an inch shorter than me, which makes her a good six inches shorter than Sophie. But they have the same handshake, cool and firm.

"Thank you for taking my daughter shopping," she says. "I was at total loss of what to get. Sophie says you're the expert."

I smile. She's mentioned me? "Not really."

Katerina glances into the kitchen, where the opera is really starting to reach a strong crescendo. "*Rusalka*, eh?" she says, affection in her voice, and leaves us and her briefcase in the entryway.

"My mom's from the Czech Republic," Sophie says, answering the question I haven't asked yet. "She does… something with data for drug companies. I don't really know what."

There's pounding on the stairs, and then a boy who's even lankier than Sophie comes down the stairs. "Dad, can you help me with my—?" He stops short when he sees me. "Oh. Hi."

I think I recognize him as one of the freshmen that just joined concert band. "Are you in orchestra?" I ask.

"Yeah."

"Double                                                                    bass?"

"Yeah. Violin?"

"Yeah." I smile.

"That's cool." He turns to Sophie. "Can you help me with my cabinets?"

"Why? I don't know how to do this Ikea shit," says Sophie. "And my friend is here."

"I don't mind," I tell her.

We follow her brother upstairs into a room that basically looks as though someone took an electronics workshop and exploded it into an otherwise empty bedroom with a bed made with military precision. A set of cabinets is assembled but diagonal in the center of the room. "Oh, you just need me to move them?" says Sophie. "Manual labor is totally my thing."

"Yes, oaf," says her brother. "Hang on, let me just get the last drawer in."

Sophie looks at me. "You wanna see something cool?"

I nod, then whisper, "Um, what's his name?"

She smiles. "This is Willie. He's a dumbass."

Willie salutes from the floor. I've seen Sophie do that too. Watching the two of them, it's like they speak to one another with an ease that I've never seen Sophie show at school.

"We're going on the roof," she says, and goes to the window on the other side of his bedroom. She opens it up. There's no screen. She swings one of her long legs, clad in her practice shorts, over the windowsill. "Coming, Em?" she asks.

I'm still standing in the doorway of the bedroom. "Um, yeah." Tentatively, I step around all the toolbox and rolls of paper on Willie's floor. I lean out the window, where Sophie has disappeared onto the roof. There's a ledge, extending maybe three feet out from the wall.

Sophie sits on the ledge, her legs dangling over the edge and a breeze blowing some of the stray curls that have escaped her ponytail across her face. "Come sit!" she says, patting the space beside her.

I hesitate. "Is it... you know, stable?"

"I promise." She grins, extending a hand. "Here, I'll help you balance."

I take her hand and climb out. Somehow, I scramble out of the window without killing either of us. The sun has mostly set, leaving the sky behind it a pinkish orange hue full of silvery cloud wisps and plane tracks. "Whoa," I say, reluctantly letting go of the reassuring grip of her hand and holding tight to the roof instead.

"Yeah. Willie really scored with the west-facing room." She leans back against the wall, kicking her legs idly against the side of the house. "Younger siblings, amiright? He says I can sit here whenever though."

"I've never been on a roof before," I tell her.

She looks at me incredulously for a long moment. "I bet you've never ridden a roller coaster or ice skated or eaten Sour Patch Kids to the point of sickness, either," she says. "You poor deprived child."

"I've ice skated," I say, a little defensively. My life might not be as interesting as Sophie's, but there's that, at least.

"I'm kidding, Em," she says, giving me a little shoulder punch. "Still. We should do some stupid shit sometime, you know? Get you off the straight and narrow."

I smile. "Maybe."

We sit there, enjoying the sunset, until Willie pokes his head out to request Sophie's help moving the drawers. I follow her back inside, leaving the riot of colors in the sky behind.

# CHAPTER 5

"Nineteen forty-one," Harris booms, clicking his timer as Sophie crosses the finish line.

"Nineteen forty-one," I echo. A big grin spreads over my face as I record her time on my clipboard. Another female runner under twenty minutes and it's only the second meet of the season. This is too good to be true.

Jon leans over the rope of flags marking the path to the finish line and lets out a whoop. "All right, Sophie!" he calls.

She's about twenty yards away, other finishers and spectators all around her doing their own thing. She starts to bend over, the hunch of someone with ragged breath, but stops herself and stands up straight. She's learning. Oxygen flows much better in that position. She raises her hands, laces her fingers behind her head. When she hears Jon, she glances over, a tired smile crossing her face.

We're at the Zachary Taylor high school meet, much closer to home than the previous week's. Sophie's dad and brother are here. Her dad waves at me and smiles broadly when he sees me as he walks past, which makes me feel a probably disproportionate level of happiness. Willie stops by to chat about band. Maybe we'll become friends as well.

The varsity women's race—this time, the last race of the day—is wrapping up now. Sophie is wearing her new turquoise spikes and has just PRed by a good fifty seconds, an insane drop in time.

Jon and I watch the finish together. Greg, the skinny freshman who is number seven on varsity and has taken to following Jon around like a little dog, is with us. He cranes his head at the next wave of women sprinting toward the finish line. "Any sign of Kari?" he asks.

"Not yet," I reply. Sophie's walking away from the finish line. She flops down on the grass and splays out her legs, wincing as she leans over them to stretch her hamstrings. "She was with Sophie at mile one but I think she probably crashed."

"Speak of the devil," says Greg as Kari crests the hill, her face contorted with effort. Cross country isn't exactly a glamorous sport. Kari is covered in a sheen of sweat and from the pained expression on her face, it looks like she's either chafing or about to throw up.

"Twenty fifty!" Harris calls as Kari crosses the line. I mark it down, then look to Jon to comment. But he's already wandered over to Sophie and sat down on the ground next to her. Their heads are bent close together as he speaks. She smiles. I wish I knew what he was saying.

"Tessa, twenty-one seventeen!"

"Twenty-one seventeen," I mumble to myself, going back to what I know how to do.

\*

Tess is our last teammate to the finish, in a rough race with a tweaky hamstring. After, we all help pack up the tent while Harris catches up with a couple of coaches from Jefferson High, the second-best school from our district (after Pineridge). I'm in the tent, sorting through the various warm-up pants people had thrown at me earlier so I can redistribute them. Then I hear angry voices a little way from the tent. "...your problem?" Sophie asks, her normally pleasant voice immediately recognizable.

I leave my folding and peer around the corner of the tent. Kari and Sophie stand across from one other about fifteen feet away, down the hill. Sophie's arms are crossed across her chest and she looks tight, defensive. Kari leans in, shaking her head. "Obviously, you. You think you're so good with your stupid spikes, but you don't know the first thing about cross country. So, you better watch out, because I race to win."

Weirdly, Sophie just laughs. "Fuck you," she says, in a way that's light, almost casual. Kari's face grows murderous.

Before I even know what I'm doing, I'm rushing over. "Hey," I say breathlessly, before I can lose my nerve.

Sophie makes a sudden move toward Kari, who flinches. I do, too. For a second, I really think Sophie is going to hit her. After all, she's from Rhizenstein. Then I wonder when I officially became a Pineridge kid, because that was a Pineridge thought.

Sophie just raises her eyebrows at Kari's reaction. "Everything's cool, right, Kari?"

Kari glowers, thinks about saying something, doesn't. She walks away. Sophie turns to me. Now that she's alone, I see the stress of the interaction in her face, the relief of Kari's departure. It strikes a chord in me. "Sorry," she says. "That was not super mature of me."

I frown. "Seems like she was also not being a paragon of maturity."

Sophie laughs, sitting on the ground, stretching out one of her legs. "Nah, she's just competitive, it's cool. But aren't we supposed to be on the same team?"

A little hesitantly, I sit beside her. "Yeah, running can be really isolating if you don't have support."

"Yeah, and don't get me wrong, I like running, and I like running my best. But... *I race to win*. Like, who the fuck are you kidding? Winning is great and I like to win. But that's not why I race."

I tug at a tuft of grass. "Why do you run?" I ask. This stupid sport where you're constantly blistering, in pain, and heaving a breath that you think will be your last... it has its zealots. And I like knowing what makes them tick.

Sophie stops stretching, leans back on her elbows, looks me in the eyes. She smiles. "I feel like I can actually hear myself think, you know? Even if I'm tired or if I'm trying to catch someone, it's like... it's just me in here, you know?" She taps her head.

I'm nodding along.

"I just don't worry about anything else, and I feel… I just feel the most like me." She laughs shortly, lies all the way down on the ground and stretches one of her legs up toward the sky to stretch her hamstring. "Kinda dumb, but whatever."

"No!" I reply, way more emphatically than I mean to. "I completely get that. I mean, I feel that way with running sometimes, too. Or violin."

Sophie smiles again. "Willie says you're sweet at violin."

I flush. They've talked about me? It's strange to think about. "I'm fine, I guess."

"I want to hear you play sometime," she says.

I smile, staring down at the ground, the little piece of grass I've torn to shreds.

"Emily! Sophie! We're heading out!" Harris calls from the tent. I stand up, and when Sophie extends her hands, pull her to her feet. "Nice job today," I tell her a little shyly. "Um, if Kari thinks she has a shot at beating you this season she's a little delusional."

Sophie laughs. "I'll hold you to that," she says. And we walk back up the hill to our team.

*

The season continues in a rush of crisp fall days and smelly, sweaty socks. September is gone before I can even blink, and October feels like it's moving at an even faster pace. Junior year is my busiest year to date. I spend every lunch poring over yet another book from Harris's shelf, spend every band trying to relax my mind enough to play my best. By the time I come home from cross country practice, eat dinner with Mom and Peter and Rachel, practice violin, and tackle homework, it's usually close to midnight.

But I feel energized, excited by it all. The team is incredible this year. Of course, I'm proudest of Sophie, since we've worked hard together and she's running sub-twenty 5K's like it's her job. She sets her sights on sub-nineteen by the end of the season, which might even slot her a spot at nationals. Jon is within one or two seconds of his PR at most meets, though he has yet to crack it. Christa is in the "pushing it" part of her season, icing her legs after every meet. By this point, Kari has mostly made peace with her God that she's number three this season, though I imagine that the fact that both Christa and Sophie are seniors is of some comfort to her. But even aside from running, the team feels special this year. Every practice, I laugh so hard my stomach hurts at least once. I don't know if it's just that I feel more ownership over the team or just know everyone better by now, but it feels so good to be part of a community.

And then there are Sundays. Now that we have a meet every Saturday, my Sundays are for Sophie. I catch a ride with Peter back to Wisteria Manors every Sunday instead of sticking with Mom and Aunt Gretchen for gardening club, then I meet Sophie for a recovery run. We'll go long and slow, giving her muscles and brain a chance to relax and reset after the stress of a meet. I take her to my favorite trails that are within jogging distance of Wisteria Manors. After a few weeks, I tell her that I'm not supposed to drive with other teenagers and swear her to Teen Driver Secrecy. She smiles, and doesn't make fun of me, and we start driving to some of the further trails that she and her dad used to run closer to the other side of town. My fastest pace is a good match for her recovery pace, so she's making me into a stronger runner, too. It feels good to be in sync with someone, feet pounding the trails, foggy breaths coming side by side.

The end of the season sneaks up on me. There are only two meets left: district finals, and states. (Technically, nationals too, but since usually only Christa qualifies I've never gone before.)

It's the last week of October, and I can't believe how fast it's gone. It's Friday. I'm in concert band, thinking about all this as I take my time putting my violin away. I didn't get to practice as much as I wanted this week, and it showed in my playing today. We've been working on our pieces for the holiday concert, which is in Mid-December. It always sneaks up on me after cross country ends.

The stage is empty, everyone else having left. I should leave for practice soon, but I take this moment to sit and hum the piece, my eyes closed, going back over a place where my fingers had slipped and played the wrong note. I'll get it right next time, but I need to practice.

There's a creak behind me. I turn around. Rhys looms over me.

Not alone after all. I jump. "Oh my gosh!"

"Sorry, sorry." Rhys flushes. "I was going to say hi but I—sorry. Do you want to walk over to practice together? We're at the track today."

"Sure," I say.

He's already got his stuff all packed up and the drum set put away, which is weird, but okay. We walk out of the auditorium together, through the linoleum hallways filled with trophy cases at the front of the school. As expected, he says nothing, and neither do I.

Until we leave the school. "Hey, so, are you going to homecoming tonight?" he asks.

"Um...." My stomach drops. "I, uh, no."

"Me either." Rhys stares straight ahead, taking such long fast steps with his long legs that I'm having a little trouble keeping up. "But, uh, Jon and Sophie were going, and they were talking to me, and saying that maybe it would be fun if, uh, we went too. Like, with them. As friends."

"Rhys, can we slow down?"

"Oh!" He stops in his tracks. "Sorry, my bad."

We're headed toward the football stadium. Today will be a typical pre-meet practice: Harris has the team run six 200s, not at top speed, but in top form. A quick, short, muscle-loosening practice, getting people ready for the next morning.

"I, um… I'm not really allowed to go to homecoming," I say. Which isn't true in the technical sense—in that I've never asked—though I know what the answer would be. Also, it sounds a little bit terrifying. It's a little nice to have the Strict Mother Excuse in this moment. Though hanging out with Jon and Sophie would be fun.

"Oh," says Rhys. He nods, way too wholeheartedly. It's kind of funny to see him so uncomfortable. This is probably the most words we've exchanged this year. "That's fine. I don't really want to go. 'Cause of the meet."

"Yeah, definitely," I say. Part of me feels a little tiny bit stung. He didn't really want to go? But I am flattered that it meant that much to Sophie and Jon, that they were trying to persuade their most introverted friends to come to the most extroverted of events.

The rest of the walk feels… awkward. Even more awkward than usual. The October wind whips past us, and I put my hands into my sweatshirt pockets. There's rain in the forecast.

Once everyone is dressed for practice and just finishing their warm-up jogs, our coach brings everyone in for some classic Harris tough talk. "I don't want any of you out late tonight, carousing and partying and doing whatever it is you teenagers are going to be doing after this dance," he says gruffly. "You eat a good dinner, you go to your dance, which ends at 10—yes, I did check—have a fun time, then go home and go to sleep. Tomorrow is important."

Tomorrow is important indeed. The state qualifier is at Jefferson High School. Our runners can qualify in two ways: as individuals, by placing in the top ten, or Harris's preferred method, as a team. The top teams in men's' and women's bring all seven of their varsity runners to states, regardless of individual placement. We're in a good position to win the team meets, since our depth is so strong—especially on the women's side.

I'm busy with the team tent bag, doing some much needed maintenance on everyone's racing spikes, replacing the old crushed and dirt-caked ones with shiny and sharp new ones. I have one eye on the group lining up for their first strider, wondering who will obey the edict of Harris. Christa, who is decked out fully in a sweat suit, to keep her muscles warm in the cold air, definitely will. She's not going to homecoming. The meet is too important to her. Kari is going, but I hear her talking to Rhys about her plans to leave by 9. Derrick stands next to her, laughing at something Jon says. He's a total loose cannon. He's going to be out late. He and Jon would get up to some mischief for sure. Too bad Rhys isn't going, but at least that might help the varsity guys out. Tess and Emma, the gigglers, will probably be out later than they should, but they're always consistent. They're sophomores anyway, and not as likely to be wild tonight.

I study Sophie, rocking back and forth on her feet as she waits for Harris to blow the whistle. She cares about this meet. But she's from Rhizenstein. I don't know. I have a bad feeling. I almost think about going, keeping an eye on her. But the thought makes my stomach crawl with nerves.

Harris blows the whistle, and they take off for strider number one.

*

Twenty minutes later, the practice is over. It really is a quick one. "Jefferson's a good hour away!" Harris shouts. "Be in front of school at six on the dot— no. Quarter of six. We will, I repeat, will, leave without you. Varsity boys race at eight!"

The practice disperses with grumbles and moans. I'm on my hands and knees, gathering the rusted-out spike pieces that I've tossed over my shoulder and now must retrieve, when I see Sophie's familiar Nikes in front of me. I look up and smile. She's blocking the sun, so I can hardly see her face, but when she crouches down in front of me she's smiling too. "Need any help?"

I nod. "You should probably be getting ready for the dance."

"We're not leaving till seven." She sits down beside me and starts gathering the little metal pieces out of the turf and dropping them into her palm. "All I need to do is shower and calm down my hair a bit."

I look up from the turf and over at her body. She's dressed in running shorts and an old T-shirt (not nearly warm enough for the fall weather, my internal control freak says), and she looks fabulous. She could probably show up to the dance like this and everyone would fall all over her.

"So, Rhys couldn't convince you to go?" she asks, crawling over to me and dropping a little shower of metal spikes into my hands. I take them, our fingers brushing as she drops them into my palm. "I figured, maybe, you and he made sense."

I blush. "I don't think so."

"Nah?"

I shrug, putting them into my pocket. These ones are done, I need to throw them away, but it seems disrespectful to leave them out in the field. "It's just not really my favorite kind of thing."

"That's cool, that's cool," she says, perching on her heels, her hands resting on her knees. She smiles. "I was hoping you'd have a last-minute change of heart. It'd be a lot more fun if you were there."

I snort. *Fun* is probably in the bottom ten adjectives that could possibly be used to describe me. "I'm terrible at this kind of thing. It'll be better with Jon."

She shrugs. "Whatever you say, manager. Anyway, we'll hang out with Derrick and Terri."

That might spell trouble. "Just... try not to go too crazy tonight or whatever," I tell her, the wind blowing my hair into my face. "I mean, you're my dyad. We'll need you tomorrow."

"No worries, chica." She gives me a salute, the same ridiculous, overexaggerated gesture I've seen her make at least once per practice. "I better head out. See you bright and early!"

Alone in the stadium (except for Harris doing bike laps while he waits for me to finish packing the bag), I try to take her advice. No worries. It's almost the end of the season. Everything will be okay.

*

As it turns out, I maybe should have worried more.

I sense something amiss as soon as Peter, yawning spectacularly, drops me off once again at school the next morning. "This is the last meet you need a ride to, right?" he asks.

We take a team bus to an overnight for states, so yes. "Until track," I tell him.

"Until track," he sighs.

Harris stands by the front stairs of the school, checking off the names of the runners as they arrive. Various members of the team huddle in small groups, at different levels of tiredness. Christa leans against the wall, headphoned up, focused and ready. About half the team has arrived.

I glance at my watch. 5:57. We're in pretty good shape, all things considered. Automatically, I run through the lists of varsity runners in my mind by PR, the way I always do— if any of them miss this meet, we've got almost no chance of qualifying as a team for states.

Christa, check. Sophie, not here yet. Kari, Julie, yes. Terri, no. Tessa, Emma, yes. Then the guys. Jon, no, which is weird. Rhys, yes. Derrick, of course not, but he's always five minutes late. Steve and Bender, just arriving, Daniel, just arriving, Greg, yes.

A flood of people usually arrives two minutes late. I decide not to worry yet about the no-shows and instead sit down near Kari, Tess, and Emma. They all glance up at me. I realize they've stopped whispering now that I'm next to them.

I busy myself in my bag, very visibly not paying attention so that they won't think I'm eavesdropping, which I absolutely am. But it doesn't seem to be particularly exciting—who did what and drank which and said what to whom.

At least, until I hear Sophie's name. Curious, I perk up my ears. "...totally led Jon on, you know?" Kari says, her voice barely a hiss. "And he took it really, really hard."

"Aww," Emma says, much louder. Bless her heart, she is not great with secrecy. "A lot of girls wanted to go with him too."

"Right? Like, everyone on the team is going to be so pissed at her. Jon freaking loved her, God knows why—" Kari, realizing her voice is growing a little loud, reduces it to a more cautious volume. I busily untie and retie my shoe in an effort to appear uninterested. "And she was apparently just like, 'oh, I'm actually not feeling this', and..."

They close their circle. I can't make out their words anymore without leaning in too close. A bad, ugly feeling begins to settle across my stomach, the way it usually does when I sense conflict brewing.

Sophie's not interested in Jon after all. Boy, I misread that one. And apparently Jon did too, though hindsight bias is making things a little clearer. I remember how eager she was to try to have me come yesterday. Did she just want a safety net?

I feel bad that I wasn't there for that.

When I look away from the gossipers, I spot Jon, arriving with Derrick. They both look awful. But while Derrick merely looks hung over, which frankly is not an unfamiliar sight, Jon looks miserable. Or am I reading too much into his drawn face and the dark circles under his eyes? I can't help but feel a little sorry for him, although the way these girls are talking like Sophie owed him something makes me a little resentful. They certainly had been—flirting, or whatever, God, I hate that word—or at least Jon had. Maybe he just mistook Sophie's friendliness as mating plumage?

I remind myself to make them both hydrate well before the meet.

Someone plops down beside me on the stairs. Before I even look, I know it's Sophie. "Hi," she says, a slight edge in her voice.

Kari abruptly stands up and walks over to Jon. I see her murmur "You okay?" to him as she lays a hand on his arm. He tears his gaze away from Sophie to mumble something inaudible in response.

Yikes. I peer more closely at Sophie. She, too, looks awful, tired and wan. I realize I can't be mad at her, even if the rest of the team knows more about what happened. Whether she'd hurt Jon's feelings or merely his pride is up for debate, but either way, he'll get over it. There's no way Sophie would hurt him on purpose. I know that, know it in my stomach, like my bacterial gut flora are talking directly to me.

"Late night?" I ask her finally, when she doesn't say anything.

She shuts her eyes and lets out a short, harsh laugh. "A bit, yeah. I have a headache."

I shake my head, offering her my water bottle. "Hydrate, then, you goose. Today's really important."

"Yeah." She takes it gratefully. "Thanks. It was dumb to go out last night."

"Probably," I agree. Tact's never been my strong suit. "Looks like most people are in a similar state, though."

Sophie casts her eyes around the bedraggled team as she takes a long pull of water. "We're all a little worse for the wear." Her eyes trail over to Jon. She bites her lip.

"What happened last night, Soph?" I whisper.

She waves her hand vaguely. "Just... you know. Some miscommunication."

I want to press her for details, but Harris's voice interrupts my train of thought. "We got everyone and it's only 6:11!" he booms. "Sound enough work, everyone. Get on the bus!"

We all shuffle on. I file into a window seat and Sophie slides in beside me. I'm startled. Usually, she sits in the back near Jon, Rhys, and Terri. When I glance back there, Kari's taken her place. A wide range of stares come our way, from the despondent, spacey gaze of Jon to the evil eye of Kari. It's not much of a surprise she sat here when that's the alternative.

Feeling a surge of what I can only describe as protectiveness, I look back at Sophie. Her eyes are shut and her arms are crossed tightly across her chest, as though she's asleep. I know she's not, though. The muscles in her face are tense. "You okay?" I ask.

She turns her head to face me, cracking one eye open against the daylight growing brighter every minute. "Everyone seems so mad at me," she replies softly, and for the first time since I've met her, I hear some hurt in her voice.

"Don't worry about it," I tell her, filling my voice with confidence that I don't feel. "Jon has a short attention span, and so does the team. I bet no one will even care by the end of the day."

She opens her other eye and grins wryly at me. "You're a terrible liar, Em."

I shrug. "Just presenting the best-case scenario."

"What's the worst-case scenario?"

"Um, we all die in a horrific bus accident," I reply.

Sophie laughs. "I find that thought very comforting," she says, and bites back a yawn.

"You should take a nap," I tell her, even though I kind of want to keep talking.

"Excellent idea." She closes her eyes again. "Thank you, Em."

I don't say anything, but I'm glad when her face relaxes.

*

The men's meet is first, on the windiest day of the year so far. By the end of it, Harris is murmuring low curses under his breath. I'm shivering next to him in the wind when the first runner, Andrew Jorgenson from Cedar Valley, crosses the finish line. Normally, that would be Jon coming in first, but he was dogging it badly at mile two. "That might be it," says Harris, rubbing his hand across his jaw. District qualifiers for states is a small meet, with only runners from the five schools in our district. Individual placement matters.

Pineridge has won the team meets for both men and women for the last six years. If we can't pull this one out, Harris might have his second heart attack. I stand next to him, not praying exactly, but running through the numbers in my head, trying to calculate where our runners will need to place to make up for not getting first.

And then rounding the corner toward the finish line like a green flash of hope comes—not Jon, but Rhys, his face a grim slash of determination. Derrick is right behind him, wheezing, but running harder than I've ever seen him at the finish. They pass the finish line at 16:01 (Rhys) and 16:06 (Derrick), in second and third place.

After crossing the finish line, Rhys slows to a jog, then a walk, lacing his hands behind his head. He glances back at the clock and smiles, closing his eyes. It's a huge PR for him—the same as Jon's, in fact. Derrick, on the other hand, continues sprinting all the way to the nearest trash can, where he proceeds to vomit spectacularly. I wince, looking back at my sheet. I'm not just recording times, here, I'm calculating team scores in the margin at the top. The top five runners from each team receive the number of points that their placement indicates. Andrew Jorgenson gets one point for his team, Rhys and Derrick have given us two and three so far. The lowest score at the meet wins.

I watch the next finishers come in; they're coming faster now, so that it's hard to keep track. But Bender comes in with a PR for himself, too, with Daniel just behind in seventh place and tenth place respectively.

Two other runners from Cedar Valley has come in at this point. "We might make it," I tell Harris.

"Where the hell is Jon?" he asks.

In the end, Jon doesn't even score for us. He comes in as our last varsity runner, with his worst competitive 5K since sophomore year, a 19:21. He finishes, limping, holding his side. It's a pretty pathetic sight. "What do you think?" our coach asks me.

"I think we eked it out, Harris." I'm pretty sure that our top five came in before Cedar Valley's top five. Greg beat their own lanky freshman in a tight sprint at the end. But if I missed any purple uniforms in the big rush to the finish around 17:30, then we might be hosed.

Harris sighs. "Definitely made it a nail biter. Women's should go more smoothly."

I watch Jon, who sullenly walks over to Rhys. Rhys gives him a sympathy fist bump, mentioning nothing about his own excellent results. This is why I like Rhys. I wonder for a second if I should have gone to homecoming with him after all. But it just would have made things worse, probably. He pretty much saved the meet. And anyway, it didn't feel right.

I watch the wind blow Jon's hair across his red, red face.

*

Harris is right. The women's meet goes much more smoothly. Christa wins handily with an 18:30 on the dot; there's only one girl faster than her in the entire state. Can't do much about a prodigy.

And even though there are a couple non-Pineridge women in the top ten who will race at states as individuals, no other school in our district can match our women's team for depth. Christa, Sophie, Kari, and Laura represent four out of the top ten, more or less locking us in as the team champions.

Sophie doesn't PR, but she runs an interesting race against a girl from Jefferson named Clara Dunham. Clara beats her out for third place by a nose, after trailing behind her the entire run. It's a psychological race I don't expect Sophie to win, not on too little sleep and too much drama.

But as they're crossing the finish line, I overhear Harris talking to the Jefferson coach. "That Dunham girl is fast," he says.

The other coach nods. Harris and other male coaches have a real way with each other, all gruff nods and manly harrumphs. "Your girl is fast, too. What's her PR?"

"Emily?"

Harris always knows when I'm eavesdropping. "19:11," I say, not bothering to check my clipboard.

The other coach, who's probably twenty years younger than Harris, laughs. "Clara's is 19:10. Looks like we'll see you at states."

Harris can't resist a little trash talk. "Better get ready. Sophie's coming for her."

The rest of the women finish as normal, other than Terri, who was Derrick's date to homecoming and was at the same party as he and Jon and Sophie. Oof. Kari PR's, though, which is good for her mentally, especially now that she is apparently Jon's self-designated emotional guardian. She's always had a crush on him, or at least, that's the rumor. It's just like her to use this moment of vulnerability to move in. Like an autoimmune disease. We're covering cell bio in Harris's class right now.

During the awards, we find out that we indeed had a team victory on both the men's' and women's sides. The men beat Cedar Valley by exactly one point, so skinny little freshman Greg who netted us that one extra place gets a giant, roughhousing hug from the whole men's' team, especially Jon. That's pretty much the high point of the day, though. As we pack up the tent to drive home, everyone's horrible mood bubbles up to the surface. Everyone is exhausted, crabby, and wind burned, and a few raindrops are just starting to fall. It's a classic late October day: brown leaves gusting around, a storm brewing in the distance of the bruise-blue sky. People are bickering over screws and tarps, trying to find personal effects that have blown further away from where they set them down.

I help Terri remove her number, accidentally jabbing her with a safety pin when Tess drops the tent poles behind me with a clatter. "Emily, you stupid bitch," Terri snaps.

I look at her, startled.

She bursts into tears and throws her arms around my neck. "I'm so sorry, Emily, I just ran such a bad race," she sobs into my shoulder. "You're not stupid, and I'm the bitch."

I have no protocol for this. I pat her gingerly on the back. "Um…"

Derrick, who I made sit down and not move until he finished a full bottle of Gatorade, grins at me as he takes her by the arm. "Long night," he says, before wrapping an arm around her shoulder and walking away with her.

"I can tell." Terri's normally so chill. This is why I don't want anything to do with any of this drama.

But in terms of drama, the stuff with Sophie is what worries me the most. People aren't saying anything outright nasty to her, but the way that people are going out of their way to treat Jon with kid gloves suggests that sides are being taken. And Kari keeps sneaking in snide comments about her every so often while giving her an obvious cold shoulder face-to-face. During the awards, she stands next to Jon, who is quite upset about his horrible race. "It's okay, Jon Jon," she said, "It's definitely not your fault you had a rough race." Which she follows up by shooting daggers with her eyes at Sophie, who to my infinite admiration, doesn't seem to let it bother her.

But by the time we get on the bus ride home and sit down a safe twenty rows away from Kari, Sophie is overwrought and clearly upset. "I hate this," she tells me as she pulls her Rhizenstein track hoodie over her head. "Like, fuck me if any of this is Kari's business."

Hesitantly, I touch her shoulder. "It'll blow over. And nobody has anything real to complain about. I mean, Jon'll still be running at states."

"Yeah, I just… I don't know. Jon and I hooked up a couple times the last couple weeks but I didn't know he wanted it to be this whole thing, and I just… when I told him, he took it badly." She rolls her eyes. "I feel bad. But this is hella drama. I miss Rhizenstein."

I'm startled by her bluntness. "That's what happened?"

"Yeah." She glances at me, and I realize that she's maybe close to tears. It's startling. "Em, do you think that's weird? I don't want you of all people to think I'm some sort of slut, or whatever. I just... didn't like him like that after all."

"No, I..." How can I explain? I suspected all along that Sophie and Jon had something going on. Why does it bother me so much to find out they did? I mean, I've never dated, and Mom has really drilled the whole 'no dating until you're eighteen, sex is sacred and not before marriage' thing into me. "I don't know. This is sort of... beyond my area of expertise."

Sophie laughs, wiping her eyes. "Me too, maybe."

"I don't think you're a... a slut, if that's any consolation," I tell her quietly, the word feeling foreign in my mouth. "I mean, looking at the situation from a logical perspective, it doesn't seem like you've done anything dishonest."

"Logical perspective, that's how you're gonna approach this, huh?"

"It's the only way I know how." I meet her gaze, and then I have to look away. Her eyes are dark, like space. They make me think of the universe.

She sighs. "I'm glad you go to this school, Em."

I smile quietly down at my lap.

# CHAPTER 6

It's November 1st, a Monday, the day after Halloween. Rachel bounces off the walls of the kitchen on a post-Halloween sugar high while Mom does the dishes after dinner, her sleeves rolled up to her elbows. I spent Halloween in our family room working on an English paper. I'm so very glamorous. Today, I skipped practice to study for precalc. The decision almost killed me this close to states. They're this coming weekend.

I'm at the kitchen table pawing through my notes about simplifying trig identities when I find the permission slip for attending the Ohio State High School Cross Country Championships in my folder. An unusual defection from organization on my part; normally that should have gone into my cross-country clipboard. I really have been busy. "Hey Mom," I say. "Can you sign my form?"

"What is it?" she asks. Her hands are soapy, so I cross the kitchen and hold it in front of her. Her face tightens the tiniest bit as she reads the form. "An overnight?" she says.

"States are outside Cincinnati this year," I tell her. "We'll leave Friday after school and be back by Saturday evening."

Mom turns back to the dishes. "That's a long way away."

Annoyance creeps into my body, tensing my muscles. Mom gets so nervous when she doesn't know where I am or if I'm safe, and yes, I think it's from a place of having lost Dad and wanting to protect me. She didn't let me out of her sight for weeks after he died. I get it. But I'm sixteen now. "We're just gone for one night. And I'll be with Mr. Harris and the team the whole time."

Rachel has apparently invented a new game where she runs from the far wall of the foyer back into the kitchen, crashing into the granite-top island at top speed, chanting about Halloween the entire time. On Rachel's third pass, Mom clotheslines her with her arm and lifts her into the air, soapy hands and all. "Rachel. We are *calm*," she says.

Rachel giggles uncontrollably, burying her face in Mom's shoulder. I smile. "Is it okay?" I ask, glad for a little bit of a distraction.

Mom sighs. "Yes, it's okay. You've been so busy this fall."

I shift guiltily. "I'll be around Sunday," I tell her. I can take the day off from running with Sophie.

"All right," she says. She puts the wriggling, wiggling Rachel down, wipes her hands on her apron, and signs the slip. "My busy girl."

After the dishes, Rachel drags Mom into the other room. I can't focus on precalc any longer, feeling stress buzzing in my brain. I don't like making Mom nervous, I don't like feeling like a bad daughter. But I also don't like feeling trapped.

So I do what I always do when I start to feel like this: I go upstairs to practice violin.

My bedroom is too big for all my stuff, but it does mean I have a whole corner of my room to practice my violin in. I take it out of the blue velvet of its case, stroke it gently for a moment. I tuck the instrument under my chin, raise my bow, and close my eyes for a long moment. I listen to the quiet house, the faint sounds of Rachel and Mom echoing up from the foyer, the faint sounds of Peter on the phone in his office down the hall from my room. Then I run through a few scales, relishing the smooth notes that unfurl from the vibrating strings and into the air.

Something surfaces in me when I play, a lighter side shaken loose by the music. When I play, I'm not awkward or shy or self-conscious. I feel like I am my violin, just a vessel through which etudes and reels and concertos are produced. That feeling disappears as soon as I think about anybody watching, of course. But moments like these fill me with a confidence that I'm doing something right.

I play through the program for the holiday concert next month, pausing to really dig into the part of "Carol of the Bells" that's really been giving me some trouble. After I've got a good handle on it, I'm starting to consider what I might use for my spring senior solo audition when the doorbell rings.

I don't bother to stop practicing. Mom will answer and it's never for me, anyway. So I'm confused, shaken out of my focus, when I hear Mom's footsteps coming upstairs a moment later. "Emily," she calls from down the hall. "You have a visitor."

I set down my violin gently on my bed, then slide out of my bedroom onto the hardwood floor in my socks. It's one of my small pleasures in this new place. Mom is waiting in the hall. "Who is it?" I ask, a little annoyed at the interruption. Who comes to see me ever, let alone at 8:30 PM on a Thursday night?

"I'm not sure. She said she's your friend." Mom looks at me, and I can see two emotions at war in her face: the protective, *I hate that it's late on a school night, why is there a stranger on our doorstep*, and the sad and pitying *This is the first time you've had a friend over to this house*. But all these feelings disappear when I walk down the stairs. Sophie grins up at me from the foyer. "Hey, Em," she says. She's dressed in a pair of running shorts and a faded zip-up hoodie. "I'm going for a run and I think I want to do some mile repeats... can I borrow one of your timers?"

I'm already smiling. I was sad about skipping practice because it meant I couldn't check in with her. We're dyads, after all. But the fact that she's here means she remembers where I live from when she dropped me off after our last run, that she was in the neighborhood and maybe she wanted to see me? Or that she just realized she needed a timer and knew I could provide...

Either way, I'm just happy to see her. "You can use my watch," I tell her. I'm wearing my dad's. I go down the steps, undoing the strap so I can give it to her. "Some extra practice, huh?"

"Yeah, practice was light today. I feel like I need the reps if I'm going to break nineteen at states." She shakes her head. "We'll see. Harris might be out of his mind on that one."

"Who's this, Emily?" Mom asks.

I cringe inside, thinking of the time I lied about going to the shoe store, about all the times I've been in a car with Sophie when I'm supposed to never get behind the wheel of someone who is not a trusted adult or Beth. "Um, this is my friend Sophie. She runs cross country. She's really good, she's the one I've been running with on Sundays."

"Hi, Sophie," Mom says. "I'm Mrs. Samstone."

It still feels weird to hear her introduce herself that way.

"Nice to meet you," Sophie says cheerily, sticking out her hand to shake. Mom does, finally smiling a little. Then Sophie turns to me. "Want to come to the park with me? It's a gorgeous evening."

I glance at Mom, who looks a little stiff about the idea. "Can I?" I ask tentatively, wishing I hadn't just used all my boundary-pushing on the permission slip.

"How old are you?" Mom asks Sophie.

Sophie sees my panicked look. She shrugs. "I'm seventeen and I drove here, but I figured we could walk over to Asbury Park," she says. Bless her for remembering Mom's rules.

Mom looks back at Peter, who has ambled into the kitchen for a snack. He shrugs mildly. Why is she looking to him for permission? I'm her daughter. But at least it works in my favor. "Be back by nine, please," she says reluctantly.

I grin and grab my sweater off the hook. "See you later!" I call.

As we walk down the steps onto the street, where the streetlights are on and the sun has just set, Sophie looks at me. "That felt like a jailbreak."

I'm already babbling apologies. "I'm sorry about all my mom's crazy rules about driving and stuff, it's not like people are magically amazing drivers once they turn eighteen…"

"It's cool," Sophie says.

"She's just protective because of my dad," I tell Sophie.

"Oh, I figured it was maybe because I was black."

I freeze up. Sophie laughs at my facial expression. "Just messing with you," she says. "Although I gotta say she did not look super pleased to see me."

I roll my eyes. "We've been here for like two and a half years and you're the first friend that's come over. I think she was just startled. And she likes knowing where I am and having me at home."

The evening is cool, but warm for November. It's a perfect temperature for a sweatshirt, probably one of our last nice nights of the year. The streetlights cast gentle yellow light onto Sophie's face as she shakes her head. "No offense, but I don't really get that. Like, you're basically the most responsible kid I've ever met."

I smile. We turn left, toward Asbury Park. "I mean, in her worldview, children need to obey their parents and family and church are the center of everything. So she tries to keep me around."

"Yeah, but you're not like… a child." Sophie shoves her hands into the pockets of her hoodie. "You're not—are you religious, like that? I guess I haven't really asked."

"I mean, I go to church every Sunday…"

"Huh, I didn't have you pegged as the religious type." Sophie shrugs. "You're so, like, analytical."

"I mean…" I hesitate. "This is kind of a secret."

"An Emily secret? Oh shit," she says. She's smiling. "I won't tell."

"I think... I don't believe in God. And that's not just from being analytical. Like, my mom is the most logical person I know. But I feel like we're seeing the world from two totally different angles. And she thinks atheism is like, the most depressing and amoral thing ever." The words are tumbling out of my mouth much faster than I intended. "But it's making more and more sense to me, because like, the reasons for there not being a god not only seem logical but are also like the coolest most interesting things ever. Like, if there's a god, who made him, right? There would have to be something else above him, and something above that, and so on. But in a universe without a god, a universe created from the bottom up by physical laws and natural selection, complexity arises from simplicity and something can arise from nothing. It makes so much more sense. At least to me."

I stop, the lack of breathing during my tirade finally catching up to me. "Uh, sorry. That became... rant-y."

"Don't apologize!" Sophie's face is surprised. "That's really interesting. I didn't know you were so into this."

I shrug. "I've been thinking about this stuff a lot, I guess."

"You should *talk* about it more. That was like, the least douchey case for atheism I've ever heard."

"No, no," I say. "My mom would find out and it would not be good." I guess I haven't asked. But I already know.

"Wow. This is some thought police shit," Sophie says.

We're at the entrance to the park. There's a dirt track that goes around the edge of the playground and tennis courts. It's about a kilometer and a half, an awkward distance—close enough but not exactly a mile. "I mean... it's fine. I'm figuring it out, you know?"

"Good," Sophie says. She studies me for a moment. A cold breeze blows the flyaways up and down in her hair.

I suddenly feel very shy. "Um, what did you want to run?"

"Was thinking some mile repeats, but whatever you think would be best." She shrugs.

"All right, but let's not overdo it with states this weekend. Why don't you do three laps around the path. Hit them around seven minutes." I sit down on one of the swings. "I don't want you to strain your shins."

She goes to the track, flashes me a smile. "Whatever you say, manager."

I clear the timer. "On my count."

When I say "go," I watch her take off on the track, pounding the dirt with every step, all alone in the darkness. I keep watching, even after she disappears around the bend.

*

"Emily... we're here."

I open my eyes, groggy, conscious only of feeling warm and comfortable. Then I realize it's because my face is pressed into Sophie's shoulder. I jump. "Oh, geez, sorry, I fell asleep," I splutter.

Sophie is cracking up. "No big deal. Figured you'd want to get off the bus, though."

"Yeah." I try to get my bearings. Fat clouds race across the night sky through the grimy bus windows as we pull into the parking lot of a Days Inn. The meet is in Central Ohio, a four-hour drive from our district in the Northeast. We would never be able to make the 9 AM girls' meet with enough time to warm up without leaving at insane-o-clock in the morning. So the district pays for the runners' lodgings. We rolled out right after school.

These fast-moving cloud clusters have me a little worried. "It might rain tomorrow," I say through a yawn.

"I like rain running. Run raining?" Sophie says brightly. "Makes me feel faster."

Behind me, her duffel bag held to her chest as she waits to get off the bus, Kari snorts. "Thanks, Pollyanna."

Sophie turns around. "Don't like rain?" she asks. "You gonna melt?"

"No," Kari says defensively.

Out of the corner of my eye, I see the corners of Jon's mouth twitch. He can't laugh, though, since Kari was on his side in the whole Sophie debacle two weeks ago.

"Hang on a minute!" Harris yells as everyone prepares to leave the bus. "Guys need to get their room keys from me, girls from Emily! We have your room assignments!"

Sophie pokes me in the side. "Want to room with me?"

I have a bad feeling. "Uh, yeah, but I think usually Harris makes the assignments." Generally by PR. I make my way through the crowded bus over to Harris. Last year, Harris had me room with Christa so she could get her nine hours of sleep before the race. That would mean...

My suspicions are confirmed when I glance through the pile of small envelopes with room numbers and names scrawled on them. Me and Christa, then next down the list—Sophie and Kari. Alone in a room together?

"This will end poorly," I mumble to no one as the team stumbles off the bus.

We all walk through the parking lot in a messy, laughing clump. On the way in, we pass a fenced-off hotel pool. "Harris! Can we go swimming?" Terri asks.

"I want all of you in bed by nine," Harris says gruffly. "We're eating breakfast at six am tomorrow and you all need to have the race of your lives."

Disgruntled murmurs rumble through the team. "Come on, Harris, it's like eight thirty now."

Harris glances at his watch and sighs. "Nine thirty," he amends. "But I'm serious. Too many people were exhausted during the Jefferson meet. Tonight, we hydrate, stretch, and rest."

I can't help but agree. This whole week I've been accosting Derrick during Bio with bottles of water to pre-hydrate. Dehydration is dangerous.

People start clustering around me and Harris for room keys. "Room assignments by PR," I say.

Sophie's right beside me. "Sweet. So, I'm with Christa?"

"Um, Harris actually put me with Christa," I say, handing Christa the key to our room over my shoulder. "So…"

Sophie does the quick mental calculation. "Christ, I'm with Kari?" she whispers to me.

I shrug. "Um, I can talk to Harris if you want to swap…"

Sophie squares her shoulders. "No, this is stupid. I'm not the one who's gonna make this an issue."

I smile at her. "That's the spirit."

Christa and I settle into our room immediately. She's already yawning. She got up at five am this morning so that she'd feel ready to go to sleep at nine. I'm helping her stretch out her hamstrings, a two-person process requiring me to push her leg down as close to her chest as she can stand.

Someone knocks on the door. "You good?" I ask Christa.

She nods. "Thanks."

I clamber to my feet. It's Harris at the door. "Hey, girls," he says. "How you feeling, Christa?"

From her position lying down on the floor, Christa gives him a thumbs-up. "Ready to run," she says brightly.

"Well, get ready to sleep," he replies. Then he turns to me. "And you, Emily?"

I shrug. "Don't mind me, I'm fine."

Harris smiles beneath his moustache. "Knew I could rely on you two to be focused, at least. Hey Emily, would you mind helping me distribute some paperwork?" The forms for states are substantially more daunting than for any other meet we attend, with numerous medical waivers and permission slips and bib numbers required, along with special time recorders that attach to the shoelaces to get a time down to the thousandth of a second. It's pretty much a dream come true for a logistics-obsessed micromanager like myself.

"Yeah. You all good Christa?"

102

She nods at me, yawning. "Maybe I'll just sleep here, on the floor."

It's nice to hear her joking around. Assuming she's joking. I can never quite tell with Christa. I follow Harris out into the hallway. First, he hands me seven packets of paperwork. "Figured I could do the boys and you could do the girls," he tells me. "And maybe when you drop in on Sophie's room, help her stretch her shins a little—they've really been bothering her."

I'm already worried about Sophie's shins. She's not a complainer, but shin splints are the absolute worst, a sharp pain in the legs that doesn't go away without rest and stretching. "Will do," I say.

"And Emily…" Harris hands me the package in his other hand. It's an already torn open shipping packet. Inside is a balled-up varsity jacket in Pineridge green. I unroll it and shake it out. Embroidered over the breast pocket is "Emily Ferris: XC Team Manager."

"Harris… I love this," I tell him honestly. It's beautiful. It makes me feel more a legitimate member of the team I've ever felt before.

He pats me on the shoulder. "You deserve it," he says gruffly. "Good work this season."

He limps rapidly down the hallway on his bad knees. I stand there for a long moment, thinking about my dad. Wishing I could have shown him this jacket, wishing he could have known Harris. They were very different men, but they both cared about running and they both care about me. I think they could have been friends.

But a glance back down at the embroidery on the jacket reminds me that I have work to do. I shrug the jacket around my shoulders and consult my rooms list.

The first room I visit is Tess and Emma's room. They're in the middle of an intense game Uno, so I merely remind them to go to bed soon and leave their forms on the floor. Then there's Julie and Terri's room, where I find them—and Derrick—watching some spy movie on the TV. "Derrick," I say warningly. Harris had informed us all on the bus that there would be no "monkey business" of any kind, leading to a slew of increasingly inaccurate biology puns from all the seniors. The curse of the high school teacher, I suppose.

Derrick waves. "Hi Emily," he says.

"I assume you're aware of the time," I say to him.

"Oh, yeah, down to the second. It's, what, twenty-one hundred hours, seventeen minutes, forty-two seconds?"

I glance at my watch. "Not close. But it's okay. Just remember. Early start."

Terri nods. "Ugh, yes. Don't remind me. No worries, Emily, I will be chasing this kid out of here at a reasonable hour."

So I leave them alone. That leaves Kari and Sophie's room. To my dismay, but not to my surprise, I already hear angry voices as I approach their door. Or at least Sophie sounds angry. Kari merely sounds sing-songy, irritating. "I mean, there had to be some kind of reason," I hear her say clearly.

Sophie's voice is an angry murmur, though it crescendos at the end. "...your goddammed business."

"If it affects my teammate, it affects me." I know this voice. Kari pulls this all the time, same as Beth—reasonable words, sneering tone.

Sophie's a lot less likely to tolerate it than me. "Bullshit!" she yells, and I wince. Okay, that may have been audible throughout the entire hallway. I need to mediate this. But I'm too scared to knock on the door. "God, you're acting like I stabbed him in the face with a metal spike or something. He's practically over it, why aren't you?"

"He's not over it, and you know it. 'Just not my thing,' that's what he said you said. What is your thing, Sophie?" Her voice grows lower.

104

Then the door bangs open. Sophie stands in front of me, her face furious. "Em," she says.

"Um, hi. Where are you—"

"I'm going for a run," Sophie says. She shoves one of the tennis shoes in her hand onto her right foot.

Kari appears in the doorway. "Oh, it's you," she says to me. "Of course."

I hate this conversation. "Um, I have some paperwork for you guys," I say inaudibly.

Sophie drops to her knee to tie her shoes. "Thanks," she says thickly. "I'll be back in a little bit." She pushes back up to her feet and walks rapidly down the hallway. "Night, Em."

Kari holds her hands out for the paperwork. "Thanks, Emily," she says.

"Is, um, is Sophie okay?" I ask.

Kari waves a hand. "She's fine. Just tense before the race, you know how it is."

"I hope her shins are all right..." I look down the hallway, half ready to chase her down, but she's already gone. Suddenly, I'm fed up with this whole stupid situation. Barely believing my own nerve, I say, "You should go apologize, Kari."

She shrugs. "She should apologize to Jon."

I exhale in frustration. This is dumb. "I'm going to go read. I'll see you in the morning. Get some rest." With that, I return to my room.

*

Around 11:30 PM, there's yet another knock on the door of the hotel room. I'm enjoying a bit of uninterrupted reading time where I don't have to worry about throwing my book suddenly behind the couch to keep Mom from looking at what I'm reading. Christa, who conked out around two hours ago, rolls over and moans in annoyance. I set down my copy of E.O. Wilson's The Ants and go to the door.

Sophie, Kari, Tessa, and Emma are clustered in the hallway, looking giggly and nervous. "Em," Sophie blurts, "Come swimming with us."

I blink, startled by the crowd. "What?"

"We're going swimming!" Sophie grins, her hair tied back in a ponytail the way it is when she's running. "Bring Christa if she wants."

Christa does not want. "Can you guys shut the hell up? Some of us are planning on actually running tomorrow," she says.

I wish I hadn't opened the door, although it's nice to see Sophie. "Um, look, have fun, but I think I'd better stick around here." Is there something defective about me that I don't particularly enjoy breaking rules? Or getting caught. That's the real thing I don't like. "Anyway, I don't have a suit. And I'm not a good swimmer. And you all have a race tomorrow."

"Aw, Em, you have to come. Please? You can bring your book and just put your feet in." Sophie gives me a pleading look. I don't know what's been going down with her and Kari since I left, but I can just envision the game of chicken that led to this. Kari, for all her bluster, isn't much of a rule-breaker. None of us cross country kids are. But I'm guessing Sophie doesn't want to go into this without someone she knows is on her side. And as far as I know, Tessa and Emma are on Kari's side of the whole Jon debacle. I mean, he's our captain, our most popular player.

Christ. This is why I despise teenagers.

But as soon as I meet Sophie's eyes, I know I'm in. This is what having a friend means, I remind myself. I wasn't there for her during homecoming; I can be there for her now. "All right," I say, and walk out of the room, triple-checking that my room key is in the pocket of my pajamas.

The five of us walk down the hallway, Tess and Emma bringing up a giggly rear. I clutch my book at my side as a sort of security blanket. Sophie walks beside me. "Thanks for coming," she whispers in my ear. "This'll be fun, I promise."

I smile. Maybe it will, even though my heart is pounding with anxiety.

We thwop and ssssh our way down the hallway (they're all in flip-flops; I'm in socks), and out the door into the cold night air. Sophie pauses, sticking her towel in the doorway to make sure it doesn't close behind us. I shiver, thinking fond memories of my jacket back in the room. "Where's the pool?" I ask, my voice sounding loud and childish in the night air.

"There," Sophie responds, pointing at the black chain link fence. Beyond it lies the pool, white lights glowing inside the blue water.

"I'm not altogether certain I'm capable of making it over that fence," I admit, glancing back at Emma and Tess, who are also staring at the obstacle in consternation. "Maybe I'll just go back."

"What's the matter? Chicken?" asks Kari. I roll my eyes. It's such a Kari comment.

"Chill, Kar," says Sophie. It stings a little that she's suddenly decided to also nickname Kari, although I reassure myself when I realize that there's distinctly less affection in her voice when she says 'Kar' versus when she says 'Em.' "Look. I'll just hop it and let you guys in from the other side, yeah?" Without further ado, she kicks off her flip-flops, finds a foothold, and pulls herself onto the fence. She crawls up, looking like the photo of the Tokay gecko in Chapter 34 of my Bio book (we haven't gotten there yet, but I've been sneaking some peeks.). Before I can blink, her hands are already on the top rail, and she's swinging her legs over to land lightly on the other side.

Kari's expression of mingled jealousy and admiration makes me grin, almost making it worth it to come out here. Sophie lets us into the pool. I hand her the discarded flip-flops as the other girls shuffle inside. "Pretty cool trick," I tell her. "Where'd you learn that one?"

She grins. "I'm full of secrets."

The other girls are all stripping down to their underwear, Emma in a nervous fit of giggles. So that's why the lack of suits isn't a problem. I blush, staring down at my feet as Sophie undresses. "I think I'm just going to put my feet in," I say uneasily.

"Suit yourself. You're missing out though. Nothing like a good, brisk pool break-in to get your blood pumping." Turning toward the pool, which no one else has entered, Sophie goes to the diving board and dives in with zero hesitation. A splash, and then she breaks the surface, gasping "Christ! It's cold as balls in here!"

Not to be outdone, Kari dives in a moment later. Tessa and Emma both opt to take the stairs instead, squealing whenever they get to the next level down. I take off my socks and dangle my feet into the water, sucking in a breath. Sophie is right, it's freezing. Night swimming in late October in Ohio... oh, teenagers and their woefully underdeveloped prefrontal cortices.

Still, it's kind of nice sitting there, listening to the splashing and giggling, looking up at the cloudy night sky. I lick my finger to test the wind direction like Mom has shown me, try to orient where we are relative to the sunset we watched from the bus. It's an easterly wind. "It's definitely going to rain tomorrow," I say.

"Emily, you should come in!" calls Tess. "It feels really good once you get used to it!"

"I'm okay," I reply, folding my arms tightly. "I'd rather just stay here."

Kari glances at Sophie. "Seriously," Kari says, swimming over to me with a grin. "Why don't you jump in?"

I scramble back, sensing a threat. "Kari, don't..."

Before I can snatch my legs away, Kari has tugged me into the pool. I hit the water and forget how to breathe. It's unexpected that my whole body feels numb and shocked and weirdly not cold for a long moment.

But then the cold hits and I really want out of there. I struggle to the surface, feel for the wall, and drag myself out of the pool, shivering. The world is blurry and dim, and at first I think my eyes are full of water. Then I realize my glasses have fallen off. Sophie and Kari argue in the pool. "She said she didn't want to go in, are you fucking kidding                                                                me?"

"It was a joke! Anyway, I didn't push you in, why are you freaking out?"

"Guys," I say, "I can't find my glasses."

There's silence. I imagine Sophie rolling her eyes at Kari, huffing out an angry breath. But it's all just conjecture. I can't see anything except vague discrepancies in color and light. Then there's a splashing sound, a "C'mon, we have to find them."

The girls hunt for my glasses. Even without sight I can tell the moment is laden with discomfort. I clutch the side of the pool with both my hands, shivering. Then a gasp of breath as a dark shape surfaces. Sophie swims over to me and pulls herself out of the pool. "Here, Em," she says, handing me my glasses. I try to wipe them on my shirt, but it's a futile effort when the shirt is soaked through. I put them on anyway. Wet vision is better than no vision.

"Come on," Sophie says, helping me to my feet. "Let's go back."

I nod, relieved. It's freezing. "You guys should go to bed soon," I say to the girls in the pool through chattering teeth. "It's an early morning."

Kari nods. I think, against all odds, she may feel a little bad. Because instead of ignoring me as per usual, she says, "Will do, manager," and goes into some backstroke.

I stand there shivering, holding my wet socks, while Sophie pulls on her T-shirt and flip flops. I follow her inside. When we get to the door, she reaches down and grabs the towel from where it's been keeping the door open. "You should dry off," she says as she takes off one of her sandals and sticks it back in the doorway for the other girls.

I accept it gratefully, wrapping it around my shoulders while I attempt to wring out my shorts before I hit the carpeted floor. "Th-thanks," I tell her.

"No worries. God, Kari is being a bitch. I can't believe she pulled you in. That is some juvenile bullshit."

I shrug. "I think she's just trying to get a rise out of you." Truthfully, I don't care all that much. It's just one of those things I try to shrug off and keep my head down through because it's more trouble to deal with it than it's worth. But on the other hand, it feels kind of nice to have someone getting all indignant on my behalf.

"Whatever. She can be nasty to me if she wants. But not my Emily." She smiles at me as we walk back down the hallway, to my room.

"Um, here's your towel," I say once we get to my door. For a second, looking at her standing there next to me, lanky and irritable and smiling, leaning casually against the wall, I want to invite her in to come hang out. Then I remember Christa, and the race the next morning. "Go to bed! You need to rest up."

Sophie looks like she's going to say something, but then she just nods. "Will do. I'll sleep like a baby. Good night," she adds over her shoulder as she walks down the hallway to her room.

"Good night," I reply quietly as a few more drops of water fall from my shirt onto the carpeted floor.

\*

As I predicted, it rains the next morning. Score one for the basic meteorology lessons Mom has been giving me my entire life. Between five AM when thunder wakes me, until seven AM when we arrive at the meet, I'm obsessively checking the weather radar: first, with the hotel TV on mute until Christa wakes up, then on Harris's phone during the hotel breakfast.

Luckily, the lightning has been gone for almost an hour by 7:30, so the meet is still on. By the time we roll up to the golf course where the meet is to take place, there's no more thunder. Just rain, and a big yellow square that we're dead in the middle of on the weather radar.

The downpour is steady and intense, but states is exciting enough that it almost doesn't matter. The varsity girls' race is first. They struggle to warm up in sweatpants weighed down with water. The guys put up the tent as best as they can while Harris swoops through the crowds on his bike in his yellow poncho like a giant banana-colored bat. I splash around under my umbrella, wearing my new Pineridge jacket and Rhys's way-too-large flip-flops, simultaneously trying to sort out bib numbers while keeping the course map at least medium dry.

States is the most exciting meet, year after year. These are the winningest teams, the strongest runners. The finish line is a big arch with a real ribbon that will be restored for each race, not just a line spray painted on the ground. Everywhere I walk, I'm passed by matching squads of six or seven women in their uniforms, doing the best they can in the rain. The rain hasn't kept the crowds of parents and siblings and other spectators away. It's noisy, chaotic. But I know what to do and where to go.

"Em," Sophie says to me in a low voice once I splatter my way back to the tent, having turned in our team paperwork to the officials. "Can you help me stretch out my shins?"

I nod. She sits down on the floor of the tent and outstretches her legs. I kneel in front of her. It's a practiced motion at this point. Greg and Danny sit in the other corner of the tent, half-asleep, but other than that it's empty. The rain pounds on the tarp above. "You nervous?" I ask as I push against the soles of her shoes, noting her bleeding cuticles and tense shoulders.

"Yeah," she replies, straining her feet against my hands. "Yeah, I'm a little worried. The trail's gonna be absolute shit."

I nod. "Gotta go wide around the corners. The inside lane'll be soup by the end. Although barring any miracles at these other schools I think you're gonna be near the front of the pack."

"Don't tell me that," says Sophie, but she smiles.

It's true. I've done my research. There are nine runners at this race, including Christa, who have PRs that are out of Sophie's reach barring any miracles. But tenth out of three hundred would net her a spot at nationals. Pretty stellar, if she can swing it.

"Switch," I tell her, and she changes the angle of her feet.

"What's the course like?" Sophie asks, her face contorting in pain. Poor thing, her shin splints have been getting worse.

"Uh, you've got a big climb near the end of mile two. Then the second half of mile three is on paved road, so you'll get a break from the mud. But watch out for spectators there, they're everywhere and they're idiots."

Her face is pale and she looks scared, but she's still got room for jokes. "I love when you call other people idiots."

"Well, they are. This is going to be a fast race though, Sophie. If you want a shot at nationals, you're going to have to get ahead of the pack quickly. Clara Dunham from Jefferson's going to be your main competition there. I think she's got the edge on you on hills, but you've got a way better kick than her, so just stick with her and save it for the end." I smile at her, let go of her feet, and give her legs a gentle pat. "Keep it loose. And just remember to smile."

She smiles back shakily. "Endorphins and stuff, right?"

"Right."

Harris rides up like a bike messenger. He pulls down the hood on his poncho. "Varsity girls to the line! Time for some striders! Emily, I need you at mile two."

"On it," I call over my shoulder. I look at Sophie, who looks more vulnerable than maybe I've ever seen her before. "Good luck," I whisper to her before grabbing a plastic bag from the pile I set up earlier for people to store dry things, putting it over my clipboard, and squishing back out into the rain.

Taking times at the second mile is always my favorite. This is the part of the race where you can see what runners are really made of. People who have slowed down, who are tired and gasping, either pull it together for the final mile or continue a limping, prideless jog to the finish. The best athletes are gritting it out, and you can see the sparkle in their eyes when they realize the end is nearing. They blow past the mile two mark, their faces grim and determined, never breaking their stride.

I know Sophie's one of the strong ones. I've watched her in every single race this year. She hurtles through the toughest parts of every course, sometimes slowing her pace but never reducing the length of her stride. I believe in her to beat out Clara, who according to the state qualifiers' website, has a PR two seconds faster than Sophie's.

The second mile mark is around twenty meters off from where they estimated it on the map, at least according to the pedometer on my dad's watch. It's on top of a brutal hill. I blink rain from my eyes as I get to the marker. I was so focused on psyching Sophie up that I forgot my umbrella at the tent. I wipe my glasses with my sleeve and peer down the hill, hoping to see the starting line. Luckily there's a good vantage point from here. The runners are lining up, the scene a frenzy of activity that seems oddly calm and quiet from this far away. Teams do strider after strider, sprinting fifty yards out and back in an attempt to keep their muscles loose and warm. I try to spot Pineridge. We're in box 72. But there are a few teams in green uniforms and I just can't tell from here.

A few other coaches are here and more still are arriving, presumably for the same purpose as me: mile two splits. I nod at them, feeling more legitimate than ever in my Pineridge jacket. One even nods back at me like I'm a real coach. One of them is wearing a purple Jefferson High School jacket, so him I don't nod at.

Finally, only eleven seconds behind by my watch, the starting gun is fired. My stomach drops with the usual nerves as I click my timer. I'm nervous for everyone—these conditions are tough—but it's Sophie who is at the front of my mind more than anyone else. She's put months of work into this, pushed through shin splints and pain. I'm so proud of how far she's come. I want this for her, so badly that I feel my muscles twitch as though I'm running alongside her.

The one downside to waiting at mile two is that you hear the starting gun and then nothing happens for more than ten minutes. The runners are back in the wooded part of the golf course and I can't hear or see them. I watch the crowd, filtering out from the starting line and dispersing toward other parts of the course.

The first runner to make it up to mile two is Carolyn Vottero at 11:38. It's not surprising. Her PR's not within reach even for Christa, who passes by twelve seconds later. Christa looks calm, strong. I'm not worried about her.

I count the next runners. Seven of them, all soaking wet and muddy up to their thighs, all within twenty seconds of one another. "Come on, Soph," I murmur to myself. She needs to be next, or close to it, to snag that nationals spot.

I'm starting to shiver from the rain. I squint down the hill and spot two blurry figures, and then... yes, it's Sophie, barely a yard behind Clara. They attack the hill, their breath coming in foggy, synchronized puffs.

I catch my breath as I watch Sophie ascend the hill, raw determination on her face. They crest the hill together, and I forget to yell or cheer. I almost neglect to click the timer for the mile split when Sophie glances at me as she passes by. She gives me the barest hint of a smile before refocusing on her goal, and then just like that they're gone, opening their stride down the hill. I watch them until I can't see them any longer.

Soon after that comes the pack, fifty or so runners. Kari's near the front of them, Terri and Tess near the back. I click their times as they pass, cheering. Kari and Tess are both on track to PR, which is frankly impressive in this weather, their splits about seven and eleven seconds faster than I would have projected. Julie is next and finally Emma, who's struggling near the back of the pack, about twenty seconds over her normal pace, a grimace of pain on her face.

As soon as the last of the Pineridge runners pass mile two, I begin a running hopping slide down the hill, the fastest I can move in these flip flops. It's the quickest path toward the finish line. If I make a beeline I can beat the first runners. I'm panting by the time I spot the senior guys standing amid the crowd, about twenty meters shy of the finish line. "Hey," I gasp, "people finishing yet?"

Derrick makes room for me in the crowd. "Nope!"

I glance at my stopwatch. 17:39. "Any second now," I say. "Harris around?"

"He's right by the line. How's everyone doing?" Derrick shakes out his wet, curly mop of hair like a dog.

"Great! Christa's in second, Kari's gonna PR I bet, Sophie is…" I pause for a second. My gaze automatically swings over to Jon, whose gaze is carefully neutral. "Sophie's fighting for tenth."

"Sick," Derrick says, and just like that, here comes Carolyn Vottero rounding the corner to the finish line. She runs past us, moving like a superhuman. "Jesus Christ, this girl is fast," Jon says, leaning over the rope of flags that bars the onlookers from the course. He looks at the clock as she crosses the finish line. "Seventeen forty-nine, that's faster than Danny. Think Christa'll break eighteen?"

"She was twelve seconds behind at—there she is! All right, Christa!" I exclaim. Christa's looking a little worse for the wear, but she puts in a seventeen fifty-seven, her muscled, mud-stained legs pumping her way to the finish. My heart pounds, my ears ring. The finish line of a race is insane. Talking, laughing, cheers, clapping. Everything exciting happens in the next five minutes. But all I really, truly care about is happening in the next sixty seconds.

"When's Sophie coming?" Derrick asks.

I glance at Jon again, and dang it, why am I so awkward. "Her goal was sub-nineteen." We watch a few more runners finish, none finishing under eighteen minutes. "She and this girl from Jefferson were fighting it out."

"Oh, who?" asks Jon. "I have some friends—"

"There they are," says Rhys.

I accidentally drop my clipboard on the ground, but I don't care. There they are, they're close together. But something is wrong. At this point in the season, I can spot Sophie a mile away. She has darker skin and is shorter than Clara, which is insane because Sophie is so tall. But she's limping, I can see it immediately. She's a few meters behind. I catch my breath. "I think she's hurting."

The noise of the crowd is too loud for me to process. Derrick leans over the rope yelling encouragement, but I can't speak, just watch and urge Sophie on mentally as they begin the final, muddy sprint.

It's not enough.

Sophie crosses the finish line behind Clara, maybe by ten meters. I don't remember to click the timer until I glance at the race clock several seconds later. At eighteen fifty-seven. These girls have pushed each other. This is a huge PR for them both. I just wish it were enough for Sophie to crack the top ten.

Without a word to the boys, I grab the clipboard and duck back out to the edge of the crowd. I jog toward the finish line. By the time I get there, I can't find Sophie among all the other girls finishing. Harris is there, though like a yellow neon sign. "Harris," I say breathlessly. "Did you see Sophie? I think she got hurt?"

"Just talked to her. She tripped on the paved section and got pretty scraped up. She went to go take a cooldown jog. You get the mile two splits?"

I hand him the muddy clipboard. "You've got the finish times right?"

"Yep," he says.

"Can I go make sure Sophie's okay?"

He looks at me for a second. "Yes, good idea. Just make sure you're back soon. Same routine for the boys' race."

I head off in the direction he indicates, away from the crowds. I stop by our tent first to snag the first aid kit. Christa's in there. I give her a hurried congrats, but she's a little too out of it to notice, and I feel urgent about finding Sophie anyway.

It takes me a minute, but I finally spot her loose stride, her black hair, her green uniform, in that order. She's mostly beyond the crowds, and heading further away, into another part of the golf course. "Sophie!" I call, splashing through a puddle, the med kit thudding at my side. "Wait up!"

She slows to a walk, looking at me over her shoulder. I catch up. The whole left side of her body is covered in mud slowly streaking away in the rain. Her chin, left elbow, and knee are raw and red. All in all, she's such a sorry sight that I almost feel like crying.

But I hold it together. "Harris sent me to patch you up. You all right?"

She shrugs, but she's moving slowly, painfully, now. "'M alright. Fucked up my arm and leg a bit. Pretty tired."

"I'll bet. C'mon, let's go sit under that tree so I can clean you up." We splatter to a small maple on the edge of the wooded part of the golf course. It provides shelter from the rain a good two hundred feet away from the crowd.

Sophie flops to the ground, steam rising off her body in the chilly wet air. She doesn't say anything, but she covers her face with her hands.

I have a weird moment of déjà vu, remembering her first race, when she got scraped up. A lot has changed since then. But this moment, for whatever reason, feels like it follows from that one.

I take a clean, dry rag out of the med kit and begin wiping the mud off her leg as gently as I can. "You ran an excellent race," I tell her, but my voice is a little too stiff for the admiration, the sadness I want to convey.

She looks up from her hands. Her eyes are red. She shakes her head. "Eleventh. That's worse than last."

"Not true," I tell her, moving on to her elbow. "Sophie, you broke nineteen minutes. Do you know the percentage of women who do that during their high school careers? It's... small. We might even have a chance at winning the team award."

She laughs a little, takes the rag I'm offering to wipe tears and mud from her face. "Sorry, I'm just so fucking tired. And mad. If I hadn't fallen..."

"It's okay," I tell her, trying to smile while I get out the hydrogen peroxide. "It's okay. Just... take a deep breath. Stretch out your legs. This might sting a little."

She hisses when I pour hydrogen peroxide over her knee. It bubbles white over her red blood, her brown skin. "Almost done," I say, taking her elbow and pouring it onto her elbow.

"You're brutal," she says.

"All done, though. I'll give you some bandages to put on once you're dry. And we'll put Neosporin on your face."

"Okay, Doctor Em," she says, a smile flickering across her face. It doesn't quite reach her eyes, though.

"Dr. Em, I like the sound of that," I tell her, rubbing hand sanitizer on my hands before rubbing Neosporin into her scrape. She winces at first, but the ointment has numbing cream in addition to antibacterial agents. She remains obedient and unmoving as I place a bandage on her chin, more just to keep the rain from washing off the ointment than to keep anything protected. I smooth it out as gently as I can and remove my hands.

Sophie sighs. "Don't..." she says.

"What?"

She shakes her head, sets her jaw. "Never mind."

We sit in silence for several moments. I put away the supplies, carefully capping the bottles and tubes and collecting the little Band-Aid wrappers so I don't litter. She stretches her legs, leaning way over them, impossibly long and flexible, her forehead practically touching her knees. I watch goosebumps start to appear on her arms and legs. She's still only wearing the unitard and she's starting to shiver. "You want my jacket?" I ask her, quickly unzipping it.

She straightens up, takes it out of my hands, but doesn't put it on. She just looks at it for a long moment. "Em..." she says, finally, hesitantly. "Was there anything that like, you wanted so bad, but you couldn't have it?"

I'm a little taken aback by the question, but it's Sophie. "I mean, I guess. Are you talking about nationals?"

"Kind of, I guess. But I maybe could have made nationals. What about something that's completely impossible?" She looks at my face, brown eyes bright and intense.

My stomach clenches under the intensity of her gaze. For some reason, I think of my dad. I want him back and I know it's impossible, unless Mom is right about him waiting for us in the Kingdom of Heaven. I don't know what to say, but Sophie looks so desperate for me to say the right thing. I remember something I've been reading about for my independent study. "I mean, I think some things are impossible. But if you're into multiverse theory, nothing's completely impossible. Just statistically unlikely."

She lets out a breath of air that's not quite a laugh. "Yeah. I guess you're right," she says. She leans in. Before I even realize what's happening, she presses her lips to mine, her hair tickling my forehead, her hands pressed to the grass on either side of me.

I forget to breathe. Blood rushes to my face so fast it feels like it's buzzing. I draw back from her. Sophie looks at me, sees my panicked impression. "Shit," she breathes. "Sorry, Em, sorry, I just thought..."

My words are all stuck in my throat and my mind is totally blank. I want to reach out, reassure her past the panic in her eyes, but I'm paralyzed. Just like always. Fight or flight or freeze, a little rabbit scared by approaching footsteps, a deer caught in headlights.

Sophie pushes herself to her feet. "Just don't mention this to anyone," she tells me, and then bolts off, the sound of her slightly uneven strides disappearing behind me.

I listen to the slowing rain, touch my lips with my fingers. My first kiss. Sophie kissed me. I'm dimly aware of the sounds of the spectators. The women's race is coming to an end. The men are next. And Sophie, Sophia Tuzarova-Williams, just kissed me, on my lips.

I'm shaking from the cold, but I can feel a smile appearing on my face. "What on earth," I say out loud. But my mind is already spinning through a thousand different things I should have recognized, little comments, little gestures, her sudden disinterest in Jon, her conversation with Kari yesterday... I'm an idiot.

And then the feeling of being an idiot doubles, no, triples, no, this is non-linear, it's quadratic, because I maybe should have recognized Sophie's feelings, but I definitely should have recognized mine. I mean, seriously, Emily? Oh, guess what, all those stomach-twisting, thrilling moments where you really, really cared about what Sophie thought of you? Those weren't all just friendship.

I feel like fifteen percent more of an adult. Also, I feel very cold, but it's a distant feeling. I feel like I can be this cold forever, and it doesn't matter. "God," I murmur softly, running a hand through my hair. I feel like I've solved a mystery. It's like the feeling I get when I finally get the sixteenth notes right in a Mozart violin concerto, but a million—no, Emily, don't exaggerate—a thousand times more exhilarating.

I kind of like it.

And it's scary to think about it, but it's true, so true... I really like Sophie.

Who probably thinks I hate her now. She hasn't seen my magical moment of clarity. She just thinks I'm freaked out that she kissed me. I have to tell her how I feel. The thought makes me shiver with fear. Or maybe it's cold.

I wobble to my feet, and walk back toward the race course under the smoky gray sky.

\*

Sophie avoids me studiously for the rest of the meet, which throws a real wrench in my confessing-my-feelings agenda. First there's the guys' meet to attend to, and every time I try to get her alone she's surrounded by other people.

The men do well enough. Jon redeems himself somewhat from his terrible finish at district qualifiers, placing sixteenth. Rhys comes in right behind him at nineteenth. Derrick gets pushed over in the first hundred meters of the race and runs terribly, his knee swollen and painful by the time he finishes. He laughs about it ("At least now I have an excuse for this garbage time!") but I can tell he's hurting over the outcome of his last cross country race.

There's a lot to do. But every time I get a second to breathe and look around for Sophie, she's making herself busy, too: discussing the race animatedly with Christa, helping Daniel shake water off the tent, or simply nowhere to be found.

I try to let my own tasks distract me, but the whole time, my mind is only half engaged.

We attend a mercifully brief award ceremony where Christa receives her second-place medal and Harris receives seven medals because our women's team took the team award. He's elated: this has only happened once, eleven years ago. The team is elated too, but I don't think Sophie's smile is fully genuine. Or is it? Am I reading too much into this?

I dig through my bag for an ice pack and an Ace bandage for Derrick's knee, listening while Harris gathers everyone in front of him. He tells the team he is proud of every single one of them, and for those he won't be coaching in the spring for track: "Go out and do some good in the world. Oh, and you should be running track. Now saddle up! We've got a four-hour drive and I want to stop for dinner!"

The bus ride back is more or less eternal. I get on and sit at my usual place at the front of the bus, wondering for a moment if Sophie will sit with me, and what that would mean, and how I would feel about it. Then I mentally harangue myself for obsessing over such a minor detail and also for not totally knowing which I would prefer. And by that point she's already gotten on the bus and made a beeline for the back, laughing with Derrick about their disappointing races.

I spend the entire bus ride back staring out the window, watching the gray sky slowly turn black. My brain switches to other thoughts occasionally—*wow it's the end of the season, oh man I do not feel like going to church tomorrow*—but other than that it's just one screaming repeating replay of the moment where Sophie leaned in and pressed her lips to mine. I see it much more vividly than the torn vinyl of the seat in front of me.

Team dinner provides a bit of relief, particularly when Daniel and Terri prove to be especially competent at throwing peas into one another's mouths. But soon we're back on the bus, and I'm more keyed up than ever.

I don't know what to do. I've never been more confused in my life. But one thing I know for sure, know it in the same way that I know I don't like Peter's church, in the same way that I know how to keep going on mile eight of a long run: I have to tell her how I feel.

When we get back to Pineridge, most of the exhausted team groggily shaking themselves awake, I wait for her outside the bus. She gets off last, her duffel bag slung over her shoulder, her hair half escaped from her ponytail.

"Sophie, can I talk to you?" I ask in a low, low voice.

"Yeah, for sure," she says. Her voice is so completely casual that I wonder for a second if I imagined the entire thing. But then I notice her fingers anxiously twisting the strap of her backpack. Maybe this isn't just me.

A raindrop splashes onto my nose. The rain is much slower back in Pineridge, but it hasn't disappeared entirely. "Here, let's go to my car," said Sophie. We walk over. I'm too nervous to say goodbye to anyone, even Harris, but Sophie yells goodbye to a couple of people. She unlocks the car, pausing to throw her duffel bag in the back. We both get in. Sophie puts the key into the ignition, but doesn't turn it. Neither of us says anything.

My mind is jumping everywhere, my whole body tense. I automatically categorize the biological processes at work: *Adrenal glands hard at work, parasympathetic nervous system kicking up the fight-or-flight response, blood diverting from digestion and thought to pump the heart faster and faster...* I sneak a glance at Sophie, who immediately looks up at the ceiling. What is happening inside her head? What is happening inside mine? Did she really kiss me, or is this just some bizarre delusion my brain cooked up? Does she regret it? Am I supposed to be doing something right now? Am I gay? Is this what regular teenagers obsess about all the time? Is...

"Em," Sophie says.

I jump.

She looks at me, one hand on the wheel, yellow glow of the parking lot's lights coming in through her hair, head cocked in concern. "You okay?" she asks.

I twist my hands together. "Yes. How are you?"

She looks at me, with—it's a soft expression, something I've only seen on her once or twice. Her whole face relaxes into a smile, and her eyes are... nobody has ever looked at me like this before.

Outside, the storm is coming back. Thunder rumbles, but far away. Sophie turns toward me, and closes her hands around mine, smoothing them flat, palm to palm. I inhale sharply.

"Sorry, am I freaking you out?" she asks, but she doesn't move her hands.

"No," I say, although my voice is trembling.

Her smile grows a little bigger. "Are you sure?" she asks.

I'm so lightheaded. I take a giant breath. "I mean, yeah, a little bit, perhaps, but not in a bad way, in a good way, but also a scary way, because I don't really know what you're doing or what I should be doing or..."

Sophie's smile is so bright that I find myself staring down at our hands instead. She laces our fingers together. "I don't totally know what I'm doing either, to be honest," she admits. "But, okay, here's what I know. I really like you, as a friend, but also, I definitely have some feelings for you as like... more than a friend, and, uh... yeah. I don't know. I guess I want to know if you feel the same."

I'm still staring at our hands. I can barely hear her, my blood is pounding so loud in my ears. My face is hot and tingly. I can't speak. Instead, I just squeeze her hands tighter.

She lets go, reaches one hand up, lifting me by the chin. "Em?"

And it's so bizarre, so purely biological, that I can hardly believe it. I push forward and press my lips against hers, my eyes shut tight but somehow aiming right. Just for one soft moment, before I pull away. "Sorry," I say quickly, for some reason.

But Sophie laughs, gently, her hands pushing into my hair, pulling me closer. "Don't be," she says, and she kisses me back, slowly, carefully. It's the sweetest thing, and it steals my thoughts. I'm losing track of everything—the car around us, the first drops of rain hitting against the windshield, the impending approach of church tomorrow—forgetting it all, except the faintly earthy smell of Sophie's hair, still damp from the day's storm, nudging my face.

When she pulls away, I feel different. "Whoa," she says.

"Yeah," I reply. I realize I'm shaking. I pull my damp jacket tighter around myself. Outside, the rain is falling in earnest, big drops splashing on the windshield. The clock reads 8:17.

"You need to get home?" Sophie asks.

Mom expected me at eight. "Kind of, yeah," I tell her, hoping she can tell in my voice how much I don't want to, how much I want this moment to go on and on and on.

Sophie starts the car. One of her CDs starts playing in the middle of the track, a slow rap song. "Can I take you home, or will your mom... I mean, it's raining."

"Um. If you have time, that would be great." I'm staring straight ahead. I feel nervous, all of a sudden.

But she takes my hand again once she's reversed out of the spot, and it makes me feel a little better. "So, uh... I don't know. What do you want to do about all this?"

I'm already thinking about my mom. How many rules am I breaking right now? Car, kissing, and while she hasn't brought it up specifically, I am guessing she won't be particularly thrilled about the female aspect of Sophie. And even though it makes me feel a little nervous— I'm already mentally racing through the lies I'll tell when I get home—I also mostly really, really just want to keep holding Sophie's hand. "What do you mean?"

"I mean, uh... can we, like... hang out or something?" Sophie asks. This car ride, which seems so unbearably long when Peter is ferrying me from school, is way too short right now. The rain and the dark make everything feel significant. "I mean, more than we do now, or... I don't know. You know. Like, date or whatever."

She stops at a traffic light. The red glow comes into the car.

"Technically, I am not allowed to date," I tell her.

She smiles. "Oh yeah, I forgot, protective mom and all that. What if I bring flowers and ask for your hand?"

I smile back, but uneasily. "I am concerned about the outcome of that scenario."

The light turns green. "So," Sophie says, and she honestly is so impressive at keeping her voice neutral, sounding like she doesn't care a bit about what she's saying. "Are you saying that you don't want to, like, be a thing, or..."

"No no no," I blurt. "I just, um, can we keep it a secret?"

Sophie's silent. My stomach twists a little. She hates hiding things, can't keep her mouth shut when she has an opinion. But she has to realize that none of this, that somehow, she magically seems to want, can happen if my mom knows about it. It will end before it begins.

"I'm sorry," I add, a little miserably.

She's still holding my hand. She squeezes it, and then lets go. "You know what? It's fine. It's not your fault. We can keep things to ourselves for now if that'll make your life easier."

Relief floods through me. "Thank you, Sophie."

"No prob. We'll be like spies, basically. Anyway, probably a better idea to keep the team gossip chain off the trail." She rolls her eyes. "I mean, Kari would have a field day with this shit."

I remember Jon's red eyes after the homecoming debacle, his terrible, limping race. I don't want him finding out either. "Yeah."

"And we'll, you know, take it slow. Figure things out as we go. You know? This is new for me too." She taps her steering wheel in rhythm with the song, one of her scratched CD mixes.

We're into the developments, now. We roll past Four Oaks, Brookside, Whispering Pines, until she turns into Wisteria Manors. She drives slowly, taking the correct turnoff and pulling up in front of my house. Suddenly, I feel nervous to go inside.

She parks in front. "You okay?"

"Yeah, I... yeah. Would you mind just parking like, three houses down," I say. "It's the teen driver thing, not the... the other thing."

To her credit, she does, without saying anything. She rolls her head back against the seat and looks at me. "Recovery run tomorrow?"

I start to say yes, then remember that I promised Sunday to my mom. "I told my mom I would do family stuff tomorrow, but want to hang out on Monday?" I ask her.

"Sounds good," she says. "Meet up with you after practice?"

"Season's over, Sophie," I tell her.

"Oh shit. You're right." She smiles, then rolls her head back against the seat. "Ugh, I still can't believe I missed natties by one fucking place."

"It was an amazing race," I tell her, because it's true. "And an amazing season."

She catches my hand in hers, and plays with it, and it's hard to breathe. "Well, at least we have a little break."

"Track'll be here soon," I say.

"Yeah, but winter will be nice." She leans in, one last time, and when she kisses me, I realize I have no idea how I've been surviving before this, because nothing else feels like having her pressed close, her little puff of breath on my lips as she pulls away.

"Have a good night," she says.

"Um, bye," I reply, and I leave the car. For a second I start to go up the steps before I remember that I'm standing outside the wrong house. I walk two over. Sophie waits until I get inside before she drives away, which is—just, okay, really cute.

"Emily? Is that you?" Mom sits in the dark family room with Peter, watching the late re-showing of *Jeopardy!*

"I'm back," I reply, wondering if there was some glowing neon sign—I'VE BEEN KISSING A GIRL AND THOROUGHLY ENJOYING IT—on my face or body.

"I'm glad you're home, I was beginning to get worried. Who took you from school?" she asks, turning around on the couch to look at me.

I shrink a little under her gaze, even though there's nothing but mild interest in her voice. "Harris dropped me off on his way home. I'm really tired, though."

Mom smiles at me. "All right. Sleep well. Gardening club after church tomorrow?"

I can't believe she can't see the day on my face. "Sounds good," I say, and run upstairs to my bedroom, my mind already back in the dark car with rain running down the windows.

# CHAPTER 7

Monday morning at breakfast, Rachel sits next to me and bounces Horsie up and down on my legs, singing a song about Noah's ark she must've learned in Sunday school. Mom is doing the perfect housewife breakfast routine, waffles in the iron and juice on the table. She didn't do this when we lived with Grandma. Back then, we all got our own breakfast of cereal and tea whenever we got out of bed. But now she packs me and Peter a lunch, makes us waffles or pancakes before we leave the house.

Peter's on his way out the door, a waffle squeezed between his teeth. He takes it out to kiss Mom on the cheek. It reminds me of Sophie, dropping me off after the states meet Saturday, brushing a kiss across my cheek that ran shivers down my spine...

"Emily, can you help clean that up?"

I jump. Rachel has spilled a glass of milk and is close to tears. I didn't even notice. "Yeah, sorry." I sop up the spill with the cloth napkin, momentarily feel bad that I've just covered one of the items that Peter's dead wife chose ten years ago, and make a silly face at Rachel.

Mom sets a paper bag with a sandwich in front of me. "Here you go."

"Mom, you know I can make my own lunch," I say, eating my last bite of waffle.

"It's fine. Are you going to the youth group November event today?"

I almost gag on my waffle. I completely forgot about youth group. "Umm, I was going to study with my friend Sophie. You met her."

"She's the one who won the states meet, right?"

Mom's dim understanding of cross country is sort of comforting, from a woman that knows every detail of my life. Well, almost every detail. "Uh, well, she did really well. Now that the season's over, I was going to, uh... tutor her. In Biology." Shoot, I should have picked a different subject, one that I don't already have lies built up in.

Mom doesn't seem to notice or care, though. "Can you do tutoring another day of the week?" she asks. "I think this youth group could be a really good thing to help you get to know this church a little better."

My whole body tightens at the thought of sitting in a church basement with Beth and Pastor Dan and Charity the homeschooler and all the other kids from various private schools around Pineridge, applying the lessons of Jesus to Teen Issues™. Especially when I could be spending the afternoon with Sophie. "You're totally right. It's just that specifically for today I promised Sophie I would help and I don't want to go back on that." I see Mom, looking at the pile of dishes, and I remember she's trying to make this work, and I'm supposed to try and make it work. "I'll go to the December one," I say in a small voice.

"Okay," Mom says. "I don't want you to have to back out on a promise. But then will you promise me that you'll go to the next one? I really think this will help you feel more comfortable at church."

I feel a twinge of guilt as I agree, and promise. But December is a long way away. At least I've delayed the inevitable in favor of an afternoon with Sophie. Which might not sound like a great deal, but when I think about seeing her for the first time in fifty-six hours, seems more than worth it.


*

At the end of the day, I head into the auditorium for concert band. Immediately, I feel like I've been slapped in the face by Christmas. Fake pine branches and twinkly lights dangle from the rafters. Stage manager Rhys wobbles at the top of a ladder, pinning tinsel against the curtains at the back of the stage. "No, no, dear, drape it more festively. It must festoon the stage," Mrs. Porco says, like that's helpful in any way, shape or form.

It's November 6th. Our concert is a month away. "Isn't it a little early for all this?" Willie asks from behind me, lugging his double bass in behind him.

It's good to see him. It's good to see anyone I associate with Sophie. Only one more period until I get to see her. "Mrs. Porco likes to make sure we're ready for the holiday concert," I tell him. "She calls them dress rehearsals for the stage."

Willie smiles. "I hope I'm ready for this level of festivity."

We settle onto the stage. That's when I spot the giant, multi-colored sign Mrs. Porco has pinned over the bulletin board backstage, covering all existing posters and notices. *SPRING SENIOR SOLO TRYOUTS!!! DECEMBER12th!!!*

Nothing like Mrs. Porco's exuberant punctuation to get me nervous. My palms get sweaty just thinking about the idea of tryouts. But they're not for a month. "Sit down, sit down, my children," says Mrs. Porco, walking away from the bottom of Rhys's ladder and to the front of the stage. "You'll notice that these halls are being decked by the inimitable Rhys."

I grin up at him. He smiles back. It's hard not to be in a good mood. Mrs. Porco is insane, but she cares so much that a lot of that care starts to spill over. I'm happy I still get to see Rhys even though cross country is over.

Mrs. Porco isn't finished with her daily speech. "This is a reminder to us all that we have a concert coming. Over the next month, we must elevate ourselves to new heights, taking it upon ourselves to push ourselves and each other to the pinnacle of our musical                                                                skill!"

People have all settled into their seat by now. Beth comes in late, sits next to me, smoothing out her skirt over her tights.

"This is also a reminder to our seniors—and to any others that may wish to try out for a high-level solo—" Here, she looks right at me. I shrink into my seat. "—to have something prepared, something that truly showcases your specific, significant skillset." Mrs. Porco does love her alliteration. "Now, before we warm up, a short word with the woodwinds."

She sashays over to the woodwinds. Beside me, Beth snorts. "Mrs. Porco's so fucking weird."

I don't say anything. Beth's not wrong. But I like Mrs. Porco.

"Are you trying out for the solo?" Beth asks, fluffing her hair in an expert way that makes it look like new. I touch my own hair, which is full of flyaways from when I got distracted daydreaming during lunch in Harris's room and then had to run to sixth period US History.

"I, uh… I think so," I say finally. "She asked me to."

"Well, that'll probably be good practice for you, what with your stage fright and all," says Beth. "But I can't see her giving it to a junior, can you?"

I grit my teeth, thinking of Mom. We're making a family. We're doing it. The band plays.

We warm up. I pray for band practice to go quickly, and like always, it goes by in a rush. It always does. We're finally starting to sound coherent in "Carol of the Bells", though as a violin section we're still struggling a little. I'm glad for the extra practice I've gotten to put in. But every second I'm not playing, I'm watching the clock. The bell rings soon, and I look up from my sheet music eagerly. Time to see Sophie!

I leave in a rush, my sheet music bunched in my hands. Beth catches up with me as I head out the door, though. "Hey, are you coming to youth group? Your mom said you might need a ride," she asks.

My hackles rise, but then I remember I've already cleared this with Mom. "I can't today. I'm tutoring my friend."

"That's too bad," says Beth, in a way that suggests she's not upset about it at all. "It'd be good for you. Since, you know, you've been going to this church for a couple years and still don't have any friends there."

I feel myself shrinking a little at the nastiness of this comment. "At least I have you," I mumble, not without irony.

She smiles, sickeningly sweet. "That's right."

We turn down left down the hallway, Beth towards the parking lot exit, me towards my locker. "I—oh, there's my friend, I gotta go," I say, glad I actually have a friend in this stupid place.

Sophie stands by my locker, her back to me, looking down at her phone. It's the first time I've seen her since she dropped me off after states. And I genuinely can't believe it, the way my heart *literally*, not figuratively, but in my actual body, starts beating faster. I always thought that was a metaphor, but no, something about my biology really likes Sophie.

Beth says something that sounds catty, but I'm not even paying attention. "Bye," I say vaguely as I drift down the hallway. Any remaining guilt I feel about lying disappears the moment Sophie turns, sees me, and smiles. The things I would do for that smile.

\*

The end of cross country and the decorations in the auditorium make it feel like the autumn switch has been flipped to "off" and the winter switch is flipped to "on." The next month is a blur of cold weather, studying, indoor track, and practicing violin.

But the one wonderful constant through the whirlwind is Sophie. I'm with her pretty much every moment I'm not at school or at home, and those other moments, I'm thinking about her. I never realized that this is what it feels like, to be falling for someone: this desire to memorize every detail of her, the habit of connecting every facet of my life back to hers somehow.

We have indoor track together, at least. Cross country isn't technically over until Christa, her parents, and Harris make their way to nationals in mid-November. She places 24th, the highest placement by a Pineridge runner in history. The rest of us have entered into the indoor track season by then. Indoor track isn't a varsity sport but that messy, weird activity in the short season between cross country and track and field. Nobody enjoys indoor track, not even Harris. We practice by running in the hallways, on the hard linoleum floors, and everyone has mild shin splints by December. The kids who run indoor are the hardcore runners: the best of cross country and track. The cross-country kids tend to run the long-distance track events, the one and two mile, while the best sprinters start training over the winter for the 100 and 200 meter events.

I can already tell Sophie is made for the middle distance, the 400 (quarter mile) and 800 (half mile). She has the body of a sprinter and the mental fortitude of a miler. I can't wait for the one and only indoor track meet Harris has us attend every year.

Sophie attends practice twice a week. I attend on the days she does, even though there's not much Harris needs me to do this time of year. On Wednesdays, when I'm supposedly tutoring her, we hole up at her house. But the best are days when we go on long, cold runs together until it's too dark to see, just us and the quiet of a trail or a park.

Mom comments at least once a week about how busy I am, but I brush her off with vague excuses. I feel like I'm just floating through my days, like I've decided to postpone all my anxieties and fears to deal with later. And it's weird, because even though I'm busy with AP Bio and precalc and SATs and *Invisible Man*, the subject I feel like I'm studying the hardest is Sophie herself.

I learn that she likes all kinds of music, but especially seventies soft rock, Czech folk, and current rap ("chill rap, not angry rap.") I poke around the floor of her car, which is littered with random mix CDs that Willie has made for her and cassettes from PJ's previous owner.

I learn that Sophie hates elevators on the Monday after Thanksgiving when her mom forgets her laptop at home on the day that she's interviewing for a higher position at her current company. We drive downtown to deliver it to her and walk up 25 flights of stairs. That's also the very first time that I hear her speaking Czech on the phone with her mom. I almost drop my clipboard because of how startled I am to hear a foreign language coming out of her mouth as fluently as English. She spends most of the journey up that flight of stairs teaching me all the Czech swear words that she knows.

I learn that Sophie can fall asleep in literal seconds one day when Willie and I get into an animated discussion about aerodynamics (he's very into kites lately.) Sophie is uncharacteristically silent, and when I glance over at her, she's asleep on the floor of their family room.

I learn about the pale birthmark on her left shoulder blade, and the scar on her abdomen from when her appendix was removed at age six. I grow familiar with the sight of her favorite T-shirt, a blue relic from a middle school science fair her brother had won as a fifth grader. I notice the way her whole body starts to droop like a thirsty tulip when she's tired or upset. I memorize the precise cadence of her laugh when she remembers something funny that happened a few hours ago. I even take careful note of the tiny sound she makes whenever I press my lips to a certain spot, just below where her neck meets her jawline.

And most interesting of all I learn that Sophie notices things, too. I'm so focused on what's going on in my head that it's astonishing to realize she has similar thoughts regarding me. She's a lot more comfortable and knowledgeable about relationships and, well, other stuff, in a way that I'm simply not. It's a learning process, fumbling, haphazard, sometimes embarrassing. But Sophie, it turns out, is a good teacher. And I've always been a quick study.

So, unlike when we do recovery runs, I let her set the pace.

By the time the holiday concert rolls around, I'm so excited for Sophie to see me play that I don't even feel nervous. Not even when we get to the key change in "Carol of the Bells" where the violins go insane. Mom, Peter, and Rachel come too, Peter with a bouquet of winter paperwhites that I see Mom's hand in selecting. It's sweet. But not as sweet as right after the concert, when Sophie waits by the backstage doors. She pulls me into an empty classroom, kisses me softly, and hands me a packet of aster seeds. "Secret flowers," she says, smiling at her own cleverness.

I can't even speak. It's the most touching gesture I've ever been offered.

It's those seeds that I touch in my back pocket, having not even planted them yet, when I audition for the solo a week later, on the day when the violinists are taking their turn. With the confidence of Sophie in my mind, I play without mistakes and with ease.

Maybe things can always be like this.

*

Mid-December, the day after my tryouts, I'm at Sophie's house. We're always at her house when we're not running. Mom thinks I'm at youth group or indoor track practice, the importance of which I may have exaggerated to her. Either way, she's busy enough with Rachel and planning a basement renovation that she doesn't expect me till six.

We're studying. Well, I'm studying, on the floor, my biology book, notebook, handouts, and notecards arranged in the semicircular order that I prefer. Sophie's theoretically working on her college applications, but instead she's lying on her narrow bed doing a lactic acid drain, her legs pressed flat up against the wall. "Hey, Em," she says.

I don't look up; I'm switching from my green to my pink highlighter to indicate a passage about cell division that's not covered by the AP but is interesting and I want to look into more. "Mmmhmm?" I ask through the cap between my teeth.

"Do you think you're gay, or…?"

The highlighter cap falls into the spine of my book. I look up at her. Her head hangs off the bed, upside down. Her jean cuffs are slipping down from her ankles to her knees, her shinbones curving into the thin, hard muscles of her calves.

"I mean," she says, her voice a little nasally from her odd angle. "I was just wondering, since, we're, like, you know… girlfriends or whatever."

I smile. "Or whatever."

"I'm serious. Are you into girls generally or is it just a me thing or what?"

I pause. It's a good question, and one that's been keeping me awake at night in the rare moments where I'm not consumed with thoughts of Sophie specifically. It's true that I haven't really noticed much in the way of guy-crushes before now, but it's not like there were girls that I was actively pursuing. I was definitely a lot more invested in the women's cross country team than the men's', but that's just because they were better. Right? I guess maybe Kari's shoulders had been a distraction point, but I just assumed that was general envy of having a powerful, fast body.

"I don't know," I say finally. "I think maybe? Gay-ish?"

"Oh, yeah?" she says.

"I think. Admittedly, I have not been terribly consumed with crushes up until now," I tell her. "I don't have the number of data points required to answer that question with any degree of rigor."

Sophie laughs. I love that I can make her laugh just by saying the stupid stuff that goes through my head. "I'm not totally sure, either," she says. "I mean, now that I think about it, I guess I had things for girls as well as guys, but guys were the ones going after me, so I was just kind of like... whatever."

Her hair is a dark cloud bunched up behind her head, so fluffy it's practically straight out of a L'Oréal commercial. "La la la. I'm Sophie," I say. "I'm so carefree and beautiful. Guys like me all the time, it's so whatever, might as well just go with it. I—ouch." She throws a pillow at my face.

"You dick," she says. "You know, you're the first person I've ever... I don't know. Like, made the first move on."

I hug the pillow to me. "Really."

"Yeah."

"But—really?"

She lifts herself to her elbows and looks at me. "Yeah. What's up?"

I stare back down at my textbook. "Um... why," I say.

"Em? You okay?"

"Yes, I... yes, I just... why?" I say to the pages. "Why on earth would you pick me? I mean, I'm not really...anything, and you're so... everything."

There's a creak as she gets off the bed. "Em," she says. She presses a hand to each of my hot, hot cheeks, forcing me to look her straight in the eyes. It gives me a jolt. "Emily." She kisses me. "That is fucking ridiculous."

I lean in again.

A few minutes later, when we're lying on the floor underneath the duvet Sophie has pulled down onto us, I press the issue. "But seriously," I say, rolling on my side to face her, "You're very sweet, but in an objective sense, honestly, how were you even attracted to me?"

"Fishing for compliments?" she asks, brushing my hair back from my face.

"No," I say defensively.

"I know, just teasing." She becomes quiet for a moment. The soft light from her lamp filters greenly through her duvet, speckling onto her face. "You really want to know? Other than that you're cute as hell?"

"Yeah," I say.

She looks at me, her face open and a little scared. But she starts talking anyway. "So, at Rhizenstein, I had really, really good friends, but I didn't totally fit in with like, everyone. Like, there were some people who—I never felt, like, black enough. Willie, either. Since our mom's Czech and all. Like, Sophie is a white-ass name but my mom's mom is named Sofia so that's where I'm at. And then here in fricking Pineridge I feel like this alien species. Not just because of being mixed, although it is super weird being like, the only brown person in a lot of my classes." She laughs shortly. "But just... it's weird here. It feels like people are more up in your business, you know? And I just didn't totally feel like I belonged either place."

Sophie pulls the blanket down over her face. I rest my hand on her belly, leaning in further so I can hear her through the fabric.

"And even in my family, I'm like, the dumb one. And I fucking love my family but half the time when Willie is just acing his classes and I'm going as hard as I can for those B's, it just... sometimes it sucks."

I feel a twinge of guilt. I think of how Sophie got quiet when I mentioned using tutoring her as an excuse for hanging out. I wish I had come up with something else.

"And right from the second I met you, you acted like I was worth something. Like I was worth a lot." She lets out another weird little laugh. "So I don't know. That's how you cracked the Sophie code, I guess."

She says this last part with a flippant tone, a joking tone. I recognize it, another little pattern. I try to figure out the right words. "Why do you always do that?" I ask, finally.

"Do what?" she asks.

I pull the blanket back from her face. "Like, make fun of yourself. It's like you're trying to beat me to it," I tell her.

She doesn't say anything, but she looks up at me.

"I'm not going to make fun of you," I tell her. "I'm not."

She pulls me tight to her. We stay like that for a long time, hearts pounding next to each other.

*

The last week of school before Christmas break is a busy one, the week of the indoor track meet. And in the haze of getting to know Sophie better, I've completely forgotten to stress about the outcome of the solo tryouts until the day Mrs. Porco announces them.

Of course, the moment she starts to announce them, all that stress comes rushing back at once. Thanks, brain! I almost forgot what this felt like!

Mrs. Porco does not disappoint when it came to dramatics. "After a great deal of thought and introspection, I have decided that this year for our spring showcase, our cornerstone piece for our soloists will be... Drumroll, please..."

She glances at Rhys. He lets out a tiny sigh before performing a perfectly executed drumroll on the snare.

"*Danse Macabre* by the inimitable Camille Saint-Saëns!" she says. "This piece is both thrilling and chilling. It asks us all to examine our mortality, how fragile life truly is. And it asks us to dance with death itself."

Beth rolls her eyes at Mrs. Porco's theatrics, but I'm trembling in my seat. I know this piece. I've heard it before, though not for a long time. But I know it features a violin soloist.

Mrs. Porco begins distributing sheet music from her bright orange binder. Percussion parts for percussion, flute and clarinet parts for the woodwinds, one lonely packet for Willie the double bassist and Jenny Lewis the cellist. "This piece will showcase many of the unique talents that this year's orchestra has. Rhys will play the part of the skeletons on the xylophone, Annie's oboe will glow as the rooster crowing in the dawn, and Emily... will portray Death herself." She smiles at me as she hands me the first chair violin music, then Beth a different set of music.

My stomach drops. I got it? I got the solo? I ignore Beth's scorching gaze and stare down at the music. Yes, there it is, that insane violin solo, right near the beginning. At first glance, it's not the most technically challenging piece I've ever tackled, but there's a lot going on here. And I've never soloed in front of an actual audience before.

Mrs. Porco flounces her way to the front of the room. "And now, let us listen to the London Symphony Orchestra regaling us with this piece."

The first chair violin. As death. With their E string tuned to E-flat for a scary minor sound. The beginning is quiet, with some stringed instrument—is that a harp? We'll have to substitute for that, no one at Pineridge plays the harp—and soft violin chords. I remember this. It represents the sun setting.

But then in comes the solo violinist, and it's not soft. It's sharp, bold, and discordant. It makes my palms start to sweat and my heart start to pound just thinking about it, fight or flight kicking in like I'm getting chased by a predator.

But it also feels kind of... amazing.

And frankly, it also feels satisfying to know that I have something that Beth wants.

I look down at the sheet music again, following along as the song washes over me. I can't wait to tell Sophie.

*

140

That afternoon, a smattering of cross country and track runners are getting on the bus, on the way to the indoor track meet. You can tell it's the second to last day of school before break. The team is giddy, laughing and shoving each other into seats, winter coats providing some cushioning. The bus throws off heat, belching exhaust. It's already snowing. Even at 3 PM, it's already getting close to twilight. I vaguely remember that today is the solstice. Soon the earth will tip again, the days will grow longer, and the garden will be green. But for now, winter is just fine by me.

Sophie runs up, almost late. "Em! My mom's coming to the meet!" she says breathlessly, joining me in line for the bus.

Another lovely addition to the day. "That's great." Katchka's recent promotion has been keeping her late for the last few weeks. Sophie's been missing her.

"Yeah. She can't get there till five, though, so I'm hoping my events are on the late side." She glances at me anxiously as we file onto the bus after Marly and Damien, two sprinters.

"The meet's not going to get started till around four, and they're always running behind schedule at Thayer." I roll my eyes. Lackadaisical time management always brings out my inner control freak. "Harris has you in the mile and the 800. I'm guessing we won't get to the mile till at least six."

"Nice," she says We sit down in a seat, both of our backpacks and Sophie's running bag and my violin case crowded around us. In the back of the bus, Jon gives his signature birdcall. I have no idea for what. "How was your day?" Sophie asks, like the whole bus isn't chaos.

"It was good. I…" I duck my head, smiling at my lap. "I have a solo for the spring concert. A really cool one."

"But Em. Wait. That's amazing!" When I look up, Sophie is looking at me, intense, happy. For one panicked second I think she's going to grab me and kiss me on the bus in front of everyone. But she just takes my hand, between us in the seats, and holds it tight. "That's fantastic, Emily," she tells me.

"Thanks," I reply.

"Are you nervous?"

"Extremely."

She smiles. "But you're excited?"

"I… I think so."

Sophie peers into my carefully neutral face. "Understatement of the century. Well, I'm really fucking excited. When's the concert? March, right?"

"Yeah."

The bus rumbles along, going slowly in the falling snow. Pineridge only attends one indoor track meet per year. It's mostly so Harris can try people out in different events before the spring track season, confirm his hypotheses about who will be better for sprint events and who will run the distance events. Sophie and I talk quietly until she wants to start to get focused for the meet. I stare out the window, my fingers still laced in hers underneath our jackets.

The meet isn't far away, but in the snow and weird winter light, traffic moves at a snail's pace. Thinking about snails makes me think about mollusks, which we're getting to soon now that we're almost done with cell bio in Harris's class. (I've been skipping ahead a little.) Earlier this week, I sat down to give Harris an update on my independent study. "I have all my notes compiled," I tell him. "I just need to synthesize them into a coherent report delineating the history and scientific merit of various origin stories."

Harris had laughed. "Okay, Emily. I'm sure it's very good. I'll sign off on it whenever you want."

Harris is two years from retirement. I know he doesn't care a ton about this investigation into theories about the origin of the universe, not really any more than Mom does. She just wants to believe that I'm getting my Bible in alongside my bio book. Still, this has felt good, researching this, trying to decide what I believe.

We pull up to Thayer University, which is hosting the meet. No high school in Northeast Ohio has its own indoor track. The bus driver gets turned around a couple times trying to find the appropriate drop-off point, with Harris sitting behind him directing. They snap at each other and even though I'm feeling a little sick from the fumes and stop-and-start pace, it's Harris enough that I can smile.

Finally, we crank to a stop. The team leaves the bus in a flurry of sweatpants, hats, and mittens. The streetlights glow a gentle orange as we walk across the parking lot, not adequately preparing me for the burst of fluorescent light that greets us as we go in through the double doors. An enormous windowless room surrounds us, the smells of rubber and concrete permeating the air.

Beside me, Sophie shudders. "Ugh. This is even worse than running the second-floor hallway."

"At least you have a track here. It'll be better on your shins," I say.

Jon, who's been keeping a somewhat frosty distance between himself and Sophie for weeks since homecoming, speaks from right behind us. I jump. "I agree with Sophie. It's so… industrial here."

Sophie smiles, surprised. "Right?"

"I guess," I say. It makes sense that they'd agree. Sophie and Jon both love being outdoors, hate being stuck in an enclosed environment. Really, they have compatible personalities. I still feel a little guilty when I think about Sophie and Jon, even if they never really dated. And part of me feels the tiniest bit jealous.

But it's a track meet! There's already so much to do. Harris hands me a duffel bag of bib numbers "Emily! Can you get these out?"

I take a breath. This is where I belong. First, I distribute the racing bibs and safety pins. Track meets are even busier than cross-country meets. We're entered in eight different running events tonight. In the spring, we'll also have people entered in the field events as well—triple jump, high jump, shot put— but those will be the purview of Ms. Declan, the field coach for track and field.

rris and I stick with the running events. It's enough trouble
e that everybody's ready for their heats when different ones
few minutes. Making sure we record times on top of that is
a lot. "Four by eight up first, Greg, Derrick, Stephen, JJ, come get your
bibs." Harris yells, and I distribute bibs for the men in the 4 x 800
relay. Hundreds of runners, coaches, officials, spectators, all crowd up
in the stands and round the track. Something about the space makes
sound carry strangely. The acoustics are terrible. The chaos pulses in
my brain. I feel a headache forming.

But once we're going, and the starting gun for the first race has
fired, I feel much calmer. I give Laura a granola bar, who forgot to
bring lunch today, and tell Derrick to put his sweatpants back on in
between events, and take down the times of the 100-meter dash.

About an hour later, Katchka finds me on the ground near the
track. "Emily! I didn't know the meet had already begun. Have I
missed Sophie's race?"

"No, she's running the mile in around fifteen minutes." I smile
at the tiny Czech woman. "You haven't missed much, but you might
have a better view from the bleachers."

She waves me off. "It is more exciting down here," she says
airily, staring up at the faraway rafters and horrible fluorescent lights.

"I'll let her know you're here," I tell her. It's nice to see her
excited instead of stressed.

I set off to find Sophie, but I end up missing most of her
performance during the mile. The men's mile is right before it, and I
spend most of the women's mile helping Jon stretch a nasty hamstring
cramp and then finding him a banana to eat. Still, Sophie finishes well,
a 5:56, according to Harris. He's excited to try her in some shorter
events, too. "She has a kick like you wouldn't believe at the end,
Emily!" he tells me.

I'm determined to at least watch her during the 800, the half-mile. It's near the end, and I'm starting to get tired and overwhelmed by that point. But I can't wait to watch this. I'm so excited to see Sophie in the middle-long distance. She has a pretty strong PR from Rhizenstein in the 800, but after a season of cross country I'm excited to see what she can do. She won't need to pace herself with as much discipline, wouldn't need to conserve long-term energy the way she needed to during cross-country. Not many girls will be able to match the length of her stride nor her momentum once she began sprinting.

I haven't gotten a chance to watch her race since states. I'm a little startled to realize how much I miss it. It's one of the reasons I... It's one of the reasons I feel about her the way I do. She puts in her heart and her soul and it makes my breath catch when I watch her.

Tonight is no exception. I stand with Harris at the finish line, watching Sophie tear around the two-hundred-meter track four times. "The eight hundred is her event," Harris says as we watch her pass the girl from Vale who won last year. "Maybe we want to get her on the four, too, come springtime."

I can't respond. I don't take my eyes off her the entire time, not until she takes first place in her heat, not until Harris says "2:17, if you don't mind, Emily," and I write it down.

When I glance up, she's no longer in my sight. "Are you all right here for a sec, Harris?"

"Yep," he says. "Two hundred next. I'll go make sure Donny's got his ass in gear."

I weave through the crowd to find her. Sophie has an alarming tendency to disappear after races that I've forgotten about since cross country. She just runs herself into such exhaustion that she can't even face people in the immediate aftermath. Her face was contorted during her last two laps and I know her shins are bothering her more than she says. I need to find her.

Instead, I find Katchka, sitting on a bench against the wall and looking around with mild interest. "Have you seen Sophie, Katchka?"

"She was having some trouble breathing, so she went to get some fresh air. She said she was okay. She ran a very good race, yes?"

"It was really impressive," I tell her.

"I think I will take her home after she comes back," Katchka says.

"I'll go find her. I'm, uh, glad you came, Katchka," I say, feeling a little shy. She smiles at me, and I leave to find Sophie. When I find her pile of stuff, it confirms what I've already guessed: She's gone out into the snow without any warm clothes.

I grab her jacket, and shrug on my own coat and scarf before heading out into the winter evening. Snow is still falling, harder now than before. A cold breeze blows white flakes into my eyes and nose. The dark sky is a relief after the horrible lighting inside.

I spot Sophie instantly, sagging against one of the streetlights in the parking lot in her unitard. "Soph!" I call, hurrying over to her, my arms full of her clothes.

She looks up at me wearily, and smiles. "Hey, beautiful," she says.

I shiver a little. "It's freezing," I tell her, though my reaction is not even a little bit related to the cold. "You need more clothes."

"It feels good out here."

"I know it's hot in there, but it's awful for your muscles to go from so warm to so cold all at once." I hand over her coat, and as she slips it around her shoulders, I take off my scarf and tuck it around her neck. She catches my hands as I let go. "Em," she says, holding them at her heart. "Emily, you know I love you, right?"

I'm speechless. Around me, the snow falls harder.

"Like, a lot," she adds softly. "I can't even think about how lucky I am right now."

I want to say the words, but they're stuck somewhere, behind the layers and layers of emotion building up in my throat. All I can do is press myself against her. She pulls me into her arms and we stand there under the streetlight's orange glow, the snow lightly landing all around us.

# CHAPTER 8

The next day, which was supposed to be the last day of school before winter break, school gets cancelled because of the snow. When I look out my bedroom window, Wisteria Manors is a sparkling sea of white, silent and cold other than an occasional rush of wind. Snow has settled onto our holly bush in the backyard. I feel proud of the hearty plant. Mom and I know the holly at least will thrive in the winter while the perennials sleep under the snow.

The prospect of an extra day of vacation is too good to waste. The first thing I do after I wake up is call Sophie. "I need to sleep for like four more hours, Em," she says in response to my eight AM phone call. I smile at the sleepiness in her voice as we make plans for later. Snow running, then Christmas shopping. We'll meet later that afternoon.

After breakfast, Mom, Rachel, and I spend the morning on a giant snowman with holly berries for tiny, beady eyes. Rachel is high on the upcoming Christmas holiday and can't stop bursting out into carols, which makes the morning incredibly fun. That is, until Mom glances at her watch. "Beth will be here to pick you up for youth group in an hour," she says. "You'd better go shower and get ready."

I'm not much for cursing, but my brain has lately been saying, *Aw, fuck* in the same intonation that Sophie uses sometimes. It's like all the goodness of the morning seeps away as I imagine getting into Beth's car, listening to her say nasty things to me, and going to church or doing whatever the hell they're doing today.

"I was going to hang out with my friend today," I tell Mom. Thinking about Sophie at last night's meet, all I want is to be with her right now. Sophie knows I get shy and tongue-tied, so I don't think she read too much into the fact that I wasn't able to return the "I love you" she told me last night. But if it seems like I'm avoiding her today...

"You promised you would go to this one, Emily," Mom says, her voice stern. Frustration rises inside of me. I did promise, but that was Past Emily's decision, not mine. I'm about to argue, but Rachel flings herself into a pile of snow right at Mom's feet. I don't want to ruin everyone's morning.

I go inside and get ready to call Sophie, melting snow dripping from my hair. Except when I take the cordless phone up to my room, I spot the shoebox where I've been keeping my bio notes. It reminds me that I really don't want to go to this youth group.

A seed of a plan starts to sprout in my mind. I dial Sophie's number by heart. "What's up?" she asks.

"Can you pick me up at Asbury Park instead of at home?"

"Uh, sure. Everything okay?"

"Yeah," I tell her. "You're helping spring me from youth group."

She laughs. "I'll be your getaway car anytime."

So, giddy with my plans, I get ready to leave. "Mom, I'm heading over to Beth's!" I call, clattering down into the foyer in my running shoes that I've attached little treads to specifically for snow running

Mom glances at the clock. She and Rachel are making hot chocolate at the stove, flushed with cold. "Aren't you early?" she asks.

My brain auto-supplies a lie straight to my mouth. "We're doing a run-through of the new pieces for concert band. They're pretty complicated."

"Don't you need your violin?" Mom asks, turning back to the stove. I can tell by her body language that she's not suspicious; she's just trying to take care of me. Somehow, piling a lie on top of another lie feels worse, not better. But I say the words through a tight throat. "I'll use Beth's extra so I don't have to drag mine along to youth group."

"All right," she says. "Have fun!"

I book it out of the house before any last-minute questions occur to her, then run to Asbury Park. Through the snow, it's more of a galloping, tripping sort of motion. The further I get from home, the more free and silly I feel.

Sophie's waiting in the parking lot by the time I get there, her car blessedly warm other than the stream of cold air that comes in through the back window that's permanently stuck about a quarter inch open. "Hi," she says, and kisses me.

I'm so happy to see her that I almost forget Phase 2 of my deception. But not quite. "Can I borrow your phone?" I say once she starts driving out of the lot.

She hands it over, focusing on the icy roads with a much greater level of attention than usual.

I text Beth from Sophie's phone, my fingers clumsy at the process. But Beth will see through me immediately if I call her.

*Hey Beth, it's Emily. I can't make it to youth group today, I'm*

Sick? No, then why would I be texting her from a random number? I'm gambling on the fact that she hasn't said much to me since I got the solo. I'm hoping that she hopes to minimize our interactions as much as I do. I settle on tutoring.

*I'm tutoring. You can go ahead without me.*

The whole car ride, I'm feeling nervous about a response—will she ask more questions? Demand to know who I'm with? Even Sophie loudly and terribly singing "I Saw Three Ships Come Sailing in On Christmas Day" doesn't cheer me up, not even when she runs out of verses she knows and starts making up her own verses about seeing three Emilys coming in.

Her phone buzzes. I grab it. "*k*" says Beth's text.

My stomach untwists. I grab Sophie's hand. She stops singing to smile at me. It's going to be a good day.

\*

Our run ends up being more of a romp, since snow blankets the trails at Emerson Nature Preserve in a layer several inches thick. We only make it a mile out and a mile back. Sophie instigates a snowball war that takes the better part of twenty minutes to resolve, with me kamikaze-attacking her into a snowdrift by tackling her. When we finally leave, very tired and still laughing, Sophie drives us to a place I hate almost as much as I love this nature preserve: the mall.

In December, Pineridge Mall is always packed. Shoppers, Christmas-clad temp workers pulled in to accommodate the extra traffic, parents pushing strollers loaded with screaming toddlers... all while "Have a Holly Jolly Christmas" unspools like tinsel into everyone's skulls.

"You Grinch," says Sophie when I try to explain these feelings to her.

"You're not bothered by all this?" I ask, gesturing down at the Santa's Village. We're on the second-floor mezzanine, peering down at the shoppers below.

"What, the crowds?"

"Not just the crowds. The... materialism. You know, the hordes bowing down to worship Santa in exchange for piles and piles of presents."

Sophie laughs. "You're such a fucking weirdo," she says, but in a voice that's warm. She bumps me with her shoulder. Yes, it's crowded, but I feel anonymous. Mom hates this place more than I do. I lean into Sophie a little as we watch the kids and parents waiting to take photos with Santa.

She glances at me, with something soft in her expression, but continues talking like this is normal. "I mean, one, they're not hordes, they're children. In an orderly line."

"Devastating hordes," I tell her.

"Sure. Fine. Devastating hordes. But posing for a photo their parents are going to, like, treasure, isn't exactly bowing down to worship him."

"What ever happened to Jesus?" I ask. As much as I've been thinking lately that Christianity is missing the mark, I loved the Christmas Eve service Mom and Dad and I used to go to. There was something—I guess *holy* is the technical term—about being pressed between my parents, still in my sheep costume from the Christmas pageant, while the chamber choir sang Silent Night and We Three Kings.

Sophie leans down and pushes my hair back. I jump, but all she does is whisper, "You're still a Grinch," her breath a tickle in my ear.

I laugh. "Jingle Bell Rock" comes on the radio. Sophie grabs my arm. "C'mon, Grinchy McScrooge, let's go shopping."

We're buying gifts for family, friends. I get Rachel a couple of big-eyed stuffed animals (after Sophie talks me out of this Junior Scientist kit when she points out I'm shopping for Rachel, not myself.) Sophie gets Willie a book about how to make kites, at my recommendation. Then she gets really secretive. "We need to divide and conquer," she tells me after we've stopped at the Dairy Queen for sustenance.

"But I hate the mall," I say through a mouthful of vanilla ice cream.

"Sucks to suck. I need to buy certain gifts for… certain people. Certain person." She grins.

"Fine. I suppose I should do the same," I tell her, to throw her off. Her gift's already at home.

She pushes back from our table. "Meet you outside in half an hour?"

"If I don't die here."

She rolls her eyes. I watch her re-enter the crowd, her hair spilling over her green t-shirt, her windbreaker tied around her waist. I watch her till she disappears, then keep watching the crowd. All day, I've been trying to think of the perfect time to tell Sophie that I love her, too. But every time I get close—pressed closed to her laughing in the snow, listening to her take in a big breath as she prepares to butcher another Christmas carol—I get shy and my mouth clams up.

But I can't sit in this crowded food court forever. A couple of overglossed preteens are eying my table with a predatory intensity. Like prey, I take off.

I wander through the mall, a bit of holiday cheer beginning to steal over me against all odds. I should get Sophie something to go with her gift. I've been growing her a plant, a little pot of sage that I planted in soil I stole from the Bowl. It's tough, like her. But maybe I should get her a book or something to go with it. Or a necklace. Some kind of jewelry. Girls like jewelry, right? I don't, so obviously there's a flaw in that line of deduction.

That's when I hit on it: I can write her a note. A letter. Where I say everything I want to tell her, in my own words, without having to worry about my voice shaking or getting shy. Something she can hold onto, tangible evidence that she is the greatest person in my world despite my terrible lack of verbal communication.

I turn into the bookstore. Just to look, maybe find some nice stationary. Just like everywhere, it's crowded. The urge for me to try and find an area where I can have some blessed, blessed personal space is strong. I push toward the children's section...

And immediately regret it when I come face-to-face with Beth. "Emily!" she says. "What are you doing here?"

My stomach twists. Okay, back in lying mode, sooner than I thought. "Um, tutoring."

"At the mall?" she asks.

For someone I don't consider to be very intelligent, Beth is very dangerous. Because she is mean. And even if she can't name every major genus in the Ranunculaceae family, she is very crafty when it comes to knowing when someone is lying, or uncomfortable, or otherwise vulnerable.

I have to throw her off the trail. "We had to pick up a book. I'm sorry I couldn't make it to youth group, just scheduling fluke."

"Yeah, that sucks," says Beth, like she doesn't actually think it sucks at all. "What book do you need?"

I'm panicking a little. "SAT prep," which, okay, good one, Em. Suitably boring. I can do this.

"How'd you get here?"

This is the real trap, because she knows as well as I do that Mom doesn't let anyone under eighteen except her drive me around. I do some mental calculations. "Sophie's dad dropped us off... I actually have to go, we're meeting in like five minutes."

Beth narrows her eyes. "Well, don't forget your prep book," she says, and turns away, heading back to her friends in the magazine section.

I'm so freaked out by a) my stupidity in coming to the mall, Beth's natural habitat, and b) the fact that Beth's gaze keeps flipping back to me, that I go ahead and drop thirty-five dollars on a prep book I already own. I rush out to wait on a bench outside the JC Penny in the freezing cold. I'm shivering, staring at the ground by the time Sophie gets there. She sits down close to me even though the bench is empty. "Hey Grinchy," she says.

Her warmth feels good, but instead of leaning in, I scoot away and cover my face.

"Hey, what's up?" she says. "I take too long?"

"No," I say through my mittens. "Beth saw me."

"The shitty cousin?"

"Yeah. I think she came here right after youth group."

"Christ," Sophie says. "That is like, the opposite of a Christmas miracle."

There's a long pause. I swear to god, I can still hear Christmas music. Maybe it's from the mall or maybe I'm just going moderately insane. One of her hands lifts, as though she's going to take my hand or cover my knee, but then she just slides it against her other hand. "She gonna tell your mom?"

I shrug. "I got out of it for now."

"You okay?"

I shrug again.

"Okay, let's just head back to the car and we can talk about it there. I'm sure it'll be fine," she says.

And it's Sophie, so I kind of believe her. Still, I'm relieved when we climb into PJ and pull out of the crowded parking lot.

*

"Emmy, wake up! Santa came!"

I roll over, groggy with sleep, then jump. Rachel is peering into my face. It's almost completely dark, and she's only visible to me as a blurry charcoal-blue blob. "Rach, it's still dark out. You gotta go back to bed."

I can't see her, but I can hear the pout in her voice clear as day. "That's what Momma Ruth said."

"Then it's true." I throw the blankets over my face.

Rachel taps me on the part of my head that is poking out of the top of my quilt. "Please can you wake up?"

I sigh. "Tell you what. You can stay here, but we have to wait until the adults are up, okay?"

She giggles and hops up onto the bed. "But I'm not tired."

"Okay, then let's tell a story," I mumble, eyes closed. "Once upon a time, there was a... there was a..."

"A princess."

"Sure. A princess. A beautiful princess. Who was a beautiful fast runner." I smile sleepily, thinking of Sophie.

Rachel nestles in beside me. "Does she live in a castle?"

"Of course, not a huge one, but a very very nice one."

"Way out in the middle of the forest," says Rachel.

"Yeah." I yawn. "But she was sad."

"Why?" Rachel wants to know.

"She's in love with someone, but nobody can know."

"A prince?"

"Sure," I reply. I can feel myself dropping off. "I guess. Why don't you take it from here, Rach?"

"The prince was sad too, because the queen wouldn't let anyone see him. And she put a big thorn in front of the prince's castle, and a river, and a big fire, and a bunch of knights, and, and..."

"Geez, isn't that enough for this poor princess to deal with?" I mumble.

"Well, that's the whole point," Rachel says, annoyed as only a know-it-all six-year-old can be. "That way when they live happily ever after, it's special."

"I sure hope so," I whisper before I fade out entirely.

\*

Peter's family arrives promptly at ten am in a flurry of food, hugs, and presents. To my horror, Beth lugs her violin case, confirming my fears that we may have to regale the family with Christmas duets like we've had to since Mom and I joined the Samstone clan. I'll have to watch her like a hawk to steer conversation away from youth group. Uncle Terry and Aunt Gretchen are sporting matching Christmas sweaters, one of which reads "Holly" and the other, correspondingly, "Jolly."

Nana, Peter's mom, hobbles slowly up the walk, holding onto her walker in the snow. Mom rushes out to help her inside. I know she misses her mother today, and I kind of do too, even though Grandma is a pretty scary lady. It would be sort of fun to see her put the fear of God into these people, with their sweaters and mistletoe and decorative light-up nativity scenes. But Grandma's spending all day in church and Nana Samstone is representing the elderly widow contingent today.

The low-level vitriol I've been feeling around the holidays surprises me a little. I mean, I can feel myself slipping more and more into heathendom every day. I haven't prayed in weeks, haven't thought about anything except Sophie and maybe sometimes my Monday weekly biology quizzes during church. But it's strange, sitting here, caught in this state between wishing people would be more reverent and less reverent at the same time. Mom, Dad, and I exchanged presents when I was little, but the focus was always the joy of the birth of Jesus and imagining the wonder that the wise men and the shepherds must have felt, to know that their savior had been born. It feels a little far from the current living room, where Terry and Peter are talking about a recent fluke in the markets that apparently did excellent things that I don't fully understand for their stock portfolios, while Mom and Gretchen put together appetizers in the kitchen and Beth sits in the corner on her phone.

But it's fun at least having Rachel around, who believes that Santa came in the night, dragging Horsie from present to present willingly distributing gifts.

I end up on the couch next to Nana Samstone. "Emily! It's lovely to see you," she says. "You've put on some weight."

I'm instantly scarlet. "Uh, hi, Nana?"

"No, no, in a good way, dear. You're finally starting to fill out."

I cross my arms across my chest. "Oh, um... oh."

"Rachel, child, come bring that small package over," Nana says. Rachel, ever obedient and doting of her granny, brings over a pink-wrapped package. Nana hands it to me with trembling hands. I open it. It's a small makeup kit. "For when you start dating, now that you're a young lady."

Boy, is this conversation in a nosedive. "Nana, I'm really just trying to focus on my studies these days."

"Nonsense. Beth has a beau and she couldn't be happier." I glance over at Beth. She's on her phone. She looks pretty cloudy. But Nana Samstone presses on, undeterred. "Now, my friend Naomi's grandson is just the nicest boy, wouldn't hurt a fly, quite dashing as well…" She gives me a wink.

"I really don't think…"

"Nonsense, a girl like you needs to have some fun! I'll call Naomi this week, we'll have a little powwow…"

Mom rescues me from this conversation when she calls me into the kitchen to help with the smoked salmon crackers.

After brunch and presents, I'm feeling a little happier. I know I make fun of Aunt Gretchen, but she makes a truly tasty quiche. That's when Uncle Terry booms out, "I think our girls owe us a song!"

I stiffen, mouth full of quiche. Beth rolls her eyes. "I'm going to the bathroom," she says. Internally, and maybe for the first time in my life, I thank her.

"After that, though, Good King Wenceslaus," says Peter. I almost roll my eyes, too. "From our resident soloist and understudy!" he adds. Beth pauses for a moment, her face darkening, before leaving the room.

I smile uncomfortably. Even though Peter and Terry's weird brotherly competitiveness kind of freaks me out. Especially when me and Beth are involved. I can never quite tell how much of it is in jest and how much of it runs deep. I sink back into the couch, wishing I had packets of chromatophores embedded in my skin like a chameleon so that I could fade into the white and pink paisley couch.

The doorbell rings. "I'll get it!" I say, thrilled for a chance to leave the room. I leap to my feet, run out of the living room, and slide into the foyer in my sock feet, grateful for the interruption.

But that's nothing compared to what I feel when I open the door and Sophie's there, her face flushed in the cold, a bright smile on her face, her entire presence a bright spot of color against the white Christmas scene developing into something postcard-worthy behind her in the front yard. "Merry Christmas, Em!" she says, and holds out a package of cheerful Christmas wrapping duct taped around a book.

I smile. For the first time all day, it's real and from deep inside me. "Merry Christmas," I tell her. My family's in the next room, but I hug her anyway, leaning out into the snow, hugging her around her winter jacket.

"Emily? Who is it?" Mom asks from behind me.

I let go of Sophie, hoping to God or the universe or whatever actually exists out there that my face is a shade of red less guilty than crimson. "Um, Mom, you've met Sophie before, right?"

"Yes, briefly," Mom says, frowning.

Sophie, of course, is cool as a cucumber. "Hi, Mrs. Samstone!" she says, cheerful, polite, and bless her for getting the name right, too. "Merry Christmas!"

"Merry Christmas, Sophie," Mom says. "How is your tutoring going?"

Sophie glances at me. I stare at the ground. "Oh, it's going all right," she says. I think only I can detect the sarcasm. "Sorry to interrupt the holiday, my brother and I are driving around handing out gifts."

"Mom, can we just run upstairs really quick? I have something for Sophie."

Mom nods. "Sure. Would you mind taking off your boots first, Sophie?"

Once Sophie has de-booted, we go up the stairs. As soon as we're safely on the second floor, I grab her hand. "Thanks for coming. Sorry about the tutoring thing."

"It's okay. I can only stay a minute, Willie's waiting in the car." She pulls me in for a moment, and we kiss, softly, quickly, conscious of the people downstairs. But if I've counted correctly, everyone is otherwise occupied. "You're welcome to come drive to Rhizenstein with us if you want though, we're not doing stuff at home till later."

"I can't, I have family stuff," I tell her. "But I'm glad you came, I have something for you."

"Oh yeah?" she asks, smiling, leaning into me.

"Yeah. And I, uh, I wrote you a letter, since... I don't know, I'm bad at saying my feelings."

Sophie smiles. "You didn't have to do that," she says softly.

"But I did, because... you said such nice things, and I uh... I really do love you, Sophie," I say, finally, blurring it out in a rush while staring at my feet.

She pulls up my chin, looks at me for a long moment, and kisses me. "I love you too," she says. "Now come on, let's open presents."

Giggling with the adrenaline of successfully telling Sophie my feelings, I pull her into my room, only to feel every muscle in my body tense up. Beth sits on the floor next to my bed, with my papers spread all around her, the secret shoebox where I normally keep them hidden wide open beside her. And worst of all, my letter to Sophie in her hands.

Beth glances up, just as startled. A look of guilt flashes across her face for one tiny second, until she sees Sophie over my shoulder. She smiles. "I should have known," she says.

Stupid, stupid, stupid. My whole body feels frozen, cold, but I manage to open my mouth. "What are you doing?"

She looks pleased as a cat. I guess that makes me the mouse. She says, "I fucking knew you were lying about youth group. And I wanted to know why." She glances up at Sophie, who is pressed right behind me. "But you have a lot more secrets than I would have figured, Emily." She waves the letter I wrote Sophie, then grabs it and shoves it into her purse, along with one of Harris's books full of my careful annotations, notecards, and highlights.

I can't speak. "Give those back," says Sophie, her voice fierce.

"What do you think, Emmy?" Beth says, the nickname said with extra vitriol. "I could give these back, or I could run them downstairs right now…"

My heart is beating so loudly that I can't process any of this. But I don't want Sophie here. This is already the most humiliating moment of my life. "You should go," I tell her.

"But Em—"

"Please." I can feel tears about to trickle from my eyes, so I shut them tight for a moment.

Sophie reaches out a hand like she's going to touch my face, drops it, and glares at Beth like murder is on her mind. "Call later," she says to me, and disappears out of the door of my room.

Beth has been watching this whole thing with a look of delighted incredulity. "Wow. How long has that been going on?"

"Beth, I need that stuff back," I say shakily, trying to make my voice reasonable, normal.

"I know, and I'll give it back." I reach out my hand, but she just smiles and tucks her purse under her arm. "After the spring concert."

"W-what?"

"Emily, that solo should be mine and you know it. I'm a senior, it's my last chance." Beth looks me square in the face. "Porco loves you. You get me the solo, I'll give you this stuff back. But otherwise, I'm giving it all to my favorite step-aunt."

"Beth, you can't, please—"

"Just get me the solo, then we'll talk." She pushes herself to her feet. "You should put this stuff away. But come down soon. I think they wanted a round of Good King Wenceslaus?"

She leaves, her purse stuffed with my secrets. I sit on my bed, surrounded by the notes that she has disarrayed. Too humiliated to cry, too shocked to do anything except pick up a pillow and hold it on my lap.

\*

That night, the second we get back from the Christmas evening service, I grab the cordless phone from the kitchen.

Mom looks over at me from where she and Peter are making gooey eyes at each other under the mistletoe. Which is weird. "Everything okay?"

"Just... homework." That's not right, it's Christmas. I self-correct. "There's a big project I want to get a jump on starting tomorrow." I've been so keyed up all day that my lies are jarring and hollow, even to me.

"Homework on Christmas, you've raised quite an industrious girl," Peter says to Mom, and there's something almost loving in his voice. She smiles up at him, and it makes my stomach sink even further. At least they're distracted.

"Proud of you, Emily," Mom says, which is pretty much the straw breaking the camel's back of my ability to not feel terrible.

So I just let out a hurried "G'night," and sprint upstairs. I go back to my room, which I hastily cleaned up this afternoon. My notes and books are all in my backpack, which is going to be a pain in the butt (or the back, rather) to carry back to school, but maybe Harris will let me keep my notes in his classroom. Not that it matters. Everything Beth has is incriminating enough.

I dial Sophie's cell phone number and sit in my closet, a dress that I haven't worn in years draping over my face. The small, dark space feels safe, and Mom won't be able to hear me if she happens to walk past my room.

Sophie answers on the first ring. "Em?"

"Hi," I say in a small voice.

"Are you okay? What happened? What did she tell your mom? I'm going to fucking murder Beth in her sleep," she says in a huge rush.

I smile a tiny bit. "She didn't tell my mom anything." I explain to her about the concert bargain she and I struck. "So overall, pretty much a net positive. Since Beth's the understudy, I can just skip the concert. I'm sorry she took your letter, though."

Sophie is silent, uncharacteristically so. Finally, she sighs, a rush of static in my ear. "Em," she says softly, finally. "You were so excited about that solo."

I haven't really allowed myself to think about that loss yet, and I kind of don't plan to. Still, a tear slips down my cheek. "I know."

"Have you thought that maybe this might be a good time to… tell people about us?" Sophie asks hesitantly.

I laugh, thinking she's kidding.

"Em, I'm serious. You'd take away Beth's stupid fucking bargaining chip or whatever. Don't let her blackmail you."

The thought of Mom finding out about all the lies I had piled up, from all the car rides I've snuck with Sophie to the biology project to her knowing I'm in love with a girl… it makes my whole body feel like lead. "Easy for you to say. Your family wouldn't care."

"It is easier for me to say, but Emily… I really think you should take control of the situation."

I close my eyes in frustration, leaning down to the floor of the closet, my head resting on an old pair of patent leather shoes. "I can't," I reply over the lump in my throat. "Sophie, I can't. I can't because I would lose you, okay?"

She's quiet.

"Look, if my family finds out, I have no idea what they'll do, but I'll be in huge trouble and they won't let me see you anymore. I know it. And you're the only... I can't lose you." I choke back a sob.

"Em..." Sophie says gently. There's a long pause. I press the phone to my ear like I can crawl through the cord and hug her. "Look, they won't take you away from me, right? First of all, you have choices, second of all, I would come find you. No matter what. Okay?"

"Okay," I squeak.

"You can tell them when you're ready, okay? No worries."

"Okay."

"Do you want me to get my Rhizenstein friends together and beat the living shit out of Beth?"

I sniffle. "Kind of."

"'Cause that bitch has my letter. Anyway, they wouldn't even have to touch her to scare the pants off a little suburban princess like her. It'd be pretty funny."

A small giggle escapes me, though it's more like half a sob.

"Seriously. She would be so freaked out she wouldn't even touch the solo." Sophie's voice is joking, but she grows serious again. "Em, keep practicing for it, in case you change your mind."

I shrug, then remember she can't see me. "I guess."

"Whatever, it's not for a few months. Maybe Beth will get hit by a fourteen-wheeler by then."

I laugh again.

"Chin up, girl. I love you."

I lower my voice. "I love you, too."

At least I crossed that bridge. It's the most honest thing I've said all day.

# CHAPTER 9

January and February go by in a stressful blur. Sophie is a ball of anxiety over college applications. She's using just missing nationals as the core of her essay, and writing about that is hard on her.

I've stopped my biology project now that I know how incriminating it is. On January 14th, I tell Harris that I need to stop working on it. "Working on what?" he asks.

"The independent study project," I tell him.

"Oh, you were still going on that? Sure, whatever keeps your mom out of my classroom," he says, and winks.

I'm sure he's joking, but it still makes me cringe inside.

Indoor track is still happening, but only as a stopgap until track begins. Harris has been including me in his meetings with Ms. Declan, the coach for field events, as we figure out which runners will try which events. So at least I'm learning a lot about the coaching side of things. But my own running is another story.

On January 21st, Sophie and I drive out to the nature preserve, bundled up in our warmest running clothes for a nice LSD run, our first in a few weeks. Half a mile in and I'm gasping for breath, a stitch in my side. Sophie stops when she realizes I'm no longer beside her. She comes back to where I'm standing on the path with my hands on my hips, breathing hard. "You okay?" she asks.

I can't seem to catch my breath. "Something's wrong," I say.

"Shit, do you need a doctor or something?" she asks, putting her arm around me.

"No, I just—give me a sec." I feel like crying. I can't hear it—the voice inside of me that says *just keep going*, the one that tells me to stay calm and relax into the run. All I feel is scared.

We stand there in the snowy woods for what feels like several minutes. Finally, gamely, I suggest pushing on, but less than a quarter mile later and I'm gasping again. I lean over, my hands on my knees. "Can we go?" I ask finally, trying to speak cheerfully and normally over the lump in my throat and the breathlessness persisting in my lungs.

Sophie looks like she wants to say something, but she doesn't. "Yeah, let's go back," she says. We walk the half mile back out of the park together, ice crunching under our feet.

After that, we don't go running together anymore. Sophie asks me a couple of times, but I find excuses, and she gets the hint that we should spend time together in other ways. She goes to indoor track practice, and I come around to help, but I don't run. I attempt it two or three times by myself at Asbury Park, starting slow, thinking that I'm just out of shape and need to ease myself back into cardiovascular exercise. But every time it's the same—before I even hit a mile, I slow down, gasping for breath, every part of me screaming to stop. And I give up.

I think it comes from the fear. Since Beth found out about us, something has changed, broken, with me and Sophie. The bubble of safe, pure happiness I felt has popped. It's the worst possible timing, because things are getting more intense. All I want is to be next to her, listen to her talk, watch her face light up when I make her laugh, learn about her and from her and with her. We barely touch in public, always feeling every eye in the room on us. Real or imagined, it's vivid enough to deter us.

In private, things are a little better, but even the safest places don't feel safe anymore.

Like Sophie's TV room. Her mom's promotion keeps her at work late, and on Thursdays her dad is usually volunteering at a battered women's shelter back in Rhizenstein. February 14th, a rare Thursday when neither of us has anything to do, since running is the last thing I want to do right now, we end up there. What starts as me reading Sophie's final draft of her college essay (she's already sent in all her applications; she's only just now letting me read her essay) ends up with us making out on her couch. Things are moving fast, not the farthest we've gone, but rapidly approaching the border—when we hear footsteps on the stairs.

"Shit," Sophie gasps, leaping away from me in such a way that she flips off the couch and lands face down on the ground. "Ouch. Fuck."

I tug my shirt down and hug a throw pillow to my chest so it's not too obvious I'm not wearing a bra underneath my white t-shirt. As Willie walks into the room, Sophie punches the remote. The TV turns on, flipping to some random channel.

"You guys, there are thirty mile per hour wind gusts today," Willie tells us, a kite under each arm. "Wanna come fly?"

Sophie is flustered, and I can't even speak. "You don't have Science Bowl today?" she asks, pulling her hair back into some semblance of order.

"Canceled. Miller's sick." Willie peers at her face. "You okay, Soph?"

"I'm chill," she says, overly brightly. "You just startled me."

To my utter horror, I notice my bra sticking out from underneath the couch. Sophie spots it the same second I do, and shoves it behind her. "We're just watching this dope show."

Willie glances at the TV. On screen, several nuns are murmuring Hail Mary's. "Weird religious local access channels?"

Sophie smiles weakly. "You know how I think nuns... are awesome."

"Whatever." Willie looks at me. "Up for a little kite-ing, Em? It's snowing, but the wind'll be great."

Barely able to get the words out, I mumble, "No thanks."

He shrugs. "You guys are lame."

"It's like negative a billion degrees," Sophie points out.

"It's hot in here. Look, Em's so red," Willie says. It's true. If my face were any redder, I'm sure it would leave the visible light spectrum and go to infrared.

"She's fine. We're just gonna keep on… praying and stuff," says Sophie.

"Aight, see you later." Willie leaves without further ado, taking the steps two at a time on the way out. Sophie and I just stare at each other.

Finally, she takes a deep breath, in and out. "Okay. I think we definitely fooled him."

I can't speak.

"Anyway, Willie wouldn't tell anyone. Em…" Sophie clambers up next to me on the couch. "This sucks."

I nod. It does.


*


The first day of March is a Wednesday. Sophie has to spend the afternoon with her actual precalc tutor due to an upcoming exam. I catch the bus and go right home after school for the first time in weeks. When I get there, Mom's in the garden, turning over the winter dirt and clearing out some winter detritus. "Emily," she says in surprise. "I thought you were tutoring today."

"Canceled today," I say automatically, barely even registering the twinge of guilt anymore. "Sophie had practice. Where's Rachel?"

"Playdate with her friend Johnny. I figured I'd use the chance to get ready for spring." She extends the shovel to me. "Want to help?"

It's chilly, but the sun is breaking through the clouds. Days are getting longer again, and for the first time, I feel a little anxiety lift off my chest. I run inside to don my dirtiest hoodie and worn gardening gloves, then follow Mom out into the backyard. I haven't spent time with her, or even in the garden, in months. I've been begging out of gardening club, too, blaming homework but mostly just worried Mrs. Glenwood will ask me if I'm ever going to show up to youth group in front of Mom.

We work in silence for several minutes, lost in our own worlds of dead brown and the occasional resilient sprig of green in our holly or our mint. When I glance at Mom, her expression is the same as the one I feel on my own face, biting her lip in concentration as she pulls at a particularly robust set of roots that have set in. Mom's like me in so many ways: wholly focused on her task, no need to fill every gap with chatter. It's so nice to be with Mom in a situation where I don't feel irritated about her restrictions or stressed about my lies.

Apparently, Mom thinks so too. About half an hour later she sits back on her heels and wipes her brow with her sleeve. "It's nice to be back out here with you," she says to me.

"Yeah, I've really missed the garden," I reply, setting down my trowel.

"I've missed *you,*" Mom says. "I feel like I've hardly seen you lately."

I feel a slight misgiving. "Junior year is so crazy. I've had stuff like every day."

"You've been stretched pretty thin," Mom agrees. I sigh in relief. Until she turns around and asks, "How are you liking the youth group?"

A cold breeze blows across my hot face. This is dangerous territory. I try to remember which youth group sessions I've legitimately gotten out of and which ones I've just lied about attending. I was definitely supposed to be at the February meeting. "It's been a little stressful on top of the other stuff I have going on but, you know, it's been good for me to, uh, get to know people at the church a little better."

"It's so important to prioritize that," Mom says. "I know how important school and running are to you, but your spiritual health is so vital to every other aspect of life."

I fucking hate how sincere Mom is sometimes. I think about the afternoons I've spent with Sophie, running or studying or even just lazing around watching TV, instead of going to a youth group event. I wouldn't trade those afternoon for anything, not even the greatest spiritual clarity that I've never seemed to be able to find. "Yeah, for sure," I say mindlessly.

"Are you looking forward to the overnight Friday night?" Mom asks.

My stomach drops. I've been so out of it. What? "Uh, yeah, it'll be great. That's Friday?"

"Yes. I spoke to Aunt Gretchen. Beth will pick you up tomorrow and take you over."

Fuck. Now that Gretchen's involved, I really am going to have to go. "Sounds awesome. Um, we have a special track practice all day Saturday, though." This, for once, is actually true. The first practice of track season, we do a "practice meet" so that everyone can get used to the complex structure and timing of events at a track meet.

"I saw on the track calendar. But you'll still be able to make the Friday night," she says. It's clear from her tone that there will be no arguing or objections to this.

"Mom, I…" *I hate Beth. I hate church. I hate lying. I can't do this much longer.*

"Yes, Emily?" Mom looks at me expectantly.

I can't break her heart. "I think we should put in more zinnias this year. We got so many butterflies last year with just one type," I say weakly, hating myself.

She looks at our empty flowerbed and smiles. "That's a great idea. Let's make a list for spring planting. We've got a lot to clear out here."

I look down at the wet brown leaves crushed beneath my knees, fighting back the urge to cry.

\*

On Friday afternoon when we're talking on the phone, Sophie offers to pick me up from the church retreat at eight am on Saturday for the special weekend practice. The retreat ends at noon, so I'm at least getting away a little early.

"You don't think that might, uh, arouse suspicion? Us driving together to practice that early?" I ask her.

Sophie laughs, but I can tell she's a little hurt. "I think you're getting paranoid, Em."

Instantly, I feel terrible. "Yeah, sorry. Thank you for the ride. I just feel stressed about this church thing."

Sophie, once again, lets me off the hook. "Dude, are you going to, like, perform exorcisms?" she asks. "The power of Christ compels you! The power of Christ compels you!"

Mom calls up the stairs. "Emily, Beth's here!"

"I gotta go," I tell Sophie. "I love you."

"You too. See you tomorrow."

At least I have that to look forward to as I grab my bag, kiss Mom on the cheek, and walk out to Beth's Hyundai. She's redoing her lip gloss in the mirror. Beth makes me want to never stop rolling my eyes. This is the one teen driver Mom has approved?

But she's family. I grit my teeth.

"Hi Emily," Beth says as I get into the passenger seat.

I don't say anything. I don't think I've said one word to her since she blackmailed me, since I try to minimize the interactions that make me want to throw myself off a bridge. But we still sit next to each other in band every day. And in the fantasy world of lies that I have been building for my mom, we are cousins and friends and youth group carpool buddies.

"So you finally had to come to one of these things," Beth says.

I shrug. The one good thing about this whole blackmail thing is that now Beth is also on the hook to keep my youth group truancy a secret. If she blows the lid on me now there would be no point to giving her the solo. It's a good thing we've been learning about evolutionary game theory in biology.

"You should keep an open mind," Beth says, pulling out of our subdevelopment onto the main drag. "From reading your little note to Sophie, you really need this."

The thought of her reading my letter to Sophie makes my whole body hot with rage. I press my head backward into my seat, fantasizing about grabbing the steering wheel and steering us into oncoming traffic.

"You still practicing for the solo?" Beth asks.

I roll my head toward her, stare at her in what I hope conveys my utter and complete loathing. The concert is on a Saturday near the end of March, the same day as our first track meet of the season. "It would be pretty suspicious if I didn't, don't you think?"

"Yeah, keep doing that. But I'm practicing too." She stops at a stoplight and shoots me a dirty look. "You know I deserve it."

"Yeah, sure," I say, staring outside the window at the darkening gray sky and occasional slush patches on the side of the road. We don't speak again until we pull into the church parking lot. It's mostly empty. Pineridge Baptist church has a congregation of around four hundred, perhaps twelve percent of whom are teenage offspring with cars at their disposal.

I follow Beth into the church, dragging my feet with every step. The first floor is silent and empty, and I catch a glimpse of the dark, empty nave, the pews empty, the shadows long. Our footsteps echo as we walk past. That, to me, is almost holy.

But then we turn down the steps into a brightly lit basement filled with voices and my stomach clenches. Hefting my backpack, which contains my biology textbook (in case there's time to study), my change of underwear and shirt for the next day, my toothbrush, and my clipboards and timers for tomorrow's meets, I follow my step-cousin down into the dungeon. I mean, the basement.

There are thirty, thirty-five kids there, more than I anticipated, mostly milling around in quiet groups around the snack tables like ungulates at an oasis. (We just got to biomes in Bio.) Pastor Dan is holding court in the center of the room, animatedly chatting with four people.

While Beth and I get in line to sign in with Mrs. Glenwood, I watch him, trying to put into a rational, logical argument why I do not like him. He officiated Mom and Peter's wedding, Rachel loves him, he has been nothing but solicitous and kind to me. No, not kind. Harris is kind. Sophie is kind. Pastor Dan is nice. But I don't trust him. Something about his perfect hair and smooth voice bring to mind a car salesman, one who will say anything to sell you the shiny red sports car in the corner that half his bonus rides on.

Mrs. Glenwood, of gardening club fame, sits behind a table handing out blank nametags. "Hello, girls," she says merrily. "I'm so happy you're here. Emily, we missed you at the last volunteer event!"

I wish I knew what it was. "Yeah, I was busy, unfortunately." Busy hanging out with Sophie, probably, but I don't really want to think about Mrs. Glenwood's hypothetical reaction to that. "I actually have to head out early tomorrow for track practice."

She pushes some nametags across the table and marks off boxes next to our names on a checklist. I bite my lip, wondering if there's a whole series of attendance sheets somewhere in the church office with my name very much not checked off on any of them.

There's a big box of colorful markers so that we can express ourselves on our nametags. Beth is already carefully printing her name in bright pink, in her obnoxious, stupid, fat handwriting, doodling an insufferable little heart next to the B.

*Easy there, Em*, I picture Sophie admonishing me. No need to make the evening any worse by finding creative new reasons to hate Beth. There are plenty as is. And now that we're here, I can blend into the crowd and pretend she doesn't exist.

I write my name slowly, making my normally messy scrawl unusually neat. I have no idea what to do with myself once I finish my nametag. Beth has already slapped her label right onto her chest and gone to chat with a couple inane girls I recognize from my gym class. I smooth my label carefully over my thigh, not wanting to put it right over my boobs, and sigh. Time to strategize.

I weigh the various costs and benefits of joining the fringes of a group so as to not look like a total social outcast versus just sitting alone in a corner with my textbook. For a tiny second, I'm almost tempted to follow Beth, the one person I actually sort of know. But I'd rather eat a dirty sock full of nails than listen to she and her friends talking about… what is it? I overhear a phrase. "Dustin's party." Yeah, that.

I'm making a beeline for a bright red beanbag chair in the corner when I'm stopped by the sound of one man clapping. Pastor Dan stands up. "Alrighty, friends," he calls cheerily, "It's about time to get started! Let's all make a circle!"

The circle takes several minutes to form, geometry apparently not being the strong suit of many of my co-churchgoers. It's probably a spatial reasoning problem due to underdeveloped teenage prefrontal cortices.

Pastor Dan opens with a prayer, asking Jesus to bless the evening's activities or something. I'm occupying myself by trying to figure out the base unit of the complex hexagonal linoleum tiles. I'm pulled back to the present by the next announcement.

"First, we're going to play a couple name games to get to know each other better. That's really what this is all about!" Pastor Dan claps his hands again. I don't know what he does to get such a loud sound out of it. Maybe it's the power of Christ. "Let's start by everyone saying their name as we go around the circle. Loud and proud, if you please! Charity, why don't you start?"

Charity doesn't go to Pineridge, but I've met her at church. She is what Sophie would call "very home-schooled." She's neither loud nor proud as she whispers her name to the group, staring shyly at the floor and scuffing her shoes. My heart sort of aches for her, and frankly, also for myself, because I know I will sound almost as painfully shy. But whatever, I plan on executing my strategy for the evening: Say and do as little as possible. Count the minutes until Sophie picks me up the next morning. Current count: six hundred and 12 minutes.

The name games go on for a while. I mostly stare into space, except when I have to give my name, and later, a correspondingly alliterative animal and activity. Emu and emancipation are my words of choice.

After the name games there are a series of playful diversions that I suppose are intended to bond us together. Most of them are varieties on tag or musical chairs that involve a lot of running around and laughing, if you're engaged, which, you know, I'm not. Not particularly.

Around nine-thirty, after a blessed snack break where I go back to chat with Mrs. Glenwood with plans for her spring garden, Pastor Dan invites us all to pull up for the first "Teen Talk" discussion of the evening. "We're going to talk about some of the troubles facing today's youth," he announces. "And then brainstorm solutions in small breakout groups."

I sigh in relief. A discussion will be infinitely easier to not participate in than a running game where I needed to be constantly on the lookout for rambunctious individuals careening into me.

Pastor Dan pulls out a poster board and a fat red marker from beneath his seat. "So, let's talk problems," he says, his voice deep and reassuring as though none of these theoretical problems could have any effect on us here. "Who has an idea? What's a negative factor that could harm the young people of today?"

Chelsea, a reasonably intelligent and quite outspoken girl I remember from last year's English class, immediately raises her hand. "Pollution," she says confidently. "It negatively impacts everyone's health, and it leaves behind a dirtier world for us to take over."

Pastor Dan nods. "Excellent start, Chelsea." He writes "Pollution" on the board in teachery handwriting. "What else?"

"Homework!" blurts out some guy I don't recognize, Michael, according to his nametag. A few people laugh. I almost do, too. It's sort of nice to have someone not take this seriously. I'm starting to feel a little bad about my inner snark.

Pastor Dan, showing that he is One of Us, guffaws like everyone else. "Maybe you should go back to the drawing board on that one, Mike. I'll call on someone else. Let's see, ah... Beth."

I glance up from my lap. Beth sits almost directly across the circle from me, her back straight, her arm raised. I sat there because the full diameter was physically the farthest I could be from her.

Beth looks right at me, lowering her hand. "Homosexuality," she says, meeting my eyes.

I feel my entire body freeze up. Panic. I barely notice the murmurs around the room that indicate that Beth has selected a controversial topic.

When I dare to look up again, Pastor Dan is nodding, writing on the poster. "Hey!" Chelsea exclaims. "I don't think that should go on                                                   there!"

When I look around the circle, sneakily, not wanting anyone to notice how freaked out I am, I see one or two people nodding along with her. Many more look like I imagine I do: deeply uncomfortable.

"Are you kidding, Chelsea?" Beth asks incredulously. "It's a sin, and it's a serious threat to America's integrity right now." She pauses, as though to let everyone admire her use of a word with four syllables. "The sacredness of the family is being destroyed."

Charity, the homeschooler, nods along with Beth, her eyes huge. "Not to mention eternal hellfire," she says in a high-pitched voice that betrays not an ounce of amusement or irony. Any sympathy I had for her earlier vanishes.

Someone giggles, nervously, but Chelsea is pissed. "My uncle is gay," she says loudly. "And he's one of the kindest, most Christian people I know."

"Well, he's going to hell. You can't be gay *and* Christian..." Beth is winding up for a rant.

But Pastor Dan cuts her off. "Now, there's no need for vitriol, Beth," he says, and for a second I think maybe he's going to stand up for Chelsea. Nope! "We must love the sinner and hate the sin, pray for those thousands of people who stray onto that wicked path..."

*13 squared is 169. 14 squared is 196. 15 squared is 225...* I can't listen to this, so I square numbers instead. Tears threaten to spill out of my eyes. All I want is to glance beside me and see Sophie, ready to take down Pastor Dan with a cutting comment, expose Beth for the sniveling little snot she is...

At some point, the conversation breaks away from gay people and onto other equally pressing threats to the youths of America. When I sneak a glance at Beth, she's grinning at me with such malice that I cringe. *25 squared is 625... 26 squared is 676...*

Eventually, we split off into small groups, somehow or other, I'm not paying attention. My group, thank whatever probably nonexistent God, gets pollution as our topic. I glance at my watch. Eleven more hours. I glance at Beth and Chelsea, who are having it out in another group.

I can't do this. Not without exploding.

"Hey, Carla, can I borrow your phone?" I ask the girl next to me, who I know from my freshman gym class.

She nods effusively. "Sure thing, Emily!" she says. I kind of want to smack her for being so cheerful right now, even though she's being nice.

Instead I force a smile onto my face as she hands me her phone. I walk out of the room and a safe distance down the hallway, a little clumsy with the touch screen but Sophie's cell number easily coming to my fingers. It's ten pm. Where would she be?

She answers on the fifth ring. "Mmmmph?"

I lean against the wall, speaking in a low voice. "Sorry, did I wake you up?"

"Just a quick nap. I need to get up anyway, I'm going out soon." She pauses to yawn, and I picture her curled up on her bed, her long limbs tangled up in her green comforter.

"Going out this late? Don't you have practice in the morning, missy?"

"I'll be fine. What's up with you, m'dear?"

"Where's your thing?"

"Some of my Rhizenstein friends are having a party, so I was gonna head over there around eleven, just for a little while." Her sleepy voice is so calm and melodic that I can already feel my angry pulse slowing down.

I think about it for zero seconds before I say it. "Can I come?"

"What? Um, sure." I can hear the frown in Sophie's voice.

"I mean, if it'd be awkward for me to be around your Rhizenstein friends…" I say quickly, sliding down the wall to sit there in the dark end of the hallway.

"No, actually, there are some people I want you to meet. It just never… this didn't seem like your thing." Sophie pauses. "You okay, Em?"

"I'm fine," I say automatically. Then I say, "Well, no, not really. I hate youth group and I just really… I want to see you."

"Awesome," she says, and I picture her grin. "Where should I pick you up?"

"Pineridge Baptist on Phillips." My mind is already racing with plans, excuses for leaving the retreat.

"Sick. I'll be there in like half an hour, that okay?"

"Perfect." We say our goodbyes and hang up. I sit there in the dark hallway, my heart pounding—this time, instead of with fear and anxiety, it's with excitement and... well, anxiety. But I feel free. I'm doing it. I'm getting out of a situation I hate instead of just sitting around and hating myself. All I need are a few lies.

Slowly, I wander back to the retreat, my plan forming. The small groups have dispersed, apparently having remedied all the problems facing America's youth. People mill around the church basement. Someone had turned the radio to the upbeat encouraging Christian rock station Peter always listens to.

I find Mrs. Glenwood at the front of the room, gathering up some pretzel snacks to distribute with a wide smile on her face. I wonder if lying to her will be tough. "Um, I'm feeling really sick," I tell her, trying my best to sound weak. It's not hard, my voice is already a little shaky from nerves.

"Oh, honey, you look very flushed," she tells me. "Do you feel feverish?"

"Yeah, and I'm kind of having chills, and... a headache, and I'm sort of nauseous," I tell her, hoping this is an appropriate assortment of maladies. "I think I need to go home."

Mrs. Glenwood clucks. "Oh, dear. Do you need me to call your mother?"

"No," I say, panicking. "Just called my stepdad for a ride." I hold up Carla's phone.

"Oh, well... I'm sorry you're feeling so poorly," she says, frowning.

"Yeah. I feel kind of warm... I'm going to go wait outside."

After reassuring Mrs. Glenwood that she doesn't need to wait outside with me, and returning Carla's phone, I'm swinging my bag over my shoulder and trying to resist the urge to jog up the steps. As I walk up, catching a glimpse of Beth watching me curiously, Pastor Dan begins the opening strums of a song on his guitar. Feeling giddy and glorious, I burst out of the church into the night. Is it really this easy? I guess, as long as everyone thinks of you as obedient.

I sit on the front steps, pulling my Pineridge Cross Country jacket tightly around my shoulders. Though spring has nearly sprung, it's still cold at night. The sky is clear, and a vivid half-moon shines above the still-bare trees. I feel scared, and cold, and alive, and free.

About twenty minutes later, when my wild feelings have mostly numbed down to just cold, Sophie arrives in Patricia Junior. She's recognizable from a half mile away thanks to her dim left headlight and the music leaking out of the window that only closes partway. Eager to make my getaway, I jump up, jog down the steps, and yank open the passenger door. "Thanks for coming," I say breathlessly, "I'm sorry to—"

Before I can finish my sentence, Sophie leans over and grabs me in a tight hug. For the first time all night, I feel myself relax.

"Sorry to interrupt," she says when she releases me. "You looked like you needed that."

"Yeah." I put on my seatbelt as she pulls away from the church. "God, what a horrible evening."

"What happened?" she asks, turning down her music.

I explain the whole Beth fiasco to her, watching her face gradually grow more and more livid. "And I just wanted to leave, so I pretended I was sick, which was a little impulsive but I don't think I'll get in trouble unless Mrs. Glenwood mentions it to Mom, but I think I can head that off at the pass if I start going back to gardening club and steer the conversation a little…"

Sophie is shaking her head. "Fucking Beth. I don't like to use the C-word lightly, but she is a flaming one."

I'm so startled that I laugh. Sophie grins, glad to get a rise out of me. "Where are we going?" I ask.

"My friend Myron's parents are out of town so he's having a thing. Told him I'd stop by." Sophie glances at me. "That cool by you?"

"Sure," I reply, feeling reckless. "Might as well break all the rules at once."

"Oh, that can be arranged," Sophie says, turning the music back up. It's a song she loves, an old one from the sixties. One I've heard often enough in her car that I know at least seventy-five percent of the words by now.

We belt out the song together, racing to the other side of town in the moonlight.

\*

It's not until Sophie parks in front of a tiny house crammed between two other tiny houses that I begin to feel nervous. Shyness is shyness and teenagers are teenagers whether they're sitting in a basement singing songs about Jesus or engaging in underage substance abuse.

The front yard is full of dandelions and crabgrass. "Um, so, you know there's going to be people drinking and stuff here," Sophie says as we approach the door. "Are you okay with that?"

I shrug, though truthfully, I feel a little uncomfortable. Just leaving the church retreat is in the top ten most disobedient things I've done in my life. Actually, other than my inner thoughts about God, pretty much every other item on that list has been with Sophie.

And I kind of love her for it, even though I'm scared.

"It's totally cool if you don't want to, you know, partake," Sophie says quickly. "I'm not drinking tonight, obviously, I'm driving. But even if I was, there'd be no pressure." She grins. "Unless you want to. I'd be curious to see drunk Emily."

I laugh. Her speech makes me feel a little better. "Probably not."

Sophie ruffles my hair, then walks me to the side of the house. She knocks on the basement window and waves at someone in a dark, crowded room. Then she leads me around to the back door. A bass line throbs inside the house.

We wait in front of the back door for what feels like a long time. I feel so nervous. "Sophie," I say. "What if your friends don't like me?"

Sophie looks at me incredulously, but before she has time to answer, there's a noise so loud it makes me jump. It's like a high-pitched whine, followed by a steady rumbling growing louder. I realize we're right by the train tracks. A few houses away, the train speeds by. Sophie was right—it does look nicer from far away.

The door opens. "Sophie!" A guy with an alarming amount of hair and beard exclaims as he throws his arms around her.

Sophie laughs. "Jesus Christ, Myron, knock me over, why don't you." She pats him on the back. "It's been forever."

"Yeah, it's been a hot sec. You too good for us now?"

She snorts. "As if. I brought the only cool person at Pineridge here with me."

Myron gives me a friendly wave. "Hi, cool person at Pineridge!"

"Um, hi."

"Okay, well everyone's downstairs," Myron says.

I can't seem to escape basements tonight. I follow Sophie and Myron down to a crowded, dimly lit room. A shock of loud, slow rap music and acrid smoke hits all my senses like I've walked into a wall. I'm guessing there are fifteen people in there, and my stomach twists again.

But Sophie is grinning. "Wanna meet some people?" she yells over the music.

I nod, unsure I'll be able to get my voice loud enough. I stay close beside her, hoping she's not going to be worried about looking uncool next to her dorky Pineridge friend.

But it's so clear that she feels completely at ease as she drags me over to two girls and a guy right by the speakers. "Ima!" she says, grabbing one of the girls in a hug.

The girl shrieks. "Sophie! What are you doing here?"

"Myron finally remembered I exist." Sophie rolls her eyes, and she laughs, and she looks... natural. She pulls me over. "Em, this is Imanuela, the best 200 runner at Rhizenstein. Ima, this is Em."

The girl throws her arms around me, smelling of smoke. "Hi," she says, and I wonder if she's drunk. But she seems nice. I am suddenly acutely aware of how little I know about Sophie's life in Rhizenstein.

But against all odds, I end up having fun meeting Sophie's friends. At Pineridge, she sticks out like a sore thumb, but here, her mannerisms, her way of speaking, they fit in and blend. I'm the sore thumb.

Sophie takes me around the basement, introducing other friends—one or two from track, one or two from class, but mostly just people she grew up with. She's in the corner, talking to a Myron, when someone I haven't met yet taps me on the shoulder.

I turn around and look up at a tall white guy with longish black hair. "Hey," he says. A quieter song is playing now, so he's not yelling, thank God. "Can I, uh, grab you a drink?"

I automatically glance at Sophie, but she, David, and Imanuela are engrossed in a conversation about someone's cousin. "Uh, no thanks."

"Oh, okay. Name's Tim," he says, grinning at me.

"Um, I'm Emily." Okay. Meeting new people. Conversations. I can do this.

"You don't go to Rhizenstein, do you?" he asks, leaning against the wall.

"N-no, Pineridge."

"Oh, cool." He nods to himself, like I'm saying something very deep and meaningful. "Very cool." He reaches toward my face, and I flinch back, startled. He laughs gently. "You just have some hair in your face."

"Tim!" I hear Sophie snap from behind me, in her voice that's 50% joke, 50% threat. The one I've heard her use on Kari a hundred times. "Quit hitting on my girlfriend!"

I glance up at her sharply. It's just out in the open? Just like that?

Tim, too, looks surprised. "What? Sophie, you guys are together?"

"Like, together together?" Imanuela chimes in.

Sophie claps a hand over her mouth, belatedly. "Shit, Em. I'm really sorry. That just slipped out."

I look around, but the world hasn't ended. The basement looks the same, although Tim, Myron, and Imanuela are looking at me. Sophie is too, anxiously.

I shrug. "It's fine," I say, waving a hand vaguely. I feel a little giddy.

Sophie's smile is huge. "Great," she says, snaking an arm around my waist. "Let me actually introduce you. Guys, this is my girlfriend, Emily."

Tim shakes his head. "Sorry, dude," he says to Sophie. "You have good taste though."

"Creepy!" Sophie says brightly.

"Don't mind Tim," Imanuela says, hanging on his elbow. "He thinks he's a player."

"It was an honest mistake," he protests. I laugh.

The night wears on, and I eventually begin yawning. When I check my watch, I'm startled to realize it's two in the morning.

"You ready to go?" Sophie asks, next to me on the couch.

I nod. "You have practice tomorrow. Have you been drinking enough water?"

Sophie grins. "Emily Ferris, on the job 24/7. We out."

184

She says goodbye to her friends, some of whom are pretty drunk at this point, but they say goodbye to me, too, and I smile. I learn what it is like to be engulfed by a Myron hug.

We leave into the cold night. The air feels fresh and clean and suddenly I feel wide awake again. "So what'd you think of your first sketchy-ass high school party?" Sophie asks me.

"I really like your friends," I say.

"Ima and Myron liked you," she says as we get into her car. "They're the ones that matter. I've gotta hang out with them more before we all graduate. I forgot how much I missed just like... hanging out."

I watch her closely as we walk away. "I'm sorry Pineridge sucks," I tell her.

"It's not all bad," she says. "Teachers are better, and I don't know, there's this girl..." I smile, leaning into her as we approach PJ. She coughs, then adds, "It was, um, nice to not have to... you know. Lie about us."

It *had* been nice, safe in that enclosed, dark space. "Too bad it's not always like that," I say, getting into the car.

Sophie gives me a weird look. "Uh, yeah, too bad." She starts PJ, who protests with a guttural, choking whine before shuddering to life. "So, 'm I taking you home?"

"I am technically accounted for until after the meet."

"Right on, stay at my place." She sniffs the air. "Probably wouldn't be a good idea to take you home anyway. We reek of pot."

I raise my eyebrows. "That's what that is?"

Sophie rolls her eyes. "Damn, we really need to get you back out here more often," she says, as we weave our way back to Pineridge. The train whistles, long and lonely, behind us.

# CHAPTER 10

Two weeks later, and it's the end of March. Almost time for our first track meet of the season.

I'm at practice with the team. Track and field practice is nothing like cross country practice. We're at the 400-meter track surrounding the football field every day. It's crowded— about twice as many kids run track as cross country—and the style of how we run is very different.

The field team is on the football field with Ms. Declan, working on shot put and high jump. The long jumpers are off in the sandpit. And the runners are with me and Harris, running sixteen 200s. This is a pretty brutal workout, even for the cool day. All the cross-county kids, the ones I know best, grumble about the low rest between reps. The sprinter kids, the ones who only do indoor and outdoor and who are a very different breed, grumble about the high volume. Nobody's happy and everyone's miserable! Just the way Harris likes his workouts.

Me, I'm also miserable, even though all I'm doing is standing with a timer, making sure they start each rep every two minutes on the dot. I'm finalizing my plans in my head about how to get out of the spring concert, which is the same day as the first track meet of the season. I have the solution. I know Sophie's not going to like it, but it's the only thing I can think of to make this work.

I mention this to Sophie while she's in between her fourteenth and fifteenth intervals of 200-repeats. It's a distracting enough time that I hope she'll forget about it until the day of and we can just cross that bridge when we get to it. But when she's dropping me off at home (well, at the house two doors down from mine, our usual drop-off point), she dashes my hopes. "So, about this whole plan for the concert..."

"It's pretty simple. We'll drive to the track meet separately from the bus so we can leave right after your last event for the concert. Rhys and Tevyn are driving separately to the concert as well, so that's not suspicious at all." I absent-mindedly open and close a CD case over and over. "I'll tell my mom I'm planning to take the bus straight back to the school. But then, we'll say the meet goes later than intended, so I get in the car with you. And, um, we'll just not go to the concert. We can say we had car trouble. Which, frankly, is not all that unbelievable with this car. I think we'll get away with it."

Sophie's voice has an uncharacteristic note of irritation in it. "Wow. Military precision." I probably shouldn't have insulted her car. "That's some Napoleonic shit there, Emily."

"What, you think it's a bad plan?"

"No, I mean... you're kind of blaming me for not making it to the concert."

I look up at her, and there's no anger, but there's sort of a....resignation. It makes me feel horrible. She looks sad, but more importantly, she looks *used* to it.

I stare back down at my lap.

"I mean, yeah, it's a plan that will probably work, and yeah, you can throw me under the bus, whatever, but... Em. Is this really what you want?"

My throat is tight. I feel like crying. "I don't know. I just can't go to the concert, so Beth has to take my solo."

"Yeah, I know, Beth said she's gonna out you to your Mom and it'll be a huge fucking mess. I get it. But what's to stop her from doing it even if you do give her the solo? Or just holding something else over you after?"

"I'll deal with that when it comes up," I say, pulling a thread out of PJ's passenger seat.

"And the other thing..." She grabs my hand, holds it in hers. "I really wanted to see you play. And Willie."

One of the tears that have been brimming on the surface slips onto my cheek, splashes onto our hands.

"You okay?" she asks.

I lean forward and sag into her, waiting for her arms to circle around me, sighing with relief when they do. She smells like track practice. The sweatpants and sweatshirt that I've gotten her to start wearing during warmups and cooldown are soft against my arm.

"Em?"

"I just don't... want this to end," I say, so soft it's more of a breath than a sentence.

We stay there, huddled against each other. It's getting dark later and later now, but the sun is pale and weak this early in the spring. I think about the meet on Saturday, the concert after it. The one I won't be at. How I'll explain it all to Mom, how she'll be all too willing to believe it because I was in a car with a *teenager*, and how could that possibly not go wrong?

It won't be the ideal scenario for her to get to know Sophie better, that's for sure, but I don't think that ideal scenario even exists. And maybe it's better—lose this battle (forfeit the solo, get in trouble for driving with an unapproved driver), but win the war (keep my larger secrets hidden from my mom, get to keep seeing Sophie). At least, that's what I'm telling myself.

Finally, she sighs. "Okay, Em, we can do it your way if that's what you really want. I just... make sure it's really what you want, right?"

"Yeah," I say. "Of course."

"Okay. Good." She leans in to kiss me. "I gotta go. Mom's actually home for dinner for once and Dad's making wienerschnitzel."

"Tell her hi," I say as I get out to leave.

"Your Mom too," Sophie says. "Oh, wait, she barely knows who I am."

I look at her.

"Sorry, sorry. Long day. Love you. See you tomorrow."

"See you," I say, my stomach twisting up more than ever.

\*

It's the day of the first track meet of the year. We're all straggling into the stadium in groups of two and three. Harris mandates that everyone gets there for the beginning of the day, but track meets last all day, and he's okay with people leaving when their events are over. I love track meets. I think I like cross country more, since we're out in nature for it. But for track meets, with hundreds of people packed into a stadium, events happening every five minutes, race officials swapping out hurdles and sorting runners into heats…there's a lot to do.

"Sophie, I want you anchoring on the four by four," says Harris, in the middle of a long list of races for the day while we're all assembling on the twenty-five-yard line of the football field inside the track. "Kari, you'll lead off, Chelsea second, Carly third. For the men…"

Sophie yanks out her earbuds and looks at me. "You're in the relay," I tell her. "Four runners each run a 400. You're anchoring—that means you go last out of the four."

"I know what anchoring is, Em," Sophie reminds me. "I have actually run on a track before."

"Yeah, but you never ran a relay." I smile at her.

"How do you know that?"

"I may have already looked into your PRs from Rhizenstein," I tell her.

She laughs, puts her earbuds back in. "You nerd," she says.

I go for a walk, seeing where I might be needed. The mile is first, and Jon's running it. I make sure his numbers are set, and Christa's too, because her heat of the women's mile is right after Jon's. This meet is huge, with runners from schools all over Ohio. Christa takes first in her heat of the women's mile, but other than that we're scraping to place against some of the bigger schools.

The day goes by in a rush of heats and races. Tevyn, one of our sprinters (the one who always beats Jon at Scrabble), takes a nasty spill on the 400 hurdles. I spend a good 45 minutes helping him clean up his face and arms. He's playing clarinet in the concert tonight. He'll have to do it with a big, painful scrape on his face. Sophie runs in the 800 and 400 and does well in both, particularly in the quarter mile. She comes in second in both, though, which I know she finds hard to handle.

I'm distracted all day, though. I mix up Kari and Carly's times in the two-mile, and drop my clipboard more than once. It's hard not to think about the plan. "What's with you?" Harris asks me near the end of the day.

I shrug, but I'm feeling some pressure in my chest, like when I've been trying to run lately. I check my dad's watch. Almost time for Sophie's last event. I'm separated from the track by the chain link fence. I walk alongside it, running my fingers over the metal, pressing close to give a Vale runner on crutches room to maneuver. Finally, I'm near enough the starting line. Sophie and the other sprinters are loosening up, laughing, joking, a green spot amid the reds, blues, and yellows of the others schools' uniforms. I press my forehead against the fence. Just seeing her makes me feel a little better. "Soph," I call.

My voice is just one of many in the crowd, but Sophie hears me right away. She looks over and smiles. Leaving the others behind, she jogs over. "Hey," she says.

"You nervous?" I ask.

She takes out her hair band, redoes her ponytail. "Nah. Sprint events are way easier than distance. This'll be over in, well, I hope around a minute."

"I will be very surprised if it isn't," I tell her. It's true. Sophie's great at distance, but she's a sprinter in her muscles. Watching her at practice is like watching a deer in the forest. I imagine. There aren't tons of deer where we live.

"The anticipation is way worse for cross-country." She leans against the fence, trying to glance down at my watch. "What time is it?"

"Close to five." My stomach tenses up.

Sophie sees my expression change. "You know, there'll still be time to make it to school after the meet," she says quietly.

I shake my head. Sophie glances around. The stadium is crowded, loud. Spectators carrying hot dogs, runners putting their sweatpants on. It's nearly the end of the day. Everything is chaos. No one is watching. She plants a soft, furtive kiss on my forehead. "Your call," she tells me.

"Runners to the line!" The race official calls.

I feel a little shaky, like when I have a fever. "Time for your race," I tell her. "Good luck."

She gives me a sad smile. "Thanks."

Kari leads off for Pineridge. She has a killer start, I'll say that much for her. Once the starting gun is fired, I jog over to Harris. We'll take down our own splits for the four runners in the 4x400, since they're just going to get a combined time. "Hi Emily," Harris says without taking his eyes off the race. "You get all the splits for the men's' four by four?"

"Yeah, Dar PRed—"

"Here comes Kari!" Harris interrupts, whipping out his stopwatch. "Sixty-two twelve," he tells me, clicking the split button as she hands off the metal baton to Chelsea and comes to a stop, lacing her hands behind her head.

I record the time, at last a smile finding its way onto my face. Nothing fires Harris up like a relay. Chelsea, a sprinter who typically runs the 200 and the 400, is already around the first turn by the time I look back up. "Good handoff," Harris murmurs appreciatively to me. Kari and Chelsea have the most complicated job because they have to change lanes, but all Carly and Sophie will have to do is take the baton and then sprint.

I glance over at Sophie, who is jogging in place, staying warm. A four-hundred puts screaming effort on the fast-twitch muscle groups, but it takes mental grit as much as it takes brawn. She smiles at me, and gives me a thumbs-up. She gets into her lane right after Chelsea and Carly perform the handoff. Kari gave us a lead and Chelsea only increased it. Carly is probably our weakest link in this 400 team, but she doesn't lose the lead. Still, the runner from Vale is only a few steps behind Carly by the time they're making the final turn.

Sophie stretches out her arm for the baton, her head turned over her shoulder as she watches Carly sprint down the straightaway. She takes a few steps into a jog—she'll need to be moving a little during the handoff so there's not a total halt of momentum. Then Carly's there, all heavy breathing and urgency. Sophie's fingers brush across the metallic surface of the baton, but as Carly lets go, it slips from Sophie's grasp and bounces to the ground.

Harris swears. Sophie leans down, scrambles for the baton as the Vale girl blows past her, then sets off at a sprint. She's uneven and stumbling on the first few steps, but she settles into her loose, loping stride by the time she hits the curve.

"How much time do you think we lost there?" I ask Harris.

"Two, maybe three seconds. Lost the lead, though." Harris shrugs. "Well, it's Sophie's first relay. And Carly was coming in hot."

I don't respond. I'm watching Sophie, unable to breathe. They're already around the first curve, heading down the straightaway. Sophie's strides are timed eerily in sync with the Vale girl's, but her legs are longer. "Come on, Soph," I murmur.

Slowly but surely, she's making up ground. "She might do it," Harris says incredulously as they start to round the second curve. The Vale girl takes the inside lane—she's good, this is clearly not her first race—but Sophie is riding her close, and Vale girl's flagging a little. By the time they're out of the curve and onto the straightaway, Sophie has edged into the lead.

My heartbeat is pounding in my ears. Harris and I are situated on the football field by the finish line. I can already see Sophie's wild panicked race expression. Vale girl puts up a good fight, but Sophie's got two or three meters on her by the time they cross the finish line, her momentum carrying her well past the finish. Harris is telling me their final time, but I'm already running to the gap in the fence. I duck underneath and jog to where Sophie has peeled off onto the football field.

She's kneeling on the turf, head resting on the ground. As soon as I reach her, I kneel down and place a hand on her back. "You good?" I ask.

She lets out a muffled moan. "Trying not to throw up."

I pull my water bottle from my bag—insulated, so it's still cold—and pour a little onto my hand before pressing it to her neck. She sighs in relief. "Your legs are going to cramp if you don't stretch them out," I tell her.

"Just give me a sec." She takes a huge, shuddering breath, and unclenches her hands against the fake grass. I just crouch beside her, rubbing her back, unable to contain a smile. Sophie's never going to stop surprising me. I've never seen a finish like that before.

"Sophie!" Kari calls, jogging over. 400's are weird. People are a mess in the immediate aftermath, but it's a short distance—a couple minutes and they're fine. It's not like cross country, where people can really be out of it for a while.

Harris is right behind her. I remove my hand, and Sophie flops over onto her side. "Sick finish," says Kari. "Don't drop the baton next time."

"Yup," Sophie says. "My bad. Nice leadoff."

"Hell of a race, Williams," says Harris. "Pineridge hasn't beaten Vale at any of these in a while. We might be able to get 'em at states if you don't muff the handoff."

"Sure," says Sophie, flopping an arm over her eyes against the late afternoon sun. "Em, would you mind stretching my hamstrings?"

I nod, and she lies down, raising one long leg vertically into the air. "Harris," she says as I push her leg down toward her chest. "Is it cool if me and Em skip out a little early? I'm giving her a lift to the concert, and she needs to get there in time for their rehearsal. I think Rhys and Tev already headed out."

"Of course," says Harris. "I'll be booking it back to the school myself. Can't wait to see it, Emily."

I smile over my guilt. Everything according to plan.

\*

Sophie and I walk out of the stadium while they start handing out medals, me holding her bag while she wriggles into a wrinkled sundress. "Sorry you're missing the awards," I tell her.

Sophie emerges from the top of the sundress, tugs it down, and shakes out her ponytail. She looks tired and windburnt and lovely. "Sorry you're missing your concert." She takes my hand as we head through the lonely parking lot, the lights coming on. It's six pm, and it's still light, but the air is the fiery red of the sunset.

I shrug, checking to make sure no one is looking. It's okay, though, her car is twenty feet away. "What do you want to do? Are you exhausted?"

"Yeah, but I'm up for anything that involves me sitting down." She laughs, breathlessly. "Wanna just drive around till we figure out something fun?"

She takes Bayer Street going west—straight into the setting sun—instead of east. Now we're officially traveling in the opposite direction of Pineridge High School. I stare out the window, squinting in the bright red light.

"So," Sophie says overly brightly, taking her eyes off the road to look at me. "What are you feeling? Drive through? Catch a movie?"

And it's weird to be in the middle of my plan right now, to be doing what I've laid out and what I'm supposed to be doing, but feeling so... shaky.

"Em?"

"I don't care. You should probably eat something after your race," I say, and stare out the window.

"Okay, well, luckily I think we have our pick of Taco Bells," she says. It's her sarcasm voice, and I can tell she's trying to make me laugh. Valiantly, I look over at her and attempt to lift the corners of my mouth.

"Or—hey, look! There's a park up here!" She keeps glancing at me. "We could sit around, watch the sunset, maybe you can play me your piece out here. You know, with the nature and stuff."

I nod, eying my violin case in the rearview mirror. It's buckled into the backseat like a little kid. I think of the bag Mom helped me pack this morning, the dark blue blouse she carefully folded so it wouldn't be wrinkled for the concert. "Um, sounds good," I say, and check dad's watch. 6:17. The concert starts in thirteen minutes. Bayer's a good half hour from Pineridge.

An ache starts to form in my stomach as I run through the list of everyone who wanted to see me perform, who I wanted to show something beautiful to: Sophie, Mom, Harris, Rachel, the Tuzarova-Williamses... A tear trickles down my cheek.

Sophie looks at me. Quickly, I hide my face.

We're at a red light, her fingers drumming on the steering wheel. When it turns green, she checks her mirrors, glances over her shoulder. "Fuck it." she says. Before I can react, she whips the car to the left in a U-turn, careening around the median on the highway so suddenly that I get pressed into the car door by the physical force of my inertia.

The driver behind us leans on the horn, but we're already zooming back down Bayer Street with the sun at our backs.

Sophie is laughing. "Holy shit! That was fun! You okay?"

I gulp down air once I realize I've stopped breathing. "What are you doing?" I ask once I can spit real words out.

Sophie's eyes flicker back and forth between me and the road. "Em. You need to play this concert." She presses on the gas, passes a minivan. "It's literally unfair to deprive people of your talents, let alone depriving yourself of the opportunity. And…" She takes a breath. "You won that solo, and I know you want to play it, I know you do. Don't let that fucking bitchnozzle Beth keep you from doing it because she thinks she can blackmail you, or whatever, because you know that she'll just come up with something worse after tonight." We slam to a stop at a light. She looks at me, pleading. Brown eyes, so intense, waiting for me.

I take a shaky breath, my stomach quivering. "We don't have enough time."

"I'll get us there, I promise. Look, the chorus is first, right, then the show choir. I bet you guys don't even go on till like seven." She grabs my hand, presses my fingertips to her lips. "Tell me to keep driving."

And I don't know if it's something in her face or something in my insides, but all of a sudden, my love of music (and for Sophie) is greater than my fear of failure. So that's what makes me smile. "Okay, Soph, keep driving, but watch the road."

The light turns green, and she whoops. "Pineridge here we come!"

The streets are crowded at this hour, but Sophie weaves in and out of traffic, jolting to a stop at every light. She slows down a little when I unbuckle my seatbelt and climb into the back seat to change into my concert outfit: dark blue blouse, black skirt, stockings. "Thought you wanted me to watch the road," Sophie says with a wicked grin when I clamber back up to the front, shiny black shoes in hand.

"Shut up," I say, but I'm smiling through my blushing face.

We're off the highway now, back in the residential streets of Pineridge, the sun fully set but the sky not yet dark. Sophie screeches into the full parking lot. It's 6:44. Oh, God, I hope concert band isn't on yet. "Quick, go in!" she says, slamming to a stop in front of the school. "I gotta park and then I'll head in."

"Hang on, I have to get my shoes on." Adrenaline courses through my veins. Fight or flight again. This time I'm going to fight, I guess. My hands shake as I pull on my patent leather shoes. How am I going to play if I can't even control my hands? "Sophie, I'm scared," I blurt out as I straighten up and grab my violin case.

"Em. Emily. You're going to be so amazing, so splendid that I can't even…" Her encouragement is muffled by my lips, when I lean in and kiss her.

"Thank you," I say softly when I finally draw away.

"Go! Go!" she tells me, shooing me away.

I run into the school lobby and past the trophy cases, my violin case banging against my knee and my shoes tapping on the linoleum. The front entrance to the auditorium is just down the hall. The faint strains of the show choir in the middle of their medley of selections from *Cats* leaks out of the doors. Internally, I shudder. I hate that musical. But I have a mission. Mrs. Porco needs to know I'm here.

I speed off down the hallway, my shoes pinching my toes. The backstage entrance to the auditorium is across from my precalc classroom. I slip through, into the dark, where I immediately spot Mrs. Porco having a hasty, whispered conversation with Jared Fischer about lighting. When I come over, she gives a little shriek and then claps a hand over her mouth. "Emily," she gasps, "Where have you been?"

"Car trouble," I mumble. That old chestnut.

"I'll have to let Beth know! She was going to take your place in the solo, you know," Mrs. Porco says, putting a hand to her forehead.

The chorus finishes the reprise of "Jellicle Cats," and the audience applauds. The sound makes my heart jump in my chest.

Mrs. Porco squeezes my shoulders. "Are you warmed up? The show choir has two more numbers. You can go run some scales in Mr. Gerard's classroom."

I nod.

"I'm so excited you're here, Emily dear," she says, before Jared takes her attention once more. I smile uneasily, hefting my violin case (it suddenly feels very heavy) as I leave for the empty classroom.

My heart is working hard, but all the blood is going to my head, my adrenal glands. My hands feel limp, floppy. My fingers shaking, I open the clasps on my violin case, run a finger down the varnished wood. Mom got me this, my next birthday after Dad died, the next size up. It took me a little while to grow into it, but now it's the perfect size for me. It's the thing I know how to use best.

But I can't quite bring myself to pick it up. That is, until another song ends and the audience claps once more, the applause sounding like faint rain from down the hallway. I grab it and fumble through a warm up, my fingers tripping on the strings, my bow slipping in my sweaty palm. All I can think about is standing up there, on stage, and forgetting everything. To reassure myself, I run through the first few lines of my solo, but there's no hint of the inner quiet that usually comes to the surface when I play.

Maybe I can just run out of the school. If Sophie's not here yet, I can cut her off at the entrance, get her to take me home. No, she won't let me. Mom? She might, if I tell her how scared I am. But how am I supposed to explain that I just got here, haven't warmed up with the band? There are woods behind the school. I could go hide in those, live off the land. Except the only thing that grows back there is kudzu, strangling the life out of anything except the tallest trees. Not exactly the best sustenance.

Why am I planning my life as a hermit right now? I'm not even breathing. Holding the violin isn't helping. I put it away. I walk into the hallway, and enter the auditorium—the audience, this time. The student performers are seated in front. I walk slowly down the aisle toward them, scared I will be noticed. Then I spot Rhys, right in the front corner. I sit down next to him. "Hi," I whisper.

"Saved you a seat," he says.

I smile. That, at least, makes me feel a little better, reminds me that I'm supposed to be here. "Thanks. I miss anything good?"

He shakes his head as the audience applauds. Our show choir is... kind of its own thing. I turn around in my seat, craning my neck to see if Sophie's arrived yet.

I can't see her, but there's Harris, a few rows back with his wife. He really must have booked it back. Although he probably didn't drive twenty minutes in the wrong direction first. He gives me a friendly wave when he sees me looking. I wave back, but continue searching the crowd. I can't find Mom and Peter, but there's Nana, Terry, and Gretchen. Here to watch their daughter. Their daughter who's supposed to be the soloist tonight. But no. I'm the soloist. She's the understudy.

I take a breath.

Once the chorus is gone, Mrs. Porco walks onto the stage, her all black outfit flowing and undulating around her. "Ladies and gentlemen," she says, pausing after every word. "I am so very, *very* overjoyed to present to you the Pineridge orchestra!"

My stomach drops. There's not enough time. Feeling weirdly like I'm in a dream, I file onstage with the rest of the orchestra, my violin and bow in my shaking hands, the stage lights hot against my skin. As in rehearsal, as in the holiday concert, my seat is near the front of the stage. First chair, first violin. Why does this feel so different? I stand in front of it, trembling.

Beth, in the second row, leans over to me. "I won't forget this," she whispers in my ear.

I close my eyes. Oh, yeah. That's why.

When Mrs. Porco nods to us, we sit in unison (more or less). "The students have worked so hard this year…"

I fade out again, searching for Sophie. It's hard—the bright stage lights pop in my brain, rendering the audience a dark mass. Finally, going row by row, I spot her parents near the back. I glance over at Willie, who winks at me from behind his double bass. It makes me feel better.

And then I see Sophie, standing in the very back, by the door. She must have just gotten inside. She sees me looking immediately, and gives me a double thumbs-up and a goofy grin. I try to smile back. I'm sure it looks more like a grimace.

Mrs. Porco introduces the first piece, the Mozart concertino. Time is moving weirdly, fast and slow at the same time. But I'm so worried about *Dance Macabre* that I play the Mozart robotically, raw muscle memory plowing through my fear. I'm hardly aware of the notes I'm so focused on the audience. The second piece goes even more quickly, and I flub the penultimate note. The applause is like rain on a roof.

"And now," says Mrs. Porco. "For our final piece, it is my utmost honor to present our soloists: Rhys Kosowsky, Emily Ferris, and Annie Gladstone! They are some of the most talented and dedicated musicians that Pineridge has ever seen."

Reluctantly, every muscle in my legs fighting against it, I stand. Poor Annie has to stand as well, even though her solo isn't until near the end of the song. I wish I could see Rhys at his xylophone, but he's behind me. And I'm supposed to be "gazing into the middle space," as Mrs. Porco has told me a thousand times.

The orchestra starts. My first notes are twenty-four measures away. I search out Sophie in the dark audience again, but I can't quite see her. Still, I can imagine her face. I know what she would say to me. *Smile, chica. Endorphins and shit.*

I inhale with difficulty, and force a smile onto my face. Twelve measures. Taking up my bow, I lift my violin to my chin. How does my part start again?

But my fingers remember. Somehow, they remember. I get through the first section, and abstractly remember that Sophie had offered the opportunity to play this outside, in the park.

I close my eyes, imagine the breeze on my face, and sink into the next theme.

# CHAPTER 11

After the concert, I shuffle backstage, holding my violin case tightly to my chest. It's crowded and dark back there, with students putting away instruments and laughing. I need to get away from everyone. I exit the stage door out into the main hallway of the school, the bright fluorescent lights making me blink. Out there, it's even more crowded: some chorus kids, and parents streaming out from the auditorium into the lobby of the school. After the concert, there's always a chaos of parents coming to grab their kids, band nerds high fiving each other, the show choir generally in the midst of some drama...

It's loud, and bright, and crowded. I feel dizzy. When I played, I found my place of focus, of calm... but I feel like I didn't breathe the entire time. I'm caught between the elation of playing and the fear of what's coming next. A couple of band kids give me quick "Congratulations" or shoulder pats as they walk past. They flow past me, barely registering. There's only one person I want to see.

I close my eyes, trembling.

Then there's a hand on my shoulder, warm and inviting, and I turn quickly, hoping it's Sophie. But it's Mrs. Porco who has found me first. She's standing next to a small man with a neat goatee and a robin's egg blue button-down. "Emily, light of my heart, you were wonderful. I want to introduce you to my friend..."

Out of the corner of my eye, several families away down the hall, I spot Mom. Technically, I spot Peter first, because Rachel's on his shoulders. But there's Mom, dark brown hair and her favorite beige skirt, looking so damn proud and happy.

"Dr. Jamison Kelly…"

I can actually feel time slowing down. Panic sets in.

"Head of the music department…"

I need to get to my mom before Beth does.

"At the university—"

I wrench my arm from Mrs. Porco. "Sorry," I say, almost no breath in my lungs. "I have to go."

Their startled faces don't even faze me as I jog toward the crush of families, my form terrible, my breathing ragged. I duck and weave through the crowd. "Mom!" I call as soon as I'm within earshot, almost walking straight into Ben McNally's French horn. Why on Earth is he still holding his French horn? "Mom!"

She turns around. Mom's not the most smiley person. But when she sees me, she beams. It makes my stomach hurt. "Emily," she says. "That was your best rendition yet."

Peter swings Rachel down so she can hug me. "Brava," he says, and hands me a bouquet of sunflowers.

The gesture completely startles me. Flowers seem so out of place in my panicked headscape, like they barely even make sense as a concept. "Thanks," I say.

"That seemed like a very challenging piece," says Mom.

"Yeah. I can hardly hear you, should we head out?" I ask, speaking too loudly, even though I can hear Mom fine. It's crowded, but she's right next to me. I'm already looking around, planning our exit. North? No, Harris and his wife are over there, talking to Rhys and his equally tall and taciturn mom. I don't want to risk another Mom vs. Harris interaction. South exit? I turn to look. There's Sophie and her family, with Willie and his freshman friend Drew. Sophie has Willie in a hug-slash-headlock, but almost like she can feel my gaze, she turns around.

We lock eyes. *You good?* she mouths.

I shake my head. But that's when Katchka spots me, smiling and walking right over. "Emily, you were wonderful!" I smile awkwardly as Katchka sweeps me into a hug, my chin against the top of her head, my sunflowers crushed against my chest.

"Is this your mother?" Katchka asks me when she pulls away.

Oh God. This cannot not be good. I meet Sophie's eyes, and hers are a reflection of mine—wide, panicked—as she follows her mom over, Willie and Ed in tow. "Um, yes."

Katchka holds her hand out to my mom. "I'm Katchka," she says. "Emily is like a part of the family."

My mom smiles, though she looks faintly bemused by that remark, coming from this tiny woman, who she's never met with her melodic accent. "And you are?"

"Oh! I'm Sophie's mother." Katchka smiles.

"Oh, the runner," Peter says. "How's tutoring going?" he asks heartily of Sophie. God dammit, Peter.

Sophie knows that I've been using tutoring as an excuse, but her family doesn't. I can see Willie getting confused. "Em's really good at bio," is all Sophie says. "Mom, can we get out of here? I'm pretty tired from the meet."

"Yeah, I want to get ice cream," Willie says. "Pleb athletes like you can come too, Sophie."

"Would you all like to join us?" Katchka asks my mom.

My mom is a little taken aback, but God help me, she's considering this. Why does Sophie's family have to be so goddammed charming?

"Ice cream!" says Rachel.

"I think we should maybe go home," I tell Mom in a low voice.

She can tell when I need alone time. She gets it. "I think we're heading out, but it was nice to meet you all," she says.

"Another time," says Katchka. The Tuzarova-Williamses leave, Sophie looking over her shoulder at me, her eyes saying everything that she can't. I look back at her, relief and regret all sweeping through my system at the same time. I'm coming close to shaking. I realize that I need to eat something. I'm deep into my glycogen storage at this point.

But I did it. We got the families apart without anything too dramatic.

That is, until Rachel behind me, like the canary in the coal mine, squeals "Bethie!"

I turn around. Beth makes a beeline for us, a giant bouquet of roses in her hands. She watches Sophie's family leave, and smiles. Aunt Gretchen and Uncle Terry are right behind her.

"Beth," my mom says warmly. "You were wonderful."

Beth just shakes her head. "Thanks, but Aunt Ruth, I need to talk to you. You know that girl that was just here?"

"Beth," I say. Nothing else. A small plea.

She shakes her head like she's at the end of some grave internal struggle. "I can't really, like, stand idly by anymore and watch you ruin your life, Emily."

Everyone's looking at her—Peter, Terry, Gretchen. Even Rachel.

But not Mom, who's looking at me, confused. I can't meet her eyes, so I stare down at my shoes. I'm trying to come up with something to say, but my mind is blank. All I feel is quivering fear. My mind goes to genus *Sylvilagus*, the cottontail rabbit. Their species-specific defense response has two parts: first they freeze. Then they take flight. I feel like that right now. That maybe if I play dead, Beth the fox won't snap me up in her jaws.

"Beth, what are you talking about?" Mom asks finally.

"Well..." Beth draws in a breath, like this is hard for her to say. "First of all. That girl Sophie who was just here? She's Emily's girlfriend."

She says it, oh, I don't know, as loudly as possible. I swear to god, the chatter around us gets a little quieter.

"Beth, I think you should…" Peter starts to say.

Beth talks over him. "This is too important. Emily is dating a girl, and I think she's an atheist, and oh yeah, she's been sneaking out of youth group."

There is… a pause.

"Emily, is this true?" Mom asks, quietly.

For one brief moment, I wonder if I can lie my way out of this. I know Mom will take my side over Beth's. Well, maybe. But I look at her, and under her direct gaze, against this genuine question of true or false, I falter. This moment of hesitation is all she needs. She knows that I'm full of shit.

"I have proof," Beth says. And just like that, she's handing Mom what is more or less my portfolio of lies. Harris's copy of *On the Origins of Species*, with all my notecards relating proofs against intelligent design, my outline for Harris for my independent study. And just inside the front cover, Beth has left my letter for Sophie, which Mom opens. She looks at it, brow furrowing like she's doing her nightly study of the New Testament.

Meanwhile, Peter and Terry are arguing, and it's starting to draw some onlookers. We're stuck between the trophy case and a crowd. "Control your daughter," Peter says, which sort of startles me.

"Sounds like you need to control *your* stepdaughter," Terry says back, and Peters face reddens. Rachel's clutching my hand, watching the adults fight. I spot Rhys looking over, craning his head over the crowd, Jenny's family next to us whispering. And Harris too…

But I forget about all of that when Mom meets my eyes over the top of the letter.

Right after Dad died, Mom wasn't right for a while. It was almost like she was confused. Startled. Like she didn't understand the way the world worked anymore. She would pick up a random object like the watering can or her keyring, and look at it like she barely recognized it. Like every natural law had been subverted and she no longer understood what things were or how they were supposed to work.

That's how she's looking at me right now.

I can't be here anymore—not with her looking at me like that, not with Beth's expression of solemn piety barely masking vindictive glee, not with a concerned Harris starting to make his way over.

I run. Like a rabbit that has seen the fox about to strike, like a scared fourteen-year-old at her first cross-country meet, like a child at a hospital that's pretty sure her dad just died and wants to get away before anyone can tell her. It's my species-specific defense response, the one for a coward. I run.

*

I sit on the floor of a stall in the empty bathroom for what must be half an hour, pretty much just crying my guts out. I want to wait for everyone to disappear before I leave. I want to have a plan before I leave. But I don't want to see my mom. I'm so scared of what she'll say. All I want is to be in Sophie's arms. So where should I go? Sophie's, obviously, but it's a solid three miles and it's after dark and I'd have to cross like two highways to get there. But maybe I can call her from the office if it's not locked.

Once my legs are getting the pins and needles that mean they're about to fall asleep, I force myself to stand up. I splash water on my blotchy face and swollen eyes before leaving the bathroom and trudging out into the hallway. I expect it to still be full and crowded, to have to avoid Mom and the family and borrow a phone. But when I get out, everyone is gone. Except the janitor. I must have been in the bathroom longer than I thought.

My stomach sinks. Where are they? I expected to have to avoid Mom. I didn't expect her to just... be gone.

I stand there for a long time, until the janitor says, "You all right?"

I panic and say, "Yeah, yeah, I'm fine, thanks," before walking purposefully down the hall like I'm catching a ride. Where's Mom? She really left me here?

I'm passing the auditorium when I hear drumbeats: a rhythm on the snare and the kick drum, with the high-hat every other downbeat. Eager to think about anything except my current situation, I open the door and peer inside. Rhys sits onstage, alone in the huge auditorium. There's a relaxed, easy grin on his face, something I've never seen on him before.

The door shuts behind me and he looks up, the rhythm abruptly halting. "Sorry," I say quickly, feeling terrible. I know what it's like to be yanked out of your own little world of music.

He shrugs. "No worries." He twirls one of the drumsticks. It hits lightly against the high-hat, a long, thin sound. He looks uncomfortable, and the normally easy silence between us just feels awkward. I'm sure he saw the scene Beth created. I don't even want to think about what might have happened after I left.

"Uh, I barely ever see you on the drum set," I mumble, trying to make conversation. Anything so that he doesn't feel a need to bring up what just happened. I cannot handle that. "I thought you were all xylophone, all the time."

He shrugs again. "Generally, Liz and Tyler want to play the drum set and snares, so I'm happy to stick with xylophone. But I like to stay around and experiment when I can."

"Oh right, stage manager privileges and all that. Um, Rhys, I'll put away the chairs and stuff for you if you can give me a ride."

The huge room is silent around us. My request hangs small and scared in the air. Rhys looks at me for a long moment. I have no idea what he's thinking about. To quote Sophie, he is "fucking inscrutable." But he nods, slowly. "Don't worry about it," he says finally. "Of course I can give you a ride."

I clamber onto the stage. "Thank you so much, this is really helpful, I can't even explain…"

"Do you want to try the drums for a minute?" he asks.

"What?" I'm already stacking chairs.

"I can do that," he says, and holds out the sticks to me. "Seriously. It's fun."

I shake my head. "I don't know how."

He walks across the stage to me. "Hell if I do. It's just nice to make a little noise sometimes, you know?"

I feel dangerously close to tears again. He presses the sticks into my hands. "Um, maybe," I say.

He starts disassembling the music stands by the violin section. "Go for it."

I walk to the drum set, sit down on the stool. I know about which drums are which because I care about music theory and Mrs. Porco makes sure we educate each other about our instruments. But I've never sat in front of them before, held the dinged and chipped sticks in my hands. "I don't really... know what to do. It's very different from violin."

"Just find a rhythm," he says, walking the music stands over to the closet behind the curtain. When he comes back, I'm still sitting there, a stick in each hand, feeling a sadness expanding so huge inside of me that it might burst out like the big bang in an ever-expanding explosion.

He gives me a small smile. "Really," he says. "It helps."

I wipe my eyes, then hit the kick drum pedal. The boom is loud and deep. I hit it again, slamming my foot on it this time, and it's even louder. It's a little satisfying. I try the high-hat. It's light and shivery. I hit it harder, and it's a crash.

Rhys busies himself putting away chairs and before long I don't feel self-conscious. I don't know what I'm doing, but I have a little idea for a rhythm and start feeling it out. I mess up a few times, missing the mark on the beat in my head, but with a little patience pretty soon things are smooth. It's slower than I want and I keep hitting the kick drum at the wrong time. It's hard coordinating both hands and a foot. But I can feel myself falling into that place I can travel to with my violin, that safe place where nothing could touch me.

The drums are satisfying in a way my violin wouldn't be right now, though, sharp and angry and dissonant in my ears, but the volume helps dull down the flashes of Mom's face that keep appearing in my mind's eye. When I've gotten the beat right several times in a row, I look up, flushed, smiling.

Rhys sits on the edge of the stage, the rest of the chairs put away, shrugging into his sweatshirt. "Sorry," I mumble.

"Just finished," he says, but I think he would have said it no matter how long it had been.

We push the drum set into the closet together, and then he turns off the auditorium lights, one at a time. I watch the stage and the audience disappear, little by little. "Ready?" Rhys asks when it's completely dark.

I breathe in, then out. "Yeah."

\*

Rhys and I are mostly silent on the way to Sophie's, the way it usually is. It's a relief to not have to say much. When he pulls up in front of Sophie's, I pause before getting out. "Um," I say, "Thank you. For, uh, yeah."

He shrugs. But when I open the door and get out, he says, "Emily... I liked your solo."

I smile, just a little. "Yours too," I whisper, then walk up the drive to Sophie's house. A few drops of rain are just beginning to fall. It'll be good for my thirsty rhododendron, I think, before thinking of the garden reminds me of home reminds me of Mom and my stomach falls all over again. I don't know what's going to happen. I'm so scared.

I ring the doorbell and cross my arms across my chest. It's starting to rain in earnest, now. There are footsteps, then there she is. She pulls me inside. "Em," she says, "What happened?"

All I can do is lean into her. She wraps her arms around me for a long time, and we stand in her entryway, silent, rocking back and forth.

"Who is it, Soph?" Ed calls from the kitchen. The house smells delicious.

"It's Em. Just a minute," she calls. She pulls me in front of her. "What happened? Tell me everything."

I stare down at the floor while I tell her what happened. The project, the youth group, the Sophie. All of it culminating in Mom looking at me like she didn't know me, walking out of the school without me. By the time I've told Sophie everything, I'm crying again. Sophie takes my face in both of her hands, brushing my tears aside with her thumbs. Her face is bright and earnest. "Em. It's going to be okay. I promise."

"How do you know?"

"Because the worst-case scenario happened and look, you're still here, you're still alive, you're still here with me." She smiles, although I think that just maybe I can see tears being held back too.

I try to take a deep breath. It's shaky, but it makes me feel better.

Sophie pulls me in, kisses my forehead, and lets me go. "If you're going through this, I want to be going through it too," she says.

My heart starts pounding again. "Sophie..."

"We've got nothing to lose, my parents are going to have to know at some point, and I'm like, really fucking proud you're my girlfriend. Come on." She grabs me by the hand and leads me into the kitchen. It smells like wienerschnitzel again. They must be celebrating the concert.

They're all three sitting around the table, but they look up when we come in. "Hi girls, are—Emily. What's wrong?" Ed says.

I remember my flushed, swollen face, but Sophie speaks up before I have time to feel embarrassed. "You guys," she says. "I, uh, family announcement. Em and I aren't just friends, we're, um, we're dating, and we're in love, and I just, uh, want you all to know that." She trails off, her voice going from confident to shaky to up at the end like she's asking a question.

I'm expecting a dramatic pause, but instead there's a clatter as Willie throws his fork down onto the table. He punches the air triumphantly. "Fucking yes! I called this shit literally months ago," he says.

Sophie laughs, then covers her mouth.

"Willie, language," Katchka snaps, setting her bottle of beer down on the table.

"I just want that on record," he says, leaning back in his seat.

Sophie wraps her arms around me. Her voice is a little more confident now. "And Em's family are kinda being wangs about this whole thing so, um, could she stay here tonight?"

Now there's the dramatic pause.

Ed and Katchka exchange glances. Finally, Ed wipes his mouth on his napkin. "Emily, Willie," he says. "Do you mind giving us the room?"

Willie scooches his chair back and sighs. "So much for family dinner. Wanna come look at the kite I made, Emily?"

I nod, looking apprehensively at Sophie. She smiles, squeezes my shoulder then pushes me toward Willie. "It's fine."

I wave awkwardly at her parents. Ed, bless his heart, waves back, but Katchka looks a little thunderstormy right now.

But I follow Willie out of the kitchen and up the steps into his room. It's exactly as full of construction materials and wiring as before, but he has more storage set up now, drawers against the walls labeled "output" "vinyl" "twine". It appeals to the neat freak in me.

Willie's kite is beautiful, made of tan canvas with some kind of LED wiring strung across it. "It's pretty heavy, so I'm probably gonna have to wait till a tornado or something, but I'm confident in my calculations that I can get it to stay aloft once it's up there."

I smile. "I'm glad you like the kit." I'm speaking through a stuffed-up nose and my eyes feel swollen, but I feel much calmer now, away from parents, in this room full of science and engineering. The moment feels easy, natural, which in itself is strange. "Did you really know Sophie and I were dating?"

"Oh, hell yeah." He hands me a tissue from next to his nightstand.

I blow my nose. "Did she tell you?"

Willie laughs. "I don't know if you guys realize this, but you are not subtle."

"Really?"

"Yeah, always exchanging all these significant glances and touching hands and shit," he says. "Also, I a hundred percent walked in on you two that one time."

Even though I'm blushing, I laugh. It feels good. "I thought we hid that pretty well."

"Nah. Sophie can't lie to me for shit," he says. He sits down on his bed, pauses for a second. "She really likes you, you know," he says finally, a little awkward.

I smile.

A few minutes later, after Willie has shown me the process of connecting tiny batteries to wires to buttons to be able to light the kite in a portable and waterproof package, there are footsteps on the stairs. I know Sophie's steps—two at a time, bouncing from one foot to the other. Sure enough, she bursts into Willie's room a second later, looking flustered but okay.

I jump up. "What happened?"

She walks over, pulls me back onto the bed with her and Willie. "It was a lot. But things are okay. They kind of wanted to ground me because I'm supposed to tell them when I'm dating someone. But I told them about how your family reacted, and they saw where I was coming from I guess. So not grounded."

I'm relieved, I'm jealous, I'm... I'm struggling a little bit.

"How'd they take the whole dating a girl thing?" Willie says.

Sophie's face gets serious. She takes my hand. "I don't know. They were both really supportive. Mom cried though."

"*Mom?*"

"Yeah. I know. She was like, 'You know your life might be a lot harder, if you live this way.'" She strokes her thumb against my palm. "It was kinda real. They were startled, I think. But they have gay friends and everything. And Dad was like, 'Well, now I'm less worried about you coming home pregnant one of these days,' and Mom hit him with her spoon, so I think things are like, eighty-five percent okay. They just need a little bit."

I smile, unsure about the waves of relief and jealousy running through me. "I wish I had your parents."

She hugs me, and Willie laughs. "Man, if your parents were our parents, this thing would be a million times weirder."

I laugh too. There's a knock on the door. Katchka looks in. Her eyes are a little red, but her voice is steady and normal. "Emily? Have you eaten, beruško? We have plenty more downstairs."

I realize that I haven't eaten all day I was so nervous about the plan. "Um, that sounds nice."

So I eat with Sophie's family. We don't talk about the events of the evening, but Sophie holds my hand under the table. Katchka notices, but she makes a point of smiling and passing me more sauerkraut. The kitchen is warm, the music Beethoven's seventh symphony, and for a few minutes, I feel safe and happy around the family of the girl that I love, that loves her too.

# CHAPTER 12

The next morning, Ed drives me home. Sophie wants to, but she has a dentist appointment at 9am. It seems bizarre that such a mundane activity could even exist in the universe of stress and emotion we've been living in for the past 24 hours, but teeth are important.

Ed and I drop her off at the dentist's office over in the Bryce strip mall and then Ed takes me home, promising to swing back to pick Sophie up.

"So what's the plan for when you get home?" Ed asks me, driving back toward my neighborhood, the houses getting bigger, the development names getting more pretentious. Oak Grove, Swan Haven, The Terrace at Poplar Lane...

"I don't know," I say, rubbing my eyes, which feel like sandpaper. I slept terribly the previous night. Sophie insisted I take her bed, and her parents insisted she sleep on the couch, but all I could think about the whole night was Mom. "I'll talk to my mom about what happened, I guess. I'll be in trouble."

Ed shrugs. "I just want to make sure you're safe."

I'm touched by his concern. I find myself fighting the tears that have been hovering constantly since the previous night. "It'll be fine. It's not like they're going to physically barricade me from the door or anything," I say.

"I can't imagine they'd do that." Ed keeps his eyes straight on the road, a much more cautious driver than his daughter. He turns into Wisteria Manors, blinking in the east-facing sun that suddenly streams through the window. "But you do know you're always welcome at our place, Emily. You don't even have to call ahead."

I smile as I gather my violin. "Thanks," I say softly, and leave the car. Ed gives a little honk as he drives away.

Our driveway is empty. For one absurd moment, I think that they've just up and abandoned me, or that I'm at the wrong house in this stupid development. Then it hits me. It's Sunday. They're at church.

For some reason, I burst out laughing. This is the first service I've missed since... since... have I been to church every Sunday since we moved in?

I unlock the door. I have the house to myself, which is a relief at first. Maybe I can figure out a way to approach the situation when Mom gets back, defuse things in some way.

But even thinking about it makes me nervous. I end up in the living room, alone on the big cushy couch that could probably seat sixteen people, watching Family Feud but too anxious to do anything but pick at my nails and wonder what will happen.

The beep of the security system goes off around noon, and I hear the door opening and closing, the sound of Mom and Peter quietly talking. No gardening club today.

Mom must spot my backpack, because immediately she calls, "Emily?"

I swallow. "In the living room," I say.

I mentally track the sound of Mom's rapid footsteps through the echoey foyer, through the kitchen, into the living room. She's wearing her second-best church outfit, but she looks terrible. Her face is red, her hands are shaking, and she's been crying, which I haven't seen in a long time. It freaks me out. It makes me feel like a little kid at the hospital again, waiting around for Mom to finish talking to the doctors about Dad.

"Where on Earth have you been?" she asks me, standing right in front of the couch, arms crossed.

"I was at Sophie's," I say in a small voice.

"We were out of our minds," Mom says, emphasizing every word. "You should have called. You should have come home."

216

"You left without me," I say. It slips out, petulantly.

"We waited for you in the parking lot!" Mom throws her hands up. "We waited for an hour. Rachel was in tears. Then Mr. Harris came over to us and said you were with a friend."

Harris. He has eyes and ears everywhere. "My friend Rhys took me to Sophie's."

"I had no idea where you were! I didn't sleep for one second! Why didn't you call us?"

"Maybe if you let me have a phone like a normal sixteen-year-old you would have been able to find out where I was," I say.

Mom looks at me like I slapped her across the face. I feel like I slapped her across the face. I've never said anything like that to her. Ever.

That's when Peter walks in. "Rachel's upstairs," he says to Mom. Then he looks at me. "Emily, we're very disappointed in you."

It's so absurd to hear anything remotely parental coming from Peter, and this bratty new Emily is taking the stage. "I'm so sure," I say.

"Your mother has rules for you, and those rules are for a good reason, and you will respect them." Peter's brow is sweaty. "But for now, there have to be consequences for your actions."

Mom is taking out the book from her purse. The notecards spill out of it onto the floor. "Shoot," she says, with the same level of vitriol that Sophie would hiss, "Fucking shit." She kneels to pick them up. "We're taking you out of Pineridge High School," Mom says. "You're going to be going to St. Mary's."

My stomach drops. I don't know what I expected, but it's not that. "What?"

"It's been nothing but bad for your development," Mom says. There are huge bags under her eyes. "I never should have let you be in that biology class with that teacher."

"Didn't he tell you where I was last night?" I might not be great at standing up for myself, but standing up for Harris? I would take a bullet for him. "He's a good person, Mom."

"He said he would work with you on this independent project and all he's done is drive you further from God." Mom spits it. "And that's not even to mention all the sneaking around you've done with youth group, and—and—this Sophie girl."

Here it is. "What else was I supposed to do?" I shout.

"Tell the truth, Emily. That's what you're supposed to do." Mom is close to shouting now.

*The truth is that I hate it here, and I'm in love with Sophie, and I'm like eighty percent sure I don't believe in god and I hope Beth gets eaten by hyenas.*

But then, out of the corner of my eye, I spot Rachel, her faded horse toy clutched to her chest, tears streaming down her cheeks. When she sees me, she flees away.

There's movement out of the corner of my eye. Rachel stands in the corner, her faded horse toy clutched to her chest, tears streaming down her cheeks. When she sees me, she flees away.

Mom looks at me, then Peter. They have some sort of wordless conversation, and then Mom goes after Rachel. It's weird to see them uniting, and it's weirder still that it's against me.

"You can finish out the school year," Peter says. He sits on the other side of the giant sofa, approximately fourteen people-spaces away from me. That thirty seconds of disciplinarian was clearly very challenging for him. "But you'll spend your senior year at St. Mary's. And you and your mother are meeting with Pastor Dan next weekend. And you are not going to see Sophie again. Emily, this is a serious betrayal of your mother's and my trust."

I feel a little bad, but mostly I just feel angry. "Whatever." Like they'll be able to enforce any of this.

"This is not whatever. This is what will happen. You'll meet your mother every day after school and come home to do homework. And we'll work on transferring you out of Mr. Harris's class."

"I can't go to track? That's so unfair!"

"You haven't earned fairness," Peter says.

That makes me really angry, because I guess I have lied a lot, but I have been a good daughter, and I have tried to make it work here. "This is fucking bullshit!" I say, like I'm Sophie.

"Go to your room," Peter says.

Well, anything is better than here. I stand up and go, trying to stomp as loud as I can on every stair in this stupid giant house.

\*

Peter drives me to school in the morning. We don't say one thing the entire drive, not until he pulls up in front of the school, surrounded by seniors parking their cars, parents dropping their kids off, school buses clustered in the parking lot. "So, your mother will pick you up in front of the school right at three," he says awkwardly.

I don't say anything, just get out of the car.

"Emmy," he says.

I pause.

"We—we're just trying to do what's best for you," he says.

I leave.

Homeroom doesn't start for nine minutes. Sophie's usually at least fifteen minutes late to school. There's not a chance she's in yet. I make a beeline for Harris's classroom, the school quiet, the linoleum echoing, the memories of Saturday night ringing loud and clear in my mind.

Harris is behind his desk when I get there. I stand in the doorway, unsure whether he'll be mad at me. "Harris," I say, and then I realize that I haven't planned anything. My throat is stuck around twenty different apologies: for the calls my mom's going to be making to the school about him, for all the track practices I'm going to miss, for the scene after the concert, for all the times I've lied, since he was someone I never really needed to lie to, which I'm only realizing now...

I realize it even more when he looks at me with an expression completely without anger, completely without judgment, just openness and forgiveness. "Well, if it isn't my biggest troublemaker," he says. But with Harris, sarcastic jokes are affection, gruff words are love.

I burst into tears.

"Come on now, Emily," he says, standing up on his bad knees and grabbing the tissue box from between his deer skull and some student from year's past diagram of DNA made of Styrofoam packing peanuts. "It's gonna be fine."

"I can't do track anymore and my mom's probably going to try to get you in trouble with the school and…" I take a tissue and blow my nose.

"She already called," said Harris. "She'd like you, uh, removed from my influence, if I recall her words exactly."

I cringe. "I'm sorry…"

Harris snorts. "You think this is the first time I've had a pissed-off parent? I'll be fine."

"Thanks for telling my mom where I was."

He shrugs. "I'm a parent, too."

Then Derrick and Jon are in the room, like they are every morning for homeroom. "Damn, Emily, you and Sophie?" Derrick yells without preamble.

The kid has no filter. "Derrick…" says Harris.

"I'm just saying! Kept that one pretty quiet." Derrick waggles his                                                                 eyebrows.

"I wonder why," Harris says drily.

I'm only really paying attention to Jon. He doesn't really look at me, just sort of stares at Boris the snake without reacting to Derrick's comments, instead of building on the joke like he usually does.

I hope we're still friends, but I still don't know if he ever got over Sophie. Maybe I'll give him some space. I throw away my tissues, tell Harris I'll be back for lunch, and leave to find out what the rest of the day has in store.

*

By last period, things are partially okay. Beth has apparently taken it as her solemn duty to spread the word about me and Sophie's relationship. Even if she hadn't, there's enough overlap between the cross-country team and orchestra that at least on the team, everyone has heard what's up. But it turns out to not be a huge deal. There are some jokes, some teasing from the cross-country people I pass—Terri, Greg—but not in a way that's any different or harsher than any of the intra-team romances that have bubbled up in the past. It's almost a little funny.

I'm tired by the time I get to orchestra, and a little weirded out that I haven't seen Sophie yet today. Usually she stops by my locker between fifth and sixth period so we can see what each other are up to after school, but I haven't seen her even once.

I watch my feet scuffing against the ground as I walk up the steps to the stage to orchestra, not wanting to see any stares after the events after the concert. However, once I sit and chance a quick look around myself, it doesn't seem like anyone is paying attention to me. Except Willie, who gives me a friendly nod while he tunes his giant double bass.

I take a deep breath. Okay. Maybe I can stop being paranoid.

Until... "Have a nice weekend, Emily?" a snide voice asks.

I cringe automatically. Beth sits, her short skirt taut over her thighs even though it's probably only fifty degrees outside, a smug grin on her face. I can't believe I'm still scared of her, but I am. Reflexes are biological, not a choice, and I still feel like a little rabbit around her.

Mrs. Porco bustles onstage, saving me temporarily from nasty remarks. "Sit down, sit down, my sweet producers of musical marvels," she says in her sing-songiest of voices. "I would like to heartily congratulate you all for your most scintillating performance on this Saturday past." She pauses to give us light golf claps, which we all reluctantly join. "A special congratulations are owed to our soloists, Emily, Annie, and Rhys," says Mrs. Porco, waving her conducting baton in Rhys's general direction as though she is bestowing a blessing upon him with a magic wand. "You all were absolutely a marvel." Then, as she waddles past me, she leans down to whisper. "I'd like to see you after class, please."

Beth snorts. I flush, remembering another apology I owe. "Mrs. Porco, I'm really sorry about not being able to talk to your friend…"

"Worry not my dear," she tells me airily, and then strides off to go speak to a clarinetist waiting patiently to speak with her about replacing a broken reed.

I watch her receding presence. What's this about, if not to reprimand me for totally brushing her off in front of her weird goateed friend?

Beth apparently thinks she knows. "She probably just wants to tell you she's even more obsessed with you now that you're, you know, a lesbian or whatever."

I stare down at my lap. Jesus, Beth is loud. The room seems to grow quieter and quieter with every word she's saying. "God, Porco's so weird., she always creeps me out. No wonder you got that solo, you two just…"

"Beth," someone says. "Shut up."

I glance up, startled. Rhys looms over Beth, his tall frame casting a shadow over her surprised face.

If the room was quiet before, it's silent now. Rhys speaking? This is an event, even if Beth mocking me isn't.

"Nobody cares, okay? Just... grow up or something." He shakes his head, and without another word, turns around and lopes back to the percussion section, where he leans over the xylophone. One of the other percussionists gives him a pat on the back.

Beth's mouth is open like one of the ill-fated guppies that lived in a tank in Harris's room freshman year. Slowly, she shuts it, the muscles around her mouth tightening in a way that reminds me of Aunt Gretchen's. She leans over, takes her violin out of her case.

I realize in that moment that Beth, who has spent the past four years torturing me, isn't scary at all. She's just a petty teenage girl. She's not inherently more powerful or dangerous than me in any way shape or form. She's not a predator. And I'm not prey.

A tiny smile tugs at my lips. Rhys. Thank you for showing me.

Mrs. Porco emerges from the backstage supply area with Tevyn the clarinetist, extra reeds in his hands. "Wonderful! Now that we are all sorted out, we may begin to produce mellifluous sounds of gold and silver," Mrs. Porco babbles nonsensically from her conducting podium.

I grin, shaking my head, and take up my violin. Suddenly, the world doesn't seem quite as threatening.

All the drama makes me forget Mrs. Porco's request to see me after class, but she doesn't forget. "Emily, dearest, can you come chat with me a moment?" she calls as the auditorium gradually empties, Beth flouncing out as quickly as possible.

I head over to Mrs. Porco. She sits in one of the empty seats left behind by the viola section, and pats the empty seat beside her. Nervously, I sit, still half-convinced that she's going to reprimand me about my behavior in front of her friend.

"Emily, you were very good in the concert on Saturday," she tells me, and for once her voice lacks its theatrical tone.

"Um, thank you."

"My friend Jamison who I tried to introduce you to..." Here, I cringe. "He was very, very impressed."

She pauses. I'm never a hundred percent sure whether her pauses are for dramatic effect or if I'm supposed to respond or what. "Uh, that's good…"

"He wants to meet with you to discuss your future as a violinist," she tells me, her eyes sparkling. "He thinks you might have the potential to study in school, maybe someday go professional, that is, with the right training."

I lift my eyebrows in surprise. "Really?"

She laughs. "Of course, I could have told him that myself. But he was terribly excited."

I'm still incredulous, but I can't help but smile back at her.

"I'll give you his email so you can get in touch with him and chat over a coffee. He's a very influential man at the university downtown, and knows a great deal about music education."

"Wow, I… wow." I feel myself smiling, which is a weird feeling based on the past thirty-six hours. "Thank you so much, Mrs. Porco."

"Not a worry, my dear," she says, giving me a wink. And for one, one, one moment, I'm so happy and proud that I played that stupid violin solo.

\*

I'm sitting on the steps of the school, waiting for my mom to come pick me up, when Sophie comes and sits beside me. She almost reaches for my hand, then hesitates. We haven't held hands at school in a long time, and never in public. "Hey," she says.

I have so much to tell her, but something in her expression stops me. "What?" I say.

"It's been, uh… a crazy day." She laughs a little. "In a lot of ways. Uh, I got into school."

My brain breaks for a second. I've been so absorbed in my own experience of the past twenty-four hours—really, the past month—that I almost forgot about Sophie's college applications. "Oh my gosh, where?"

"OSU." She shrugs. "Still waiting to hear back from a few places, but this makes it kinda real, I guess. And they actually are going to give me some money if I run cross-country."

"Congratulations," I say, and bump her with my shoulder.

"Wanna celebrate? Slash, talk about how your cousin has apparently decided that everyone in this school needs to know that we're together?" She laughs.

Automatically, I glance out at the cars waiting to pick people up. I don't see Mom in her old sedan. I grab Sophie by the elbow and walk so that we're behind a tree relative to where the cars can see us. "Um, I don't know if I can today."

She cocks her head. "Why not?"

I tell her everything: the plan to send me to St. Mary's, the fact that I'm not allowed to go to track or take AP Bio or even see her anymore. "But obviously, that's not going to happen," I tell her in a rush at the end. "I figure, you know, if we just lie low for a few days and I go talk to the pastor and tell him I've found Jesus and everything, I think I can get her to back off a little and I can see you after school and stuff."

Sophie just looks at me. Hard.

My stomach lurches, but I forge ahead. "I know it's not ideal, but it's not that different than before. We'd just have to... you know. Keep it even more on the "down low," to borrow your terminology."

Sophie lets out a bitter laugh. "Oh, yeah, and we all know how well that works."

I glance up at her sharply. "It worked fine. If I hadn't played the solo, which, by the way, you wanted me to do—"

"Of course I fucking wanted you to play it!" Sophie interrupts me. I stop short. I don't think she's ever talked over me, not once, not even when I'm lost in thought and my sentences start trailing. "Emily, fuck, come on. Don't tell me it wasn't worth it. And this whole sneaking around thing, man. It's bad for me, but honestly, I think it's so much worse for you."

There's so much pent-up anger behind her words. I feel my defenses rising, like a porcupine's quills bristling. I've tried freeze and flight. The only thing left is fight. "I mean, I don't know, I'm not the one that blurted out that we were dating in the middle of a party."

Sophie laughs, but it's not a happy laugh. "You said you didn't care about that."

"I'm just saying that keeping things hidden isn't a problem for me and I don't feel like it has to be." I'm starting to feel a little scared now. I can see her turning into Tough Sophie, who's sharp and sarcastic and absolutely closed off. I haven't seen Tough Sophie since the beginning of the year, at least not when it's just us talking.

But she's here, in full force. She huffs out a breath. "I didn't mean that you're bad at keeping shit hidden," she says, her voice full of scorn. "You're like, really fucking good at it. How does it feel to constantly be hiding everything that matters to you?"

That one hurts. My eyes fill with tears. "So, what, what am I supposed to do, just do all this stuff that my mom wants? Never see you again?"

"That's not what I'm saying, I just think that lying about everything is like... ruining your life." She's looking at me so intensely. Even now, Sophie's eyes can startle me with their power.

But I'm too hurt for it to stop the angry words tumbling from my mouth. "It honestly sounds like you're just tired of all this drama in my life and you want me out of it."

Sophie's eyes fill with tears. "That's not what I want, Jesus fucking Christ. I just fucking want you to be happy, and I don't—I don't think you can be if you keep lying about everything."

Out of the corner of my eye, I spot Mom, pulling up to the curb in front of the school. My whole body is stressed. It's different from when Beth outed me at the concert, different from the fear at the start of the race. This is Sophie, and suddenly it feels like I might lose her, and the feeling is white hot electric fear.

Sophie follows my gaze and spots Mom. "So what are you gonna do?" she says. "Go tell your mom everything is fine and you were a perfect little princess all day?"

That startles me. Sophie sees it in my face. I start walking away, and she grabs me. "God, Em, I didn't mean that, I'm just—"

I lash out, wanting to hurt her before she hurts me more. "Fuck off," I reply harshly, the words unfamiliar coming out of my mouth. But they have the desired effect. Sophie stops short. She stares at me like she doesn't know me. I've been getting that a lot lately.

Fighting back a sob, I walk toward the car. When Mom sees me, she's taken aback. "Emily, what's going on?"

"Let's just go," I say through a constricted throat. And Mom may be furious at me right now, but she does.

# CHAPTER 13

Pastor Dan's office feels like a principal's office. Well, what I imagine getting sent to the principal's office feels like. It's not like I've ever been in this much trouble before. The only time I saw the inside of the principal's office was back at Rhizenstein Catholic School right after my dad died and they wanted to make sure that I was doing okay since I didn't really talk to anyone for a week. But that was back in sixth grade and our principal was a nice nun who gave me a Dumdum and a book about dogs and let me cry a little bit. This is... different.

The past week has been horrible. No track means I come right home after school. No AP Bio means my hardest class is gone. Mom brokered a deal where my current grade in the course will be my final grade. And even if I'm not allowed to see Sophie, the worst part is that she doesn't even try. I pass her once in the hallway at school and we sort of make eye contact, but we both look away.

That's the worst part.

I've been sitting at home a lot, looking at my violin but too sad to play, looking at the garden but too listless to weed, walking around the track at Asbury Park but too anxious to run. The whole week has been an endless wave of sadness and boredom, a loneliness I haven't felt since I met Sophie, no, even since I came to Pineridge.

And now this meeting, which is pretty much the cherry on top.

Bookshelves cover the left wall filled with glossy hardcover books. A few have their front covers turned out on display, with preachers I've seen on TV, smiling in their author headshots with gleaming white teeth and nice hair. Pastor Dan matches, his tanned skin glowing against his black shirt and white collar. He does have a few Bibles, one King James and two New King James. A third one sits on the desk in front of us. A big window looks out into the church gardens. I can see the lavender I helped Mom plant when we first started volunteering in the garden, just beginning to bud for the spring.

"Thank you for meeting with us," Mom says. I get hit with the weirdest shock of déjà vu, back to the beginning of the school year, sitting in front of Harris, Mom on my left.

"Of course," Pastor Dan says. "Obviously, when I got your call I was... concerned."

Of course he was. Can't have a little deviant messing with the reputation of Pineridge Baptist.

"Well, we're all concerned," Mom says. She tries to take my hand. I cross my arms.

"How can I best help you, Ruth?" Pastor Dan asks. I hate how he always uses people's names, like, oh, I'm so special, I'm a good pastor who knows my congregation, look at me.

Mom shifts in her seat. She keeps glancing at me. The only person I can think about right now is Sophie. What would she do? Not put up with this bullshit situation. I know Sophie gets scared, but she never lets people see it. I try to adopt one of her tougher facial expressions.

I wish we weren't fighting. It makes me feel more alone right now.

"Emily has always—she's always been a good Christian. A model for me, really," Mom says, which surprises me. "But this year, she's been having—she's been doubting. And she's been lying. Constantly."

I keep my face empty, even though the inside of me is curling up. God damn Mom for her sincerity.

"And you said there was a, ah, relationship?" Pastor Dan asks, his face carefully neutral.

Mom frowns. "Yes. Emily has really lost her way. And I was hoping... I was praying... that maybe you'd have some guidance for us."

Pastor Dan lets that settle for a minute. A beam of sunlight comes in through the window and moves over his shiny blonde hair, like a benediction from the world. I roll my eyes. Come on, nature. Don't leave me hanging. "How do you feel about all this, Emily?" he asks in his 'rappin' with the teens' voice. It's much more patronizing than genuine, giving a little pause to engage with a troubled youth while very clearly planning on barreling forward with a planned speech regardless.

So for once in my mousy existence, I answer that question honestly. I open my mouth and say every single thing that's on my mind. "I feel great," I say. "Sophie is awesome and I feel a thousand times happier without believing in God." I'm startled by how much Mom's face breaks, but it feels recklessly good. She left me at the school, didn't stand up to Beth. I can feel all the anger I've been feeling since then, no, since she married Peter, no, since Dad disappeared into the hospital and then into the ground... it's all boiling out of me. And God help her for being part of it. If I even do believe in God.

"Atheism is a denial of God's power. Humility is the most important virtue of all," Pastor Dan says, and for a moment, I feel guilt, because I kind of actually believe in humility.

But it's like the voice in my head has finally figured out the route to my actual voice. I blurt out, "But isn't it more humble to believe that I know very little about the beginning of the universe than to assume it's a man who is basically obsessed with humans?"

Pastor Dan stares me down for a long moment. I stare back. Then he turns to Mom. "It's very bad," he says to her. "These kids, when they fall into these—same-sex couplings—they can be exposed to all kinds of poisonous ideas."

My face flushes. "Hang on, this has nothing to do with Sophie, I've been thinking about this since, like, I moved here."

Pastor Dan, long out of Relating to Troubled Teen mode, gets out a pamphlet. He slides it across the table to Mom like this is a business negotiation. "We know a therapist who works with our youth group—he's been known to help out with teens who are feeling these... urges."

Mom picks it up, slowly. I'm almost crying from anger and humiliation, but dammit, I'm not going to cry in front of Pastor Dan. "I don't need therapy," I say in a tiny voice. I can't say anything else or my words will shake too much.

Mom turns the pamphlet over, pauses. A smiling boy and girl hold hands and look toward the sky together. "Under God's Gaze: A Guide for Teens," the pamphlet says. Is that... that pun can't be intentional, can it? But I'm too busy watching Mom. She pages through it for a long moment. I can't believe her. I can't believe how far she's turned from me. Pastor Dan watches her, carefully avoiding my hard gaze when I turn to him.

Finally, Mom puts the pamphlet down. "Pastor Dan," she says. "Yes, Ruth?"

"This is for conversion therapy," she says.

He shifts in his seat. "Well, our left-wing radicals might call it that. But I assure you, it's a wonderful process for young people to reaffirm their commitment to Jesus."

"Then why does it quote Leviticus here? That's Old Testament." Mom asks, handing him the pamphlet as she points out a Bible passage.

"God's word is God's word," says Pastor Dan.

"This counselor you're recommending seems specifically targeted toward homosexuality," Mom says. I look up at her. I don't remember the last time I've heard her disagree with anyone. I don't think I've ever heard her say the word "homosexuality" either.

Pastor Dan looks less comfortable now, despite the nice leather of his seat. "I thought that you came to me for help with that."

"I came to you because you're the head of my family's church and my daughter has been lying, breaking rules, and doubting her faith," Mom says. Her voice is soft, but passionate, and her words are coming fast. "I wanted guidance on helping her back to God's love. I didn't come here for you to condemn homosexuals and drive her further away."

"But Leviticus..." Pastor Dan says, his finger stabbing the passage in the packet like he is squashing a bug.

Mom doesn't interrupt, but when he doesn't finish the sentence, she goes into full-on Bible study mode. "I can't believe that you're looking toward the Leviticus for your views on this," she says. "Are you forgetting your New Testament?"

Pastor Dan bristles. I'm grinning. I can't help it. I don't think he's been challenged on Scripture since he was in seminary school. "Of course I'm not forgetting my New Testament. Corinthians 6:9, Romans.1:26," he says, and pushes the Bible across the table.

Mom takes it, and flips through, finding the passages, reading them through. She knows the New Testament better than anyone else I've ever met, but she respects men of the cloth. Still, she shakes her head when she's done. "I find that interpretation to be very out of context," she says. "I can't believe you'd rather make that passage in Romans the cornerstone of your beliefs on this matter over, say, 10:4," she says. "That's the entire point of Paul's epistle to the Romans."

My anger has disappeared for the moment. It's like I'm in gardening club, watching her pierce Mrs. Derrow's judgments on something she knows so much more about: gentle, quiet, but backed up by study and experience and total conviction.

"10:4, 10:4..." says Pastor Dan, taking the book back and flipping through the book.

I know the passage she's talking about. It's the one she's always felt it's the most important in one of the books she finds to be most important. The one where Paul tells the smug Romans that they aren't good people just because they obey a list of rules. It's the passage on the magnet on our fridge, on the bookmark in her Bible. "For Christ is the end of the law for righteousness to everyone that believeth," I say quietly.

Mom looks at me, with tears in her eyes. "Christ is the end of the law," she says.

"But Corinthians," Pastor Dan starts to say.

This time, Mom does cut him off, and her voice is stronger than ever. "If you'd rather choose to make an obscure and controversially translated passage in Corinthians the center of your attempts to help us rather than the direct words of Christ, I'm not comfortable letting you minister to my daughter. Or my step-daughter, for that matter."

"Ruth, there are many scholars who would say differently," Pastor Dan says, sweating through his collar.

"That's correct, although I do question whether those scholars are motivated by faith and study or bigotry. And I question that of you, Pastor Dan," she says. "We'll be practicing our faith elsewhere. Emily?" she asks, standing up.

Holy shit. Pastor Dan tries to splutter out a coherent sentence, but doesn't manage to finish it by the time Mom has gotten to the door. She holds it open for me. We walk through the hallway, quiet, empty, the office door shutting behind us with a thud. Mom pushes open the heavy church doors and we burst out into the afternoon sun.

As soon as we're outside, Mom turns to me. "Emily," she says. "Are you alright?"

"I... yeah." I can't really form a coherent thought right now.

"Good. I cannot believe that man. We need to find another church as soon as possible."

I stop in my tracks. I don't feel like me. I feel cold despite the spring warmth. Mom stops and looks over her shoulder. "Emily?"

It's like the dam that's been holding back the flood of feelings bursts. "Oh, yeah, let's find a new church. I've only been saying that for months," I say.

Mom looks a little scared.

I'm not yelling, but I'm close. "Of course this church is terrible. You knew that. I told you that. I can't believe you."

She stands there, and covers her mouth with one hand. Then she sits, kind of crumples really, onto the short brick wall surrounding the church garden, and a suppressed sob shakes her body. A robin lands on the little dogwood tree behind her, cocks its head, and flies away.

The breeze is cool against my hot, hot face. I stand there by the wall, arms crossed. I don't know where soft, crying Emily is right now. "I don't get it. How can you be like that in there, and then..." I'm definitely yelling. "Just stand there after the concert with Beth going off on me?"

She looks up at me over her hand, her eyes red and painful. "Emily..."

"And not only that, but you left me there," I say.

"We had to get Rachel home," Mom says in a stronger voice, as if this statement gives her some courage. "Beth was making a scene, so we left and waited in the parking lot. We waited for you for over an hour."

I guess that might be true. If Harris saw me leaving with Rhys, they would have to have still been there. "It just...it felt really bad."

"I know," she says. "I'm sorry. I should have stood up for you in the school, but I was just... I felt so scared. You're my Emily. I used to know you so well, and suddenly I didn't know anything about you anymore. I could see you slipping away. It's just... the lying that I can't... the lying and the turning away from God. How could I not see that happening? We should have talked about it, we used to talk about all your questions, but... why don't we do that anymore?"

I feel something breaking open inside me, spindly wooden legs breaking under the weight of what I've been holding since Dad died. "It's because I fucking hate it here, Mom," I say, and oh, there's crying Emily, a little late but right on cue. "I hate this neighborhood and this church and this school, and I hate our family now sometimes too, and everything that I love right now is stuff that I felt like I had to hide from you, because you were trying to make things work..."

I have to pause, because I'm gasping for breath.

Mom pulls me down next to her on the wall and takes my hand. I kind of want to yank it away, but I don't. I've already been pretty mean to her. Mrs. Partridge, the very old lady from gardening club, walks past us toward the church. She starts to say hello, sees our faces, and thinks better of it.

I watch the sidewalk for a little while, watch an ant march toward a melting jolly rancher about ten feet away, six or seven ants behind it, marching toward the prize. When I tear my gaze away and glance at Mom, her eyes are closed, and I know she's praying.

She must feel me looking, though, because she opens them, and looks at me. She has the same eyes that I do. "I think I knew you felt that way. And I don't think I was willing to believe it," Mom says finally, softly.

"I just... it felt like Dad died, and then thirty seconds later we had this totally different life," I tell her.

Mom's face twists up a little, but she's done crying. I can see it in her face, the same way I saw it after Dad's funeral. "I know things moved a little fast. I hope you know that... it doesn't mean I loved your father any less."

"You married Peter like, two minutes after you met him."

Mom smiles a little, though her face just looks even sadder. "Peter and I... we needed each other," she says. "We had both lost someone we loved, but... you'll understand this someday, if you start a family. When you lose your husband, your wife, you're losing the person you love, but you're also losing the person that you built your life with. Starting a family, owning a house, keeping each other safe and healthy and well-fed and not in debt... those roles are shared, and Peter and I... well, Rachel was so young, and you're going off to college                                                          soon..."

She wipes her face. "Like I said. We needed each other."

I'm stunned. I try to imagine Peter changing one year old Rachel's diapers, putting a Band-Aid on her knee, all alone in that big empty house. I remember Mom and I, moving in with Grandma, Mom finding part-time work as a cashier but not much else, looking at her checkbook register and her expression tightening.

I try to imagine what life would be like with Sophie—a reflex, we're fighting, I remind myself. But would she cook and I work? Would I bear children and she drop them off at sports practice? I can't picture any of that. My brain feels like it's too full.

"Also... I'm sorry I didn't do a better job of protecting you in the school. I just froze," Mom says.

I smile, a little bit. Mom's species-specific defense is a lot like mine. "I hate Beth," I tell her. It feels really good to say it out loud.

Mom's face tightens. "We must love those who hurt us, for they need it the most... but it's going to take me some time with Beth," she says.

I laugh out loud. That's probably the nastiest thing I've ever heard Mom say.

Mom smiles when I laugh. "Really," she says. "I thought she was needlessly cruel, particularly in the public way she brought this up. It seemed like she didn't have your best interests in mind. "And Emily... I still think you're too young to date, but I wish we had talked about it." Mom takes a deep breath. "If you, uh... identify as homosexual... I just want you to know that there are complexities there, in the Bible, but I will love and support you no matter what."

This feels really uncomfortable, because I don't really know what I am yet, just that I love Sophie. Why are we fighting again?

But then I think about what just happened with Pastor Dan. "Where did all that stuff come from? In there? About gay people?"

Mom smiles, a little proud. "You remember your Aunt Elly? Your father's sister?"

"Yeah." I haven't seen her since Dad died, but I still get a bright, hand-painted card from her every year on my birthday.

"She is, well, she's a lesbian, and your father and I had this argument many times with his family." Mom shrugs. "We were both of the mind that anyone who—wants to make intolerance a cornerstone of their Christianity—isn't a sincere follower of Jesus Christ. So we talked about—Biblical context of homosexuality, quite a lot."

I imagine my mom and my dad, head bent over their King James Bible, pointing out particular passages, discussing, arguing, laughing together. A sudden memory, of them talking together late in the evening when I came downstairs for a drink of water. I've never seen her and Peter talk about the Bible, at least not extensively.

"So Emily, I don't want you to think... that I would judge you for that. It's the..." she purses her lips. Pauses for a long time. "I don't know how you could turn your back on God. On salvation. On the sacrifice that Jesus Christ made for you."

I feel it like a wound—the difference, between she and I. My whole life, my mom and I have been the same, and this… it doesn't feel like it's going away. I just haven't felt that connection to God, to Jesus, for a long time. I feel like that bubble has popped for me. But it's also feeling like… maybe… for the first time… it feels like I can disagree with her, and still be whole. "I don't want you to worry about me, Mom. I'm figuring it out."

She covers my hand with hers, and we sit there, looking at the garden. Things aren't okay. Not by a long shot. But everything is out there, even if it's broken. Maybe now we can start putting things back together, so we can start moving forward again.

\*

Over the next few days, it turns out that my conversation with Mom at the church was only the beginning of a conversation that we have over the next week. We talk more about Dad, for the first time in what feels like forever. I can't believe the relief of talking about it with the one person who feels his absence as much as I do.

We also talk rules and logistics. After many discussions, some cajoling from Peter, and a PowerPoint slideshow by me with statistics about the benefits of participating in extracurricular sports, Mom concedes that she has been "a little overprotective." She agrees to let me return to track, although she doesn't plan on letting me take the Biology AP exam. She's still mad at Harris for, I don't know, poisoning my mind against God or something. I'll keep having that discussion with her, maybe with a Bible in one hand and my biology textbook in the other.

And then there's the Sophie of it all. I haven't talked to her in a week and I'm really scared I'm never going to get to again. "Mom," I tell her finally one evening when we've finished Jeopardy! and Rachel and Peter are reading together in the other room. "Sophie isn't just someone I've been dating, she's my best friend, and she—she's so important. She's the one who wanted me to be honest this whole time."

The lines around Mom's mouth tighten, but she takes a breath. I think she's been praying about me a lot, which is muddling up all my feelings in a confusing way. But, baby steps. One conversation at a time. "I still think you're too young to date, but... we can talk about it."

"Can I..." I hesitate. Be honest. "We're kind of in a fight, and I really want to go see her."

Mom glances at the clock. We're trying a new thing where she doesn't freak out if I'm out until 9, and I don't tell her I'm somewhere that I'm not. "I think that's okay. Just... be safe."

I nod.

"Wait—I have something for you." Mom leaves the room. To my shock, she comes back with my letter to Sophie, the one saying more or less *Sorry I'm bad at expressing my feelings, you mean the world to me.* "You know, your father wrote me a very similar letter one time."

"Really?" I ask.

She nods. I smile. Mom's not the only person that I'm like.

\*

Sophie doesn't pick up when I call her cell phone, which makes my stomach feel nervous. I call her house. Willie picks up. "Can I talk to Sophie?" I ask him.

He hesitates. "What's the deal with you guys right now?"

"I just need to talk to her in person. Look, I'm going to go take a walk in Asbury Park. If she wants to talk, she can come join me."

"I'll let her know."

I tell Mom where I'll be, and walk the half mile to Asbury Park. I think about running around the track, but it just reminds me of the time Sophie and I came here before states to get extra reps. It hurts to remember. Also, I am very out of shape from being too stressed to run. This whole "telling the truth" thing leaves me feeling raw and vulnerable every second of every day. But Sophie was kind of right. There's freedom in it. The sun is setting—it's a "red sky at night, sailor's delight" kind of sky. I feel very alone, but also somehow freer than I have in months.

I'm sitting on the swing when I hear PJ's familiar rattle. Sophie gets out, looks around, sees me. She comes over and stands in front of me. She's wearing shorts and her old Rhizenstein track hoodie, her hands shoved into her pockets. "Hey," she says.

"Hi," I say.

We're silent. I push myself on my swing gently side to side with my foot that's resting on the ground.

Finally, we both start to speak at the same time. "You go first," I tell her.

"You know I didn't mean that I like, want you out of my life or anything, right?" she asks quietly.

"Yeah, I... yeah. God, Soph, I'm so sorry." I shake my head. "I was being horrible."    She laughs a little, takes a hand out of her pocket to tuck a few flyaways back into her ponytail. "Yeah. But I mean, I wasn't helping."

"You were right, though. I finally, uh... started telling the truth. About everything." I tell her about my mom's showdown with Pastor Dan, about the past week where it feels like I'm starting to get to know my mom again instead of just having this New Mom role she's been playing since we moved here. And letting her know me more.

Sophie listens intently. She was the first person that I ever really got practice being honest with, that let me be myself. It's like riding a bike when it comes to telling her everything. She laughs when I tell her about Rhys and Beth, scoffs when I mention Pastor Dan's attempts at conversion therapy. When I finally finish, my hands twisting together in my lap, she sits down on the swing next to mine. The chains clink on her swing as she turns toward me. "So your mom knows you're here? With me? Right now?"

I nod.

"That's cool. Are we..." She trails off, looks at me intently.

I blush. "I am if you are."

She grins, takes my hand. Using her feet and taking little steps, she scoots closer to me on her swing until she's close enough to kiss me, softly, tenderly. "I am, too."

She wraps her arms around me and we sit like that, watching the sunset, just glad to be near each other again. I know there's so much more to talk about—what will happen when she leaves, how she feels about graduation and college, whether I'll even be allowed to date her, everything that the future holds—but right now, I'm happy just being at her side.

As we're walking out, I remember to give her my letter. It's finally in the hands of the right person, and she smiles, takes it, reads it. But I realize it doesn't really matter. By this point, she already knows.

*

I return to track at the beginning of May, just in time for the last couple of weeks. Once Mom got my registration in for St. Mary's, she felt much better, as though my soul were only a few weeks and a summer away from saving. She's still angry at Harris, but I think she's starting to realize that most of the lies I told—most of my beliefs and questions—are mine and mine alone.

Even though it's only been a few weeks, I can't believe the progress everyone has made. Kari is quick to inform me that she's PRed in both the mile and the two-mile. Harris is grooming one of the sprinter freshman for cross country next year. Tevyn's face scratches have mostly healed.

The last track meet, city finals, is two weeks before the last day of school. It's weird to feel nostalgia for something that is happening in the present. But every moment of the day, whether I'm recording times next to Harris or helping Derrick stretch his recently developed shin splints, I already miss it. All the seniors look like they feel the same way, hugging one another, laughing when Harris gets into an argument with a race official about the timing of the one mile, seeing all the small annoyances of being at a track meet in a golden light.

Since we're the largest school in the district, Pineridge hosts city finals at the track that goes around the football field. It's a glorious day, clear and bright and warm. I wear a pair of Sophie's sunglasses perched over my own glasses, and hold my clipboard and pen close. The day goes quickly, as track meets always do: eight hours of nonstop activity, and by the end, I'm exhausted and happy.

Sophie has disappeared for a long warm-up jog with the other girls in the 4x400, the next and final event of the meet after the two-mile. I go to cheer on Kari and Christa in the two-mile from outside the chain link fence around the track, my clipboard out to record their mile splits. Kari is having the best season of her life—she's not even that far behind Christa. Granted, Christa's better in a 5K than she is in a two-mile, but still. The competition with Sophie this fall has really made Kari a better runner.

It hurts that I'm not going to be able to see some of these peoples' progress next year.

Someone comes up beside me and leans on the fence. When I glance up, thinking maybe it's Rhys, to my surprise, it's Jon.

"Hey, Emily, one of the spikes in my shoe partially snapped off and I can't get it out... can you help me fix it?" he asks. "I just finished warming up for the two-mile, then I realized it felt wrong..."

"Oh geez, yeah." I set my clipboard down and take the shoes and spike key he is proffering. Running the two-mile in asymmetrical spikes would be a terrible idea. We sit down in the bottom row of the bleachers. "I'll hurry."

"Thanks." He watches as Kari grimly passes a girl from Jefferson, her face contorted and fierce. "Last track meet ever. This feels so weird," he says wistfully. He's graduating with all the other seniors in just two weeks.

"Yeah," I agree cautiously as I wedge the spike key into the tiny gap between spikes. I know it was months ago, but I still feel weird that Jon and Sophie used to be a little tiny microcosmic bit of a thing. He's been a little cool to me over the past couple of weeks, just not really joking around or being friendly in Harris's classroom at lunch.

"I mean, you'll be back next year, at least."

I glance up at Jon. "Um, actually, I'm going to be at St. Mary's next year." I've felt a little too embarrassed to go into much detail with the team. Some of them had seen the Family Drama that ensued after the competition, but I had kept the St. Mary's thing mostly to myself.

"Wait, what?" Jon's voice is incredulous. "Why?"

I shrug. "Just... oof." I grunt, twisting the spike key. The broken spike falls to the bleachers with a tiny but satisfying little clink. "Just family stuff," I tell him.

"What's going on?" Derrick asks, walking over and squeezing right in between us.

"Emily's switching to the Catholic school next year," Jon tells him.

"Technically, it's a parochial school," I mumble.

But that gets lost under Derrick's exclamation of, "What? NOOOOO," in a lengthy and exaggerated tone of woe. He drops down to his knees and grabs my hand. "Say it isn't so, my dearest, say it isn't so!"

Derrick. I'm going to miss this idiot. "Derrick, you're supposed to be warming up. Your race is in..." I glance at my watch. "Derrick, your race is basically now."

"It's like eighty degrees out," he whines. "I don't need to warm up."

"You do if you don't want to pull your hamstring again." I push him in the shoulder. "Go stretch, at least."

"Fine." He stands up, pulls me to my feet, and gives me a tight hug. "Don't go to St. Mary's, Emily!"

"See, this is exactly why you can't leave," Jon says as Derrick lets go of me and runs off to go stretch before the girls' two-mile finishes up. "The team needs you. Harris will have his second heart attack, Derrick probably literally would have *died* without you this year, Sophie..." He raises his eyebrows. "Sophie will be sad," he says awkwardly.

I shrug. "I mean, she's graduating too," I say.

"Yeah, but... I don't know. I'm sad too. I... for what it's worth, I'm sorry about the way I acted. About Sophie. To you, and even to her, in the fall." He takes a deep breath. "I was mad at first, but it's not anyone's fault, really. I guess. That she liked you better."

I nod, staring down at my shoes. "Thanks, I guess. I mean, for what it's worth, Sophie likes you a lot. Not romantically, but still. She thinks you're 'pretty dope', to use her terminology. And you were one of the first people to be nice to her here. That meant a lot to her."

He shrugs. "Whatever, I'm over it. Just wanted to say, you know, sorry."

I hand him his spikes, ready to race. "Good luck," I say.

"You too, at St. Mary's," he says, and grins that easy grin that all the girls die for. Except Sophie, apparently. Oh, and me, I guess. He gives a little salute before jogging barefoot over to Derrick and sitting down to put on his spikes. It's something the team has picked up from Sophie. It makes me smile to think of Sophie and Willie's shared little gesture as something the team has picked up on.

"St. Mary's?" a loud voice asks behind me. I glance over my shoulder. It's Kari, still panting heavily from her race.

"Great run, Kari," I tell her, though I hadn't been paying much attention to the end.

"Thanks. Why are you going to St. Mary's?"

"Uh, family stuff."

She stares at me, sweat shining on her forehead. "That's crazy. Does Harris know?"

"Uh, yeah." He had brought me into the senior huddle at the beginning of the meet where he told all of us to take what we had learned on this team and use it to make the world better. He looked right at me when he said that last part, and I almost started bawling.

"That's good. You know, Emily, I've always thought you were a bit of a doormat." Kari stares at me frankly.

I have to fight back a laugh. "Uh, okay, Kari."

"Yeah. No problem. But, you know, I have a gay cousin. And I know it takes serious nads to just totally come out of the closet all at once."

"Um… okay." I didn't come out of the closet so much as get thrown out. Not to mention that that the whole term "come out of the closet" is, according to Sophie, "embarrassingly dated" when I used it one time. Still, this conversation isn't one I expected to have at all.

"So, you're tougher than I thought." She nods at me.

This is surreal. What on Earth is this nostalgia doing to people? "Thanks," I tell her.

"No problem." She turns abruptly, and walks away to go stretch with Christa.

A slender arm slides around my waist from behind. Automatically, I lean into Sophie. "You're just getting all kinds of goodbyes, aren't you?" she asks into my hair.

"Everyone is being so weird." I shake my head. "God, I'm even going to miss Kari."

"Yeah, I'm not," she says. But she laughs, and it's gentle. We stand there like that for a long moment. I'm thinking about Pineridge, without Sophie, without me.

Finally, I twist around and look up at her dazzling eyes. "You ready for your last race of the season?"

"Yeah. I'm tired of this stupid track. I want to go run around in the woods." Sophie's performance at states for cross country netted her a half-scholarship to be a varsity runner at OSU. She got into a couple other schools as well, but this one will allow her to stay within driving distance of her family and net her some scholarship money. Her cross-country training camp starts in a little over a month. I'm so proud of her, and I'm so nervous about her leaving. We haven't talked yet about what it will mean.

Sophie glances over as the starting gun goes off for the boys' one mile. She asks, "Are you going to try to work with the cross-country team at St. Mary's? Do they have one?"

"I don't know if they do... I don't know anything about anything." I especially don't know what's going to happen with her and me, and really, that's all I care about.

She senses my worry, and squeezes my shoulder. "You'll figure it out. We'll figure it out."

I smile. Maybe we will.

"Sophie! You coming to warm up handoffs?" Carly calls from the football field.

"Yeah, just a minute!" she calls. She turns to head over, then pauses. "You okay, Em?"

We've both been asking each other that a lot. Neither of us wants to fight again. "I'm fine," I tell her. "Go get 'em."

"Oh, I will." She tweaks me on the nose. I clutch the clipboard to my chest and watch her jog away. One race to go. We're near the end.

*

Mrs. Porco's friend reschedules on me several times. He's in charge of the music department at the college downtown and the end of the school year is an insane time of year for him. He finally offers to squeeze me in between a senior jazz trumpet final recital and a committee meeting, for a twenty-minute chat in his office in early June.

246

School is out. It's weird to think I won't be back to Pineridge next year. Sophie has been giving me all her tips about starting out at a new school for senior year. ("First thing, smile at people unless they're nasty to you. Second thing is act like you don't give a shit what people think about you. And share snacks if you have any.")

For my meeting with Jamison Kelly, Peter drops me off at his office. Well, technically, I drive, and he sits in the passenger seat and calmly reminds me to *brake into the turn, use your turn signal, red light Emily, red light Emily!* I only got my permit a couple of weeks ago. Even though I'm still lurching and halting at every stoplight, he's pretty patient. In fact, against all odds, he's not the worst teacher on Earth. He's certainly much better than Mom, who's sitting in the back seat and covering her face the entire time. But I'm driving!

Peter's only a little sweaty by the end of the drive, but he keeps his relief to himself when I get out of the driver's seat. "You're okay to run home?" he asks.

I nod. "Looking forward to it."

"You have your phone?" Mom asks, getting out of the back to join            Peter            up            front.

I nod. My new phone, barely a month old, is in the little backpack where I have some water and a change of clothes for running after the meeting. Like driving, the phone was also Peter's idea. Mom has always thought that phones are distractions from the things that matter in life. She still barely touches hers. But Peter's unexpectedly sound logic was that if I could call her at home and tell her where I am, she would worry about me less. Now she's more into it than I am.

I still think Peter's kind of stupid and maybe a jerk, but I also think that he feels lucky to be with Mom. I've thought so much about their relationship since all this began, and I think I understand it a little better now. I try to see the good things about it: the choices that they make about Rachel as a team, like looking for a new Sunday school for her. The fact that we've tried three different churches the past few weeks. That Peter ordered pizza last week and remembered to only put banana peppers on half. That Mom is trusting him to have some parenting input. That they're spending a little more time together.

They're going downtown to walk in the botanical gardens after dropping me off. They left Rachel with Nana Samstone, who still claims she's going to set me up with her friend Naomi's son. But that's a worry for another day.

We haven't seen Terry or Gretchen since Beth and I had our confrontation, and I haven't seen Beth since school let out. I don't think they're out of our lives forever. They're family, whatever that even means at this point. But I have overheard Mom and Peter discussing it, so we will figure it out. They're trying harder. I'm trying harder. I'm not looking forward to St. Mary's, and I hate the way Mom looks at me when I know she's worrying about my immortal soul for my treasonous thoughts… but sometimes I see her smiling, especially when I'm smiling. Things at home are starting to feel a little more—home—in a way I haven't felt in years.

\*

Dr. Jamison Kelly's office is a disaster, but it's the kind of disaster that I want to spend all afternoon in. He has built in wall shelves stuffed with books on music theory, pedagogy, and performance, many of which are partially obscured by stacks and folders of sheet music and yes, more books. A poster of a saxophonist I don't recognize hangs on the wall over the piano. One, two, no, three saxophones total are in the office, one in pieces on his desk, which is otherwise so covered in papers that I can't see the surface.

I knock on the ajar door, but no one is in there. Hesitantly, I perch on the piano bench, facing away from it and toward his desk, since the armchair is also covered in paper.

"Excuse me, Emily, I'm sorry I'm late," he says, bustling in. He's dressed in an eggplant purple button down and a lavender tie. He has a well-kept goatee. He is a very small man, but he moves into the office with a fiery but controlled energy.

I can see why he and Mrs. Porco get along.

We only have a few minutes, but he's very engaging. He tells me about his journey from busboy to renowned saxophonist (he doesn't use the term "renowned saxophonist", but I gather). He's deeply passionate about music pedagogy and has taken over as head of the music department in the past year. "That's why I always like to come out and see Evangelie's concert. We have a bit of a feeder program. She used to teach at the university, you know."

Evangelie? Oh my gosh, Mrs. Porco. "Really?"

"Yes. And you're interested in pursuing music?" he asks, without further preamble.

"Oh! Um, I honestly don't know, but potentially," I tell him, forgetting to be shy. I'm too at home in this office, too interested in his story. "After the solo, I was thinking about it a little, but I also might be interested in biology."

"They're not mutually exclusive. Although I will tell you, we do have a great bio department here as well." He smiles. "Just inserting a little advertisement."

I laugh, then hesitate. Be honest. "I'm also not totally sure I'm good enough to even consider doing anything too serious with music."

Dr. Kelly checks his watch again, but then he looks me dead in the eye. "I watch kids audition for hours and hours every fall. I am an authority on this. You are good enough for a college audition. Trust me."

Inwardly, I glow. "Really?"

"You say you're not sure about doing anything serious. I saw your solo. That was serious. Serious people, who keep working hard, sticking around for the long haul. They are the ones who make it. It's about practice, and stamina. Okay?" He looks at his watch again. "I have to run. Again, I apologize for the rudeness, but that was pretty much the extent of the message I wanted to deliver to you after I saw Evangelie's concert."

"Thank you so much."

"You're welcome. Hope to see you in auditions here next year. And give my best to Evangelie."

And he's gone again, before I can even mention that it's unlikely I'll see Mrs. Porco again. I sit there in his office, probably a little longer than is socially acceptable. I'm busy imagining what the future could look like, thinking for the future—for the first time not with anxiety, but with excitement.

Finally, when I hear footsteps and jump guiltily to my feet only to realize that there's a Saturday janitor coming in to empty the trash can, I head outside. I check my phone. I have text messages from Sophie. I'm still so slow at texting that I usually just call her, which I do now. "What's up?"

"How was the meeting?" she asks.

"Tell you about it on our run?" I tell her.

"Sounds good. Meet you at the nature preserve in an hour?"

"Yeah. Love you," I tell her.

I hear the smile in her voice. "You too. See you soon."

I'm running to Emerson Nature Preserve. Overall, it's probably going to be about ten miles for me on the day. I decided after the school year was over to train for a half marathon next fall. It'll be the first time I've run a race since freshman year. I still don't know if my new school will have cross country, but I finally feel like I can run again. I want to do something with it.

I check my dad's watch. One hour. Five miles to the preserve. I'm still a little out of shape, but it's a comfortable enough time for a long distance, at my own pace. Sophie will be waiting.

I glance up at the blue, blue sky, smile, and take off across the quad.

## Acknowledgments

Julien—thank you for being the greatest collaborator from half a planet away. I am so lucky for the talent, attention, humor, and sincerity you brought to this book as its first reader, its illustrator, and its publicist. I'm grateful that you're my friend and I'm so excited about your art. You made this project feel real. Thanks also to Filip for reading and feedback!

Wil—thank you for the website and the many hours spent hunched over our laptops working on projects. Katy and Liza, thank you for the typo-hunting, the nights on Porch, many glasses (...bottles) of wine, and an endless supply of love and patience. I love you all.

67414155R00156

Made in the USA
San Bernardino, CA
22 January 2018